[FRONTISPIECE]
Perseus went to seek the Gorgons. The sickle-sword that Hermes gave him was at his side, and on his arm he held the bronze shield that was now well polished.
See page 140.

THE STORY OF THE
GOLDEN FLEECE

PADRAIC COLUM

ILLUSTRATIONS BY
WILLY POGANY

DOVER PUBLICATIONS, INC.
MINEOLA, NEW YORK

To the Children of
Susan and Llewellyn Jones

Bibliographical Note

This Dover edition, first published in 2005, is an unabridged republica-
tion of the work originally published as *The Golden Fleece and the Heroes
Who Lived Before Achilles* by The Macmillan Company, New York, in 1921.
The color plates have been omitted. The three black-and-white illustra-
tions in the front matter have been moved from their original positions.
Captions have been provided for the illustrations.

Library of Congress Cataloging-in-Publication Data

Colum, Padraic, 1881–1972.
    [Golden Fleece and the heroes who lived before Achilles]
    The story of the Golden Fleece / Padraic Colum ; illustrations by Willy
Pogany.
        p. cm.
    Originally published: The golden fleece and the heroes who lived
before Achilles. New York : Macmillan, c1921.
    ISBN 0-486-44366-3 (pbk.)
    1. Argonauts (Greek mythology)—Juvenile literature. 2. Mythology,
Greek—Juvenile literature. I. Pogany, Willy, 1882–1955. II. Title.

BL820.A8C64 2005

2005045545

Manufactured in the United States of America
Dover Publications, Inc., 31 East 2nd Street, Mineola, N.Y. 11501

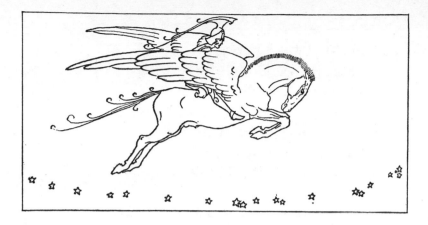

Contents

The Story
of the Golden Fleece

PART ONE
The Voyage to Colchis

I. The Youth Jason

A MAN in the garb of a slave went up the side of that mountain that is all covered with forest, the Mountain Pelion. He carried in his arms a little child.

When it was full noon the slave came into a clearing of the forest so silent that it seemed empty of all life. He laid the child down on the soft moss, and then, trembling with the fear of what might come before him, he raised a horn to his lips and blew three blasts upon it.

Then he waited. The blue sky was above him, the great trees stood away from him, and the little child lay at his feet. He waited, and then he heard the thud-thud of great hooves. And then from between the trees he saw coming toward him the strangest of all beings, one who was half man and half horse; this was Chiron the centaur.

Chiron came toward the trembling slave. Greater than any horse was Chiron, taller than any man. The hair of his head flowed back into his horse's mane, his great beard flowed over his horse's chest; in his man's hand he held a great spear.

Not swiftly he came, but the slave could see that in those great limbs of his there was speed like to the wind's. The slave fell upon his knees. And with eyes that were full of majesty and wisdom and limbs that were full of strength and speed, the king-centaur stood above him. "O my lord," the slave said, "I have come before thee sent by Æson, my master, who told me where to come and what blasts to blow upon the horn. And Æson, once King of Iol-

1

cus, bade me say to thee that if thou dost remember his
ancient friendship with thee thou wilt, perchance, take
this child and guard and foster him, and, as he grows, instruct him with thy wisdom."

"For Æson's sake I will rear and foster this child," said
Chiron the king-centaur in a deep voice.

The child lying on the moss had been looking up at the
four-footed and two-handed centaur. Now the slave lifted
him up and placed him in the centaur's arms. He said:

"Æson bade me tell thee that the child's name is Jason.
He bade me give thee this ring with the great ruby in it
that thou mayst give it to the child when he is grown. By
this ring with its ruby and the images engraved on it
Æson may know his son when they meet after many years
and many changes. And another thing Æson bade me say
to thee, O my lord Chiron: not presumptuous is he, but he
knows that this child has the regard of the immortal Goddess Hera, the wife of Zeus."

Chiron held Æson's son in his arms, and the little child
put hands into his great beard. Then the centaur said,
"Let Æson know that his son will be reared and fostered
by me, and that, when they meet again, there will be ways
by which they will be known to each other."

Saying this Chiron the centaur, holding the child in his
arms, went swiftly toward the forest arches; then the
slave took up the horn and went down the side of the
Mountain Pelion. He came to where a horse was hidden,
and he mounted and rode, first to a city, and then to a village that was beyond the city.

All this was before the famous walls of Troy were built;
before King Priam had come to the throne of his father
and while he was still known, not as Priam, but as Podarces. And the beginning of all these happenings was in
Iolcus, a city in Thessaly.

Cretheus founded the city and had ruled over it in days
before King Priam was born. He left two sons, Æson and
Pelias. Æson succeeded his father. And because he was a

"O my lord," the slave said, "I have come before thee sent by Æson, my master, who told me where to come and what blasts to blow upon the horn. . . . if thou dost remember his ancient friendship with thee thou wilt, perchance, take this child and guard and foster him, and, as he grows, instruct him with thy wisdom." *See page 1.*

mild and gentle man the men of war did not love Æson; they wanted a hard king who would lead them to conquests.

Pelias, the brother of Æson, was ever with the men of war; he knew what mind they had toward Æson and he plotted with them to overthrow his brother. This they did, and they brought Pelias to reign as king in Iolcus.

The people loved Æson and they feared Pelias. And because the people loved him and would be maddened by his slaying, Pelias and the men of war left him living. With his wife, Alcimide, and his infant son, Æson went from the city, and in a village that was at a distance from Iolcus he found a hidden house and went to dwell in it.

Æson would have lived content there were it not that he was fearful for Jason, his infant son. Jason, he knew, would grow into a strong and a bold youth, and Pelias, the king, would be made uneasy on his account. Pelias would slay the son, and perhaps would slay the father for the son's sake when his memory would come to be less loved by the people. Æson thought of such things in his hidden house, and he pondered on ways to have his son reared away from Iolcus and the dread and the power of King Pelias.

He had for a friend one who was the wisest of all creatures—Chiron the centaur; Chiron who was half man and half horse; Chiron who had lived and was yet to live measureless years. Chiron had fostered Heracles, and it might be that he would not refuse to foster Jason, Æson's child.

Away in the fastnesses of Mount Pelion Chiron dwelt; once Æson had been with him and had seen the centaur hunt with his great bow and his great spears. And Æson knew a way that one might come to him; Chiron himself had told him of the way.

Now there was a slave in his house who had been a huntsman and who knew all the ways of the Mountain Pelion. Æson talked with this slave one day, and after he had talked with him he sat for a long time over the cradle of his sleeping infant. And then he spoke to Alcimide, his wife, telling her of a parting that made her weep. That evening the slave came in and Æson took the child from the arms of the mournful-eyed mother and put him in the slave's arms. Also he gave him a horn and a ring with a great ruby in it and mystic images engraved on its gold. Then when the ways were dark the slave mounted a horse, and, with the child in his arms, rode through the city that King Pelias ruled over. In the morning he came to that mountain that is all covered with forest, the Mountain Pelion. And that evening he came back to the village and to Æson's hidden house, and he told his master how he had prospered.

Æson was content thereafter although he was lonely and although his wife was lonely in their childlessness. But the time came when they rejoiced that their child had been sent into an unreachable place. For messengers from King Pelias came inquiring about the boy. They told the king's messengers that the child had strayed off from his nurse, and that whether he had been slain by a wild beast or had been drowned in the swift River Anaurus they did not know.

The years went by and Pelias felt secure upon the throne he had taken from his brother. Once he sent to the oracle of the gods to ask of it whether he should be fearful of anything. What the oracle answered was this: that King Pelias had but one thing to dread—the coming of a half-shod man.

The centaur nourished the child Jason on roots and fruits and honey; for shelter they had a great cave that Chiron had lived in for numberless years. When he had grown big enough to leave the cave Chiron would let Jason mount on his back; with the child holding on to his great mane he would trot gently through the ways of the forest.

Jason began to know the creatures of the forest and their haunts. Sometimes Chiron would bring his great bow with him; then Jason, on his back, would hold the quiver and would hand him the arrows. The centaur would let the boy see him kill with a single arrow the bear, the boar, or the deer. And soon Jason, running beside him, hunted too.

No heroes were ever better trained than those whose childhood and youth had been spent with Chiron the king-centaur. He made them more swift of foot than any other of the children of men. He made them stronger and more ready with the spear and bow. Jason was trained by Chiron as Heracles just before him had been trained, and as Achilles was to be trained afterward.

Moreover, Chiron taught him the knowledge of the stars and the wisdom that had to do with the ways of the gods.

Once, when they were hunting together, Jason saw a form at the end of an alley of trees—the form of a woman it was—of a woman who had on her head a shining crown. Never had Jason dreamt of seeing a form so wondrous. Not very near did he come, but he thought he knew that the woman smiled upon him. She was seen no more, and Jason knew that he had looked upon one of the immortal goddesses.

All day Jason was filled with thought of her whom he had seen. At night, when the stars were out, and when they were seated outside the cave, Chiron and Jason talked together, and Chiron told the youth that she whom he had seen was none other than Hera, the wife of Zeus, who had for his father Æson and for himself an especial friendliness.

So Jason grew up upon the mountain and in the forest fastnesses. When he had reached his full height and had shown himself swift in the hunt and strong with the spear and bow, Chiron told him that the time had come when he should go back to the world of men and make his name famous by the doing of great deeds.

And when Chiron told him about his father Æson—about how he had been thrust out of the kingship by Pelias, his uncle—a great longing came upon Jason to see his father and a fierce anger grew up in his heart against Pelias.

From stone to stepping-stone she went, Jason holding on to the wood that she had drawn to her shoulders. *See page 8.*

Then the time came when he bade good-by to Chiron his great instructor; the time came when he went from the centaur's cave for the last time, and went through the wooded ways and down the side of the Mountain Pelion. He came to the river, to the swift Anaurus, and he found it high in flood. The stones by which one might cross were almost all washed over; far apart did they seem in the flood.

Now as he stood there pondering on what he might do there came up to him an old woman who had on her back a load of brushwood. "Wouldst thou cross?" asked the old woman. "Wouldst thou cross and get thee to the city of Iolcus, Jason, where so many things await thee?"

Greatly was the youth astonished to hear his name spoken by this old woman, and to hear her give the name of the city he was bound for. "Wouldst thou cross the Anaurus?" she asked again. "Then mount upon my back, holding on to the wood I carry, and I will bear thee over the river."

Jason smiled. How foolish this old woman was to think that she could bear him across the flooded river! She came near him and she took him in her arms and lifted him up on her shoulders. Then, before he knew what she was about to do, she had stepped into the water.

From stone to stepping-stone she went, Jason holding on to the wood that she had drawn to her shoulders. She left him down upon the bank. As she was lifting him down one of his feet touched the water; the swift current swept away a sandal.

He stood on the bank knowing that she who had carried him across the flooded river had strength from the gods. He looked upon her, and behold! she was transformed. Instead of an old woman there stood before him one who had on a golden robe and a shining crown. Around her was a wondrous light—the light of the sun when it is most golden. Then Jason knew that she who had carried him across the broad Anaurus was the goddess whom he had seen in the ways of the forest—Hera, great Zeus's wife.

"Go into Iolcus, Jason," said great Hera to him, "go into Iolcus, and in whatever chance doth befall thee act as one who has the eyes of the immortals upon him."

She spoke and she was seen no more. Then Jason went on his way to the city that Cretheus, his grandfather, had founded and that his father Æson had once ruled over. He came into that city, a tall, great-limbed, unknown youth, dressed in a strange fashion, and having but one sandal on.

II. King Pelias

THAT day King Pelias, walking through the streets of his city, saw coming toward him a youth who was half shod. He remembered the words of the oracle that bade him beware of a half-shod man, and straightway he gave orders to his guards to lay hands upon the youth.

But the guards wavered when they went toward him, for there was something about the youth that put them in awe of him. He came with the guards, however, and he stood before the king's judgment seat.

Fearfully did Pelias look upon him. But not fearfully did the youth look upon the king. With head lifted high he cried out, "Thou art Pelias, but I do not salute thee as king. Know that I am Jason, the son of Æson from whom thou hast taken the throne and scepter that were rightfully his."

King Pelias looked to his guards. He would have given them a sign to destroy the youth's life with their spears, but behind his guards he saw a threatening multitude— the dwellers of the city of Iolcus; they gathered around, and Pelias knew that he had become more and more hated by them. And from the multitude a cry went up, "Æson, Æson! May Æson come back to us! Jason, son of Æson! May nothing evil befall thee, brave youth!"

Then Pelias knew that the youth might not be slain. He bent his head while he plotted against him in his heart. *See page 11.*

Then Pelias knew that the youth might not be slain. He bent his head while he plotted against him in his heart. Then he raised his eyes, and looking upon Jason he said, "O goodly youth, it well may be that thou art the son of Æson, my brother. I am well pleased to see thee here. I have had hopes that I might be friends with Æson, and thy coming here may be the means to the renewal of our friendship. We two brothers may come together again. I will send for thy father now, and he will be brought to meet thee in my royal palace. Go with my guards and with this rejoicing people, and in a little while thou and I and thy father Æson will sit at a feast of friends."

So Pelias said, and Jason went with the guards and the crowd of people, and he came to the palace of the king and he was brought within. The maids led him to the bath and gave him new robes to wear. Dressed in these Jason looked a prince indeed.

But all that while King Pelias remained on his judgment seat with his crowned head bent down. When he raised his head his dark brows were gathered together and his thin lips were very close. He looked to the swords and spears of his guards, and he made a sign to the men to stand close to him. Then he left the judgment seat and he went to the palace.

III. The Golden Fleece

THEY brought Jason into a hall where Æson, his father, waited. Very strange did this old and grave-looking man appear to him. But when Æson spoke, Jason remembered the tone of his father's voice and he clasped him to him. And his father knew him even without the sight of the ruby ring which Jason had upon his finger.

Then the young man began to tell of the centaur and of his life upon the Mountain Pelion. As they were speaking together Pelias came to where they stood, Pelias in the purple robe of a king and with the crown upon his head. Æson tightly clasped Jason as if he had become fearful for his son. Pelias smilingly took the hand of the young man and the hand of his brother, and he bade them both welcome to his palace.

Then, walking between them, the king brought the two into the feasting hall. The youth who had known only the forest and the mountainside had to wonder at the beauty and the magnificence of all he saw around him. On the walls were bright pictures; the tables were of polished wood, and they had vessels of gold and dishes of silver set upon them; along the walls were vases of lovely shapes and colors, and everywhere there were baskets heaped with roses white and red.

The king's guests were already in the hall, young men and elders, and maidens went amongst them carrying roses which they strung into wreaths for the guests to put upon their heads. A soft-handed maiden gave Jason a wreath of roses and he put it on his head as he sat down at the king's table. When he looked at all the rich and lovely things in that hall, and when he saw the guests looking at him with friendly eyes, Jason felt that he was indeed far away from the dim spaces of the mountain forest and from the darkness of the centaur's cave.

Rich food and wine such as he had never dreamt of tasting were brought to the tables. He ate and drank, and his eyes followed the fair maidens who went through the hall. He thought how glorious it was to be a king. He heard Pelias speak to Æson, his father, telling him that he was old and that he was weary of ruling; that he longed to make friends, and that he would let no enmity now be between him and his brother. And he heard the king say that he, Jason, was young and courageous, and that he would call upon him to help to rule the land, and that, in a while, Jason would bear full sway over the kingdom that Cretheus had founded.

So Pelias spoke to Æson as they both sat together at

Very strange did this old and grave-looking man appear to him. But when Æson spoke, Jason remembered the tone of his father's voice and he clasped him to him. *See page 11.*

the king's high table. But Jason, looking on them both, saw that the eyes that his father turned on him were full of warnings and mistrust.

After they had eaten King Pelias made a sign, and a cupbearer bringing a richly wrought cup came and stood before the king. The king stood up, holding the cup in his hands, and all in the hall waited silently. Then Pelias put the cup into Jason's hands and he cried out in a voice that was heard all through the hall, "Drink from this cup, O nephew Jason! Drink from this cup, O man who will soon come to rule over the kingdom that Cretheus founded!"

All in the hall stood up and shouted with delight at that speech. But the king was not delighted with their delight, Jason saw. He took the cup and he drank the rich wine; pride grew in him; he looked down the hall and he saw faces all friendly to him; he felt as a king might feel, secure and triumphant. And then he heard King Pelias speaking once more.

"This is my nephew Jason, reared and fostered in the centaur's cave. He will tell you of his life in the forest and the mountains—his life that was like to the life of the half gods."

Then Jason spoke to them, telling them of his life on the Mountain Pelion. When he had spoken, Pelias said:

"I was bidden by the oracle to beware of the man whom I should see coming toward me half shod. But, as you all see, I have brought the half-shod man to my palace and my feasting hall, so little do I dread the anger of the gods.

"And I dread it little because I am blameless. This youth, the son of my brother, is strong and courageous, and I rejoice in his strength and courage, for I would have him take my place and reign over you. Ah, that I were as young as he is now! Ah, that I had been reared and fostered as he was reared and fostered by the wise centaur and under the eyes of the immortals! Then would I do that which in my youth I often dreamed of doing! Then would I perform a deed that would make my name and the name of my city famous throughout all Greece! Then would I bring from far Colchis, the famous Fleece of Gold that King Æetes keeps guard over!"

He finished speaking, and all in the hall shouted out, "The Golden Fleece, the Golden Fleece from Colchis!" Jason stood up, and his father's hand gripped him. But he did not heed the hold of his father's hand, for "The Golden Fleece, the Golden Fleece!" rang in his ears, and before his eyes were the faces of those who were all eager for the sight of the wonder that King Æetes kept guard over.

Then said Jason, "Thou hast spoken well, O King Pelias! Know, and know all here assembled, that I have heard of the Golden Fleece and of the dangers that await on any one who should strive to win it from King Æetes's care. But know, too, that I would strive to win the Fleece and bring it to Iolcus, winning fame both for myself and for the city."

When he had spoken he saw his father's stricken eyes; they were fixed upon him. But he looked from them to the shining eyes of the young men who were even then pressing around where he stood. "Jason, Jason!" they shouted. "The Golden Fleece for Iolcus!"

"King Pelias knows that the winning of the Golden Fleece is a feat most difficult," said Jason. "But if he will have built for me a ship that can make the voyage to far Colchis, and if he will send throughout all Greece the word of my adventuring so that all the heroes who would win fame might come with me, and if ye, young heroes of Iolcus, will come with me, I will peril my life to win the wonder that King Æetes keeps guard over."

He spoke and those in the hall shouted again and made clamor around him. But still his father sat gazing at him with stricken eyes.

King Pelias stood up in the hall and holding up his scepter he said, "O my nephew Jason, and O friends assembled here, I promise that I will have built for the voyage the best ship that ever sailed from a harbor in Greece. And I promise that I will send throughout all Greece a word telling of Jason's voyage so that all heroes desirous of winning fame may come to help him and to help all of you who may go with him to win from the keeping of King Æetes the famous Fleece of Gold."

So King Pelias said, but Jason, looking to the king from his father's stricken eyes, saw that he had been led by the king into the acceptance of the voyage so that he might fare far from Iolcus, and perhaps lose his life in striving to gain the wonder that King Æetes kept guarded. By the glitter in Pelias's eyes he knew the truth. Nevertheless Jason would not take back one word that he had spoken; his heart was strong within him, and he thought that with the help of the bright-eyed youths around and with the help of those who would come to him at the word of the voyage, he would bring the Golden Fleece to Iolcus and make famous for all time his own name.

IV. The Assembling of the Heroes and the Building of the Ship

FIRST there came the youths CASTOR and POLYDEUCES. They came riding on white horses, two noble-looking brothers. From Sparta they came, and their mother was Leda, who, after the twin brothers, had another child born to her—Helen, for whose sake the sons of many of Jason's friends were to wage war against the great city of Troy. These were the first heroes who came to Iolcus after the word had gone forth through Greece of Jason's adventuring in quest of the Golden Fleece.

And then there came one who had both welcome and reverence from Jason; this one came without spear or bow, bearing in his hands a lyre only. He was ORPHEUS, and he knew all the ways of the gods and all the stories of the gods; when he sang to his lyre the trees would listen and the beasts would follow him. It was Chiron who had counseled Orpheus to go with Jason; Chiron the centaur had met him as he was wandering through the forests on the Mountain Pelion and had sent him down into Iolcus.

Then there came two men well skilled in the handling of ships—TIPHYS and NAUPLIUS. Tiphys knew all about the sun and winds and stars, and all about the signs by which a ship might be steered, and Nauplius had the love of Poseidon, the god of the sea.

Afterward there came, one after the other, two who were famous for their hunting. No two could be more different than these two were. The first was ARCAS. He was dressed in the skin of a bear; he had red hair and savage-looking eyes, and for arms he carried a mighty bow with bronze-tipped arrows. The folk were watching an eagle as he came into the city—an eagle that was winging its way far, far up in the sky. Arcas drew his bow, and with one arrow he brought the eagle down.

The other hunter was a girl, ATALANTA. Tall and bright-haired was Atalanta, swift and good with the bow. She had dedicated herself to Artemis, the guardian of the wild things, and she had vowed that she would remain unwed-ded. All the heroes welcomed Atalanta as a comrade, and the maiden did all the things that the young men did.

There came a hero who was less youthful than Castor or Polydeuces; he was a man good in council named NESTOR. Afterward Nestor went to the war against Troy, and then he was the oldest of the heroes in the camp of Agamemnon.

Two brothers came who were to be special friends of Jason's—PELEUS and TELAMON. Both were still youthful and neither had yet achieved any notable deed. Afterward they were to be famous, but their sons were to be even more famous, for the son of Telamon was strong Aias, and the son of Peleus was great Achilles.

Another who came was ADMETUS; afterward he became a famous king. The God Apollo once made himself a shepherd and he kept the flocks of King Admetus.

And there came two brothers, twins, who were a wonder to all who beheld them. Zetes and Calais they were named; their mother was Oreithyia, the daughter of Erechtheus, King of Athens, and their father was Boreas, the North Wind. These two brothers had on their ankles wings that gleamed with golden scales; their black hair was thick upon their shoulders, and it was always being shaken by the wind.

With Zetes and Calais there came a youth armed with a great sword whose name was Theseus. Theseus's father was an unknown king; he had bidden the mother show their son where his sword was hidden. Under a great stone the king had hidden it before Theseus was born. Before he had grown out of his boyhood Theseus had been able to raise the stone and draw forth his father's sword. As yet he had done no great deed, but he was resolved to win fame and to find his unknown father.

On the day that the messengers had set out to bring through Greece the word of Jason's going forth in quest of the Golden Fleece the woodcutters made their way up into the forests of Mount Pelion; they began to fell trees for the timbers of the ship that was to make the voyage to far Colchis.

Great timbers were cut and brought down to Pagasæ, the harbor of Iolcus. On the night of the day he had helped to bring them down Jason had a dream. He dreamt that She whom he had seen in the forest ways and afterward by the River Anaurus appeared to him. And in his dream the goddess bade him rise early in the morning and welcome a man whom he would meet at the city's gate— a tall and gray-haired man who would have on his shoulders tools for the building of a ship.

He went to the city's gate and he met such a man. Argus was his name. He told Jason that a dream had sent him to the city of Iolcus. Jason welcomed him and lodged him in the king's palace, and that day the word went through the city that the building of the great ship would soon be begun.

And in his dream the goddess bade him rise early in the morning
and welcome a man whom he would meet at the city's gate—
a tall and gray-haired man who would have on his shoulders tools
for the building of a ship. *See page 18.*

But not with the timbers brought from Mount Pelion did Argus begin. Walking through the palace with Jason he noted a great beam in the roof. That beam, he said, had been shown him in his dream; it was from an oak tree in Dodona, the grove of Zeus. A sacred power was in the beam, and from it the prow of the ship should be fashioned. Jason had them take the beam from the roof of the palace; it was brought to where the timbers were, and that day the building of the great ship was begun.

Then all along the waterside came the noise of hammering; in the street where the metalworkers were came the noise of beating upon metals as the smiths fashioned out of bronze armor for the heroes and swords and spears. Every day, under the eyes of Argus the master, the ship that had in it the beam from Zeus's grove was built higher and wider. And those who were building the ship often felt going through it tremors as of a living creature.

When the ship was built and made ready for the voyage a name was given to it—the ARGO it was called. And naming themselves from the ship the heroes called themselves the ARGONAUTS. All was ready for the voyage, and now Jason went with his friends to view the ship before she was brought into the water.

Argus the master was on the ship, seeing to it that the last things were being done before *Argo* was launched. Very grave and wise looked Argus—Argus the builder of the ship. And wonderful to the heroes the ship looked now that Argus, for their viewing, had set up the mast with the sails and had even put the oars in their places. Wonderful to the heroes *Argo* looked with her long oars and her high sails, with her timbers painted red and gold and blue, and with a marvelous figure carved upon her prow. All over the ship Jason's eyes went. He saw a figure standing by the mast; for a moment he looked on it, and then the figure became shadowy. But Jason knew that he had looked upon the goddess whom he had seen in the ways of the forest and had seen afterward by the rough Anaurus.

Then mast and sails were taken down and the oars were left in the ship, and the *Argo* was launched into the water. The heroes went back to the palace of King Pelias to feast with the king's guests before they took their places on the ship, setting out on the voyage to far Colchis.

When they came into the palace they saw that another hero had arrived. His shield was hung in the hall; the heroes all gathered around, amazed at the size and the beauty of it. The shield shone all over with gold. In its center was the figure of Fear—of Fear that stared backward with eyes burning as with fire. The mouth was open and the teeth were shown. And other figures were wrought around the figure of Fear—Strife and Pursuit and Flight; Tumult and Panic and Slaughter. The figure of Fate was there dragging a dead man by the feet; on her shoulders Fate had a garment that was red with the blood of men.

Around these figures were heads of snakes, heads with black jaws and glittering eyes, twelve heads such as might affright any man. And on other parts of the shield were shown the horses of Ares, the grim god of war. The figure of Ares himself was shown also. He held a spear in his hand, and he was urging the warriors on.

Around the inner rim of the shield the sea was shown, wrought in white metal. Dolphins swam in the sea, fishing for little fishes that were shown there in bronze. Around the rim chariots were racing along with wheels running close together; there were men fighting and women watching from high towers. The awful figure of the Darkness of Death was shown there, too, with mournful eyes and the dust of battles upon her shoulders. The outer rim of the shield showed the Stream of Ocean, the stream that encircles the world; swans were soaring above and swimming on its surface.

All in wonder the heroes gazed on the great shield, telling each other that only one man in all the world could carry it—Heracles the son of Zeus. Could it be that Heracles had come amongst them? They went into the feasting hall and they saw one there who was tall as a pine tree, with unshorn tresses of hair upon his head. Heracles indeed it was! He turned to them a smiling face with smiling eyes. Heracles! They all gathered around the strongest hero in the world, and he took the hand of each in his mighty hand.

V. The *Argo*

THE heroes went the next day through the streets of Iolcus down to where the ship lay. The ways they went through were crowded; the heroes were splendid in their appearance, and Jason amongst them shone like a star.

The people praised him, and one told the other that it would not be long until they would win back to Iolcus, for this band of heroes was strong enough, they said, to take King Æetes's city and force him to give up to them the famous Fleece of Gold. Many of the bright-eyed youths of Iolcus went with the heroes who had come from the different parts of Greece.

As they marched past a temple a priestess came forth to speak to Jason; Iphias was her name. She had a prophecy to utter about the voyage. But Iphias was very old, and she stammered in her speech to Jason. What she said was not heard by him. The heroes went on, and ancient Iphias was left standing there as the old are left by the young.

The heroes went aboard the *Argo*. They took their seats as at an assembly. Then Jason faced them and spoke to them all.

"Heroes of the quest," said Jason, "we have come aboard the great ship that Argus has built, and all that a ship needs is in its place or is ready to our hands. All that we wait for now is the coming of the morning's breeze that will set us on our way for far Colchis.

"One thing we have first to do—that is, to choose a leader who will direct us all, one who will settle disputes amongst ourselves and who will make treaties between us and the strangers that we come amongst. We must choose such a leader now."

Jason spoke, and some looked to him and some looked to Heracles. But Heracles stood up, and, stretching out his hand, said:

"Argonauts! Let no one amongst you offer the leadership to me. I will not take it. The hero who brought us together and made all things ready for our going—it is he and no one else who should be our leader in this voyage."

So Heracles said, and the Argonauts all stood up and raised a cry for Jason. Then Jason stepped forward, and he took the hand of each Argonaut in his hand, and he swore that he would lead them with all the mind and all the courage that he possessed. And he prayed the gods that it would be given to him to lead them back safely with the Golden Fleece glittering on the mast of the *Argo*.

They drew lots for the benches they would sit at; they took the places that for the length of the voyage they would have on the ship. They made sacrifice to the gods and they waited for the breeze of the morning that would help them away from Iolcus.

And while they waited Æson, the father of Jason, sat at his own hearth, bowed and silent in his grief. Alcimide, his wife, sat near him, but she was not silent; she lamented to the women of Iolcus who were gathered around her. "I did not go down to the ship," she said, "for with my grief I would not be a bird of ill omen for the voyage. By this hearth my son took farewell of me—the only son I ever bore. From the doorway I watched him go down the street of the city, and I heard the people shout as he went amongst them, they glorying in my son's splendid appearance. Ah, that I might live to see his return and to hear the shout that will go up when the people look on Jason again! But I know that my life will not be spared so long; I will not look on my son when he comes back from the dangers he will run in the quest of the Golden Fleece."

Then the women of Iolcus asked her to tell them of the Golden Fleece, and Alcimide told them of it and of the sorrows that were upon the race of Æolus.

Cretheus, the father of Æson and Pelias, was of the race of Æolus, and of the race of Æolus, too, was Athamas, the king who ruled in Thebes at the same time that Cretheus ruled in Iolcus. And the first children of Athamas were Phrixus and Helle.

"Ah, Phrixus and ah, Helle," Alcimide lamented, "what griefs you have brought on the race of Æolus! And what griefs you yourselves suffered! The evil that Athamas, your father, did you lives to be a curse to the line of Æolus!

"Athamas was wedded first to Nephele, the mother of Phrixus and Helle, the youth and maiden. But Athamas married again while the mother of these children was still living, and Ino, the new queen, drove Nephele and her children out of the king's palace.

"And now was Nephele most unhappy. She had to live as a servant, and her children were servants to the servants of the palace. They were clad in rags and had little to eat, and they were beaten often by the servants who wished to win the favor of the new queen.

"But although they wore rags and had menial tasks to do, Phrixus and Helle looked the children of a queen. The boy was tall, and in his eyes there often came the flash of power, and the girl looked as if she would grow into a lovely maiden. And when Athamas, their father, would meet them by chance he would sigh, and Queen Ino would know by that sigh that he had still some love for them in his heart. Afterward she would have to use all the power she possessed to win the king back from thinking upon his children.

"And now Queen Ino had children of her own. She knew that the people reverenced the children of Nephele and cared nothing for her children. And because she knew this she feared that when Athamas died Phrixus and Helle, the children of Nephele, would be brought to rule in Thebes. Then she and her children would be made to change places with them.

"This made Queen Ino think on ways by which she could make Phrixus and Helle lose their lives. She thought long upon this, and at last a desperate plan came into her mind.

"When it was winter she went amongst the women of the countryside, and she gave them jewels and clothes for presents. Then she asked them to do secretly an un-heard-of thing. She asked the women to roast over their fires the grains that had been left for seed. This the women did. Then spring came on, and the men sowed in the fields the grain that had been roasted over the fires. No shoots grew up as the spring went by. In summer there was no waving greenness in the fields. Autumn came, and there was no grain for the reaping. Then the men, not knowing what had happened, went to King Athamas and told him that there would be famine in the land.

"The king sent to the temple of Artemis to ask how the people might be saved from the famine. And the guardians of the temple, having taken gold from Queen Ino, told them that there would be worse and worse famine and that all the people of Thebes would die of hunger unless the king was willing to make a great sacrifice.

"When the king asked what sacrifice he should make he was told by the guardians of the temple that he must sacrifice to the goddess his two children, Phrixus and Helle. Those who were around the king, to save themselves from famine after famine, clamored to have the children sacrificed. Athamas, to save his people, consented to the sacrifice.

"They went toward the king's palace. They found Helle by the bank of the river washing clothes. They took her and bound her. They found Phrixus, half naked, digging in a field, and they took him, too, and bound him. That night they left brother and sister in the same prison. Helle wept over Phrixus, and Phrixus wept to think that he was not able to do anything to save his sister.

"The servants of the palace went to Nephele, and they mocked at her, telling her that her children would be sacrificed on the morrow. Nephele nearly went wild in her grief. And then, suddenly, there came into her mind the thought of a creature that might be a helper to her and to her children.

"This creature was a ram that had wings and a wonderful fleece of gold. The god of the sea, Poseidon, had sent this wonderful ram to Athamas and Nephele as a marriage gift. And the ram had since been kept in a special fold.

"To that fold Nephele went. She spent the night beside the ram praying for its help. The morning came and the children were taken from their prison and dressed in white, and wreaths were put upon their heads to mark them as things for sacrifice. They were led in a procession to the temple of Artemis. Behind that procession King Athamas walked, his head bowed in shame.

"But Queen Ino's head was not bowed; rather she carried it high, for her thought was all upon her triumph. Soon Phrixus and Helle would be dead, and then, whatever happened, her own children would reign after Athamas in Thebes.

"Phrixus and Helle, thinking they were taking their last look at the sun, went on. And even then Nephele, holding the horns of the golden ram, was making her last prayer. The sun rose and as it did the ram spread out its great wings and flew through the air. It flew to the temple of Artemis. Down beside the altar came the golden ram, and it stood with its horns threatening those who came. All stopped in surprise. Still the ram stood with threatening head and great golden wings spread out. Then Phrixus ran from those who were holding him and laid his hands upon the ram. He called to Helle and she, too, came to the golden creature. Phrixus mounted on the ram and he pulled Helle up beside him. Then the golden ram flew upward. Up, up, it went, and with the children upon its back it became like a star in the day-lit sky.

"Then Queen Ino, seeing the children saved by the golden ram, shrieked and fled away from that place. Athamas ran after her. As she ran and as he followed hatred for her grew up within him. Ino ran on and on until she came to the cliffs that rose over the sea. Fearing Athamas who came behind her she plunged down. But as she fell she was changed by Poseidon, the god of the sea. She became a seagull. Athamas, who followed her, was changed also; he became the sea eagle that, with beak and talons ever ready to strike, flies above the sea.

"And the golden ram with wings outspread flew on and on. Over the sea it flew while the wind whistled around the children. On and on they went, and the children saw only the blue sea beneath them. Then poor Helle, looking downward, grew dizzy. She fell off the golden ram before her brother could take hold of her. Down she fell, and still the ram flew on and on. She was drowned in that sea. The people afterward named it in memory of her, calling it 'Hellespont'—'Helle's Sea.'

"On and on the ram flew. Over a wild and barren country it flew and toward a river. Upon that river a white city was built. Down the ram flew, and alighting on the ground, stood before the gate of that city. It was the city of Aea, in the land of Colchis.

"The king was in the street of the city, and he joined with the crowd that gathered around the strange golden creature that had a youth upon its back. The ram folded its wings and then the youth stood beside it. He spoke to the people, and then the king—Æetes was his name—spoke to him, asking him from what place he had come, and what was the strange creature upon whose back he had flown.

"To the king and to the people Phrixus told his story, weeping to tell of Helle and her fall. Then King Æetes brought him into the city, and he gave him a place in the palace, and for the golden ram he had a special fold made.

"Soon after the ram died, and then King Æetes took its golden fleece and hung it upon an oak tree that was in a place dedicated to Ares, the god of war. Phrixus wed one of the daughters of the king, and men say that afterward he went back to Thebes, his own land.

"And as for the Golden Fleece it became the greatest of King Æetes's treasures. Well indeed does he guard it, and not with armed men only, but with magic powers. Very strong and very cunning is King Æetes, and a terrible task awaits those who would take away from him that Fleece of Gold."

So Alcimide spoke, sorrowfully telling to the women the story of the Golden Fleece that her son Jason was going in quest of. So she spoke, and the night waned, and the morning of the sailing of the *Argo* came on.

And when the Argonauts beheld the dawn upon the high peaks of Pelion they arose and poured out wine in offering to Zeus, the highest of the gods. Then *Argo* herself gave forth a strange cry, for the beam from Dodona that had been formed into her prow had endued her with life. She uttered a strange cry, and as she did the heroes took their places at the benches, one after the other, as had been arranged by lot, and Tiphys, the helmsman, went to the steering place. To the sound of Orpheus's lyre they smote with oars the rushing sea water, and the surge broke over the oar blades. The sails were let out and the breeze came into them, piping shrilly, and the fishes came darting through the green sea, great and small, and followed them, gamboling along the watery paths. And Chiron, the king-centaur, came down from the Mountain Pelion, and standing with his feet in the foam cried out, "Good speed, O Argonauts, good speed, and a sorrowless return."

THE BEGINNING OF THINGS

Orpheus sang to his lyre, Orpheus the minstrel, who knew the ways and the stories of the gods; out in the open sea on the first morning of the voyage Orpheus sang to them of the beginning of things.

He sang how at first Earth and Heaven and Sea were all mixed and mingled together. There was neither Light nor Darkness then, but only a Dimness. This was Chaos. And from Chaos came forth Night and Erebus. From Night was born Æther, the Upper Air, and from Night and Erebus wedded there was born Day.

And out of Chaos came Earth, and out of Earth came the starry Heaven. And from Heaven and Earth wedded there were born the Titan gods and goddesses—Oceanus, Cœus, Crius, Hyperion, Iapetus; Theia, Rhea, Themis, Mnemosyne, gold-crowned Phœbe, and lovely Tethys. And then Heaven and Earth had for their child Cronos, the most cunning of all.

Cronos wedded Rhea, and from Cronos and Rhea were born the gods who were different from the Titan gods.

But Heaven and Earth had other children—Cottus, Briareus, and Gyes. These were giants, each with fifty heads and a hundred arms. And Heaven grew fearful when he looked on these giant children, and he hid them away in the deep places of the Earth.

Cronos hated Heaven, his father. He drove Heaven, his father, and Earth, his mother, far apart. And far apart they stay, for they have never been able to come near each other since. And Cronos married to Rhea had for children Hestia, Demeter, Hera, Aidoneus, and Poseidon, and these all belonged to the company of the deathless gods. Cronos was fearful that one of his sons would treat him as he had treated Heaven, his father. So when another child was born to him and his wife Rhea he commanded that the child be given to him so that he might swallow him. But Rhea wrapped a great stone in swaddling clothes and gave the stone to Cronos. And Cronos swallowed the stone, thinking to swallow his latest-born child.

That child was Zeus. Earth took Zeus and hid him in a deep cave and those who minded and nursed the child beat upon drums so that his cries might not be heard. His nurse was Adrastia; when he was able to play she gave him a ball to play with. All of gold was the ball, with a dark-blue spiral around it. When the boy Zeus would play with this ball it would make a track across the sky, flaming like a star.

Hyperion the Titan god wed Theia the Titan goddess, and their children were Helios, the bright Sun, and Selene, the clear Moon. And Cœus wed Phœbe, and their children were Leto, who is kind to gods and men, and Asteria of happy name, and Hecate, whom Zeus honored above all. Now the gods who were the children of Cronos and Rhea went up unto the Mountain Olympus, and there they built their shining palaces. But the Titan gods who were born of Heaven and Earth went up to the Mountain Othrys, and there they had their thrones.

Between the Olympians and the Titan gods of Othrys a war began. Neither side might prevail against the other. But now Zeus, grown up to be a youth, thought of how he might help the Olympians to overthrow the Titan gods.

He went down into the deep parts of the Earth where the giants Cottus, Briareus, and Gyes had been hidden by their father. Cronos had bound them, weighing them down with chains. But now Zeus loosed them and the hundred-armed giants in their gratitude gave him the lightning and showed him how to use the thunderbolt.

Zeus would have the giants fight against the Titan gods. But although they had mighty strength Cottus, Briareus, and Gyes had no fire of courage in their hearts. Zeus thought of a way to give them this courage; he brought the food and drink of the gods to them, ambrosia and nectar, and when they had eaten and drunk their spirits grew within the giants, and they were ready to make war upon the Titan gods.

"Sons of Earth and Heaven," said Zeus to the hundred-armed giants, "a long time now have the Dwellers on Olympus been striving with the Titan gods. Do you lend your unconquerable might to the gods and help them to overthrow the Titans."

Cottus, the eldest of the giants, answered, "Divine One, through your devising we are come back again from the murky gloom of the mid Earth and we have escaped from the hard bonds that Cronos laid upon us. Our minds are fixed to aid you in the war against the Titan gods."

So the hundred-armed giants said, and thereupon Zeus went and he gathered around him all who were born of Cronos and Rhea. Cronos himself hid from Zeus. Then the giants, with their fifty heads growing from their shoulders and their hundred hands, went forth against the Titan gods. The boundless sea rang terribly and the earth crashed loudly; wide Heaven was shaken and groaned, and high Olympus reeled from its foundation. Holding huge rocks in their hands the giants attacked the Titan gods.

Then Zeus entered the war. He hurled the lightning; the bolts flew thick and fast from his strong hand, with thunder and lightning and flame. The earth crashed around in burning, the forests crackled with fire, the ocean seethed. And hot flames wrapped the earth-born Titans all around. Three hundred rocks, one upon another, did Cottus, Briareus, and Gyes hurl upon the Titans. And when their ranks were broken the giants seized upon them and held them for Zeus.

But some of the Titan gods, seeing that the strife for them was vain, went over to the side of Zeus. These Zeus became friendly with. But the other Titans he bound in chains and he hurled them down to Tartarus.

As far as Earth is from Heaven so is Tartarus from Earth. A brazen anvil falling down from Heaven to Earth nine days and nine nights would reach the earth upon the tenth day. And again, a brazen anvil falling from Earth nine nights and nine days would reach Tartarus upon the tenth night. Around Tartarus runs a fence of bronze and Night spreads in a triple line all about it, as a necklace circles the neck. There Zeus imprisoned the Titan gods who had fought against him; they are hidden in the misty gloom, in a dank place, at the ends of the Earth. And they may not go out, for Poseidon fixed gates of bronze upon their prison, and a wall runs all round it. There Cottus, Briareus, and Gyes stay, guarding them.

And there, too, is the home of Night. Night and Day meet each other at that place, as they pass a threshold of bronze. They draw near and they greet one another, but the house never holds them both together, for while one is about to go down into the house, the other is leaving through the door. One holds Light in her hand and the other holds in her arms Sleep.

There the children of dark Night have their dwellings— Sleep, and Death, his brother. The sun never shines upon these two. Sleep may roam over the wide earth, and come upon the sea, and he is kindly to men. But Death is not kindly, and whoever he seizes upon, him he holds fast.

There, too, stands the hall of the lord of the Underworld, Aidoneus, the brother of Zeus. Zeus gave him the Underworld to be his dominion when he shared amongst the Olympians the world that Cronos had ruled over. A fearful hound guards the hall of Aidoneus: Cerberus he is called; he has three heads. On those who go within that hall Cerberus fawns, but on those who would come out of it he springs and would devour them.

Not all the Titans did Zeus send down to Tartarus. Those of them who had wisdom joined him, and by their wisdom Zeus was able to overcome Cronos. Then Cronos went to live with the friendly Titan gods, while Zeus reigned over Olympus, becoming the ruler of gods and men.

So Orpheus sang, Orpheus who knew the ways and the histories of the gods.

VI. Polydeuces' Victory and Heracles' Loss

ALL the places that the Argonauts came nigh to and went past need not be told—Melibœa, where they escaped a stormy beach; Homole, from where they were able to look on Ossa and holy Olympus; Lemnos, the island that they were to return to; the unnamed country where the Earth-born Men abide, each having six arms, two growing from his shoulders, and four fitting close to his terrible sides; and then the Mountain of the Bears, where they climbed, to make sacrifice there to Rhea, the mighty mother of the gods.

Afterward, for a whole day, no wind blew and the sail of the *Argo* hung slack. But the heroes swore to each other that they would make their ship go as swiftly as if the storm-footed steeds of Poseidon were racing to overtake her. Mightily they labored at the oars, and no one would be first to leave his rower's bench.

And then, just as the breeze of the evening came up, and just as the rest of the heroes were leaning back, spent with their labor, the oar that Heracles still pulled at broke, and half of it was carried away by the waves. Heracles sat there in ill humor, for he did not know what to do with his unlaboring hands.

All through the night they went on with a good breeze filling their sails, and next day they came to the mouth of the River Cius. There they landed so that Heracles might get himself an oar. No sooner did they set their feet upon the shore than the hero went off into the forest, to pull up a tree that he might shape into an oar.

Where they had landed was near to the country of the Bebrycians, a rude people whose king was named Amycus. Now while Heracles was away from them this king came with his followers—huge, rude men, all armed with clubs, down to where the Argonauts were lighting their fires on the beach.

He did not greet them courteously, asking them what

manner of men they were and whither they were bound, nor did he offer them hospitality. Instead, he shouted at them insolently:

"Listen to something that you rovers had better know. I am Amycus, and any stranger that comes to this land has to get into a boxing bout with me. That's the law that I have laid down. Unless you have one amongst you who can stand up to me you won't be let go back to your ship. If you don't heed my law, look out, for something's going to happen to you."

So he shouted, that insolent king, and his followers raised their clubs and growled approval of what their master said. But the Argonauts were not dismayed at the words of Amycus. One of them stepped toward the Bebrycians. He was Polydeuces, good at boxing.

"Offer us no violence, king," said Polydeuces. "We are ready to obey the law that you have laid down. Willingly do I take up your challenge, and I will box a bout with you."

The Argonauts cheered when they saw Polydeuces, the good boxer, step forward, and when they heard what he had to say. Amycus turned and shouted to his followers, and one of them brought up two pairs of boxing gauntlets—of rough cowhide they were. The Argonauts feared that Polydeuces' hands might have been made numb with pulling at the oar, and some of them went to him, and took his hands and rubbed them to make them supple; others took from off his shoulders his beautifully colored mantle.

Amycus straightway put on his gauntlets and threw off his mantle; he stood there amongst his followers with his great arms crossed, glowering at the Argonauts as a wild beast might glower. And when the two faced each other Amycus seemed like one of the Earth-born Men, dark and hugely shaped, while Helen's brother stood there light and beautiful. Polydeuces was like that star whose beams are lovely at evening-tide.

Like the wave that breaks over a ship and gives the

Like the wave that breaks over a ship and gives the sailors no respite
Amycus came on at Polydeuces. *See page 34.*

sailors no respite Amycus came on at Polydeuces. He pushed in upon him, thinking to bear him down and overwhelm him. But as the skillful steersman keeps the ship from being overwhelmed by the monstrous wave, so Polydeuces, all skill and lightness, baffled the rushes of Amycus. At last Amycus, standing on the tips of his toes and rising high above him, tried to bring down his great fist upon the head of Polydeuces. The hero swung aside and took the blow on his shoulder. Then he struck his blow. It was a strong one, and under it the king of the Bebrycians staggered and fell down. "You see," said Polydeuces, "that we keep your law."

The Argonauts shouted, but the rude Bebrycians raised their clubs to rush upon them. Then would the heroes have been hard pressed, and forced, perhaps, to get back to the *Argo*. But suddenly Heracles appeared amongst them, coming up from the forest.

He carried a pine tree in his hands with all its branches still upon it, and seeing this mighty-statured man appear with the great tree in his hands, the Bebrycians hurried off, carrying their fallen king with them. Then the Argonauts gathered around Polydeuces, saluted him as their champion, and put a crown of victory upon his head. Heracles, meanwhile, lopped off the branches of the pine tree and began to fashion it into an oar.

The fires were lighted upon the shore, and the thoughts of all were turned to supper. Then young Hylas, who used to sit by Heracles and keep bright the hero's arms and armor, took a bronze vessel and went to fetch water.

Never was there a boy so beautiful as young Hylas. He had golden curls that tumbled over his brow. He had deep blue eyes and a face that smiled at every glance that was given him, at every word that was said to him. Now as he walked through the flowering grasses, with his knees bare, and with the bright vessel swinging in his hand, he looked most lovely. Heracles had brought the boy with him from the country of the Dryopians; he would have him sit beside him on the bench of the *Argo,* and the ill humors that often came upon him would go at the words and the smile of Hylas.

Now the spring that Hylas was going toward was called Pegæ, and it was haunted by the nymphs. They were dancing around it when they heard Hylas singing. They stole softly off to watch him. Hidden behind trees the nymphs saw the boy come near, and they felt such love for him that they thought they could never let him go from their sight.

They stole back to their spring, and they sank down below its clear surface. Then came Hylas singing a song that he had heard from his mother. He bent down to the spring, and the brimming water flowed into the sounding bronze of the pitcher. Then hands came out of the water. One of the nymphs caught Hylas by the elbow; another put her arms around his neck, another took the hand that held the vessel of bronze. The pitcher sank down to the depths of the spring. The hands of the nymphs clasped Hylas tighter, tighter; the water bubbled around him as they drew him down. Down, down they drew him, and into the cold and glimmering cave where they live.

There Hylas stayed. But although the nymphs kissed him and sang to him, and showed him lovely things, Hylas was not content to be there.

Where the Argonauts were the fires burned, the moon arose, and still Hylas did not return. Then they began to fear lest a wild beast had destroyed the boy. One went to Heracles and told him that young Hylas had not come back, and that they were fearful for him. Heracles flung down the pine tree that he was fashioning into an oar, and he dashed along the way that Hylas had gone as if a gadfly were stinging him. "Hylas, Hylas," he cried. But Hylas, in the cold and glimmering cave that the nymphs had drawn him into, did not hear the call of his friend Heracles.

All the Argonauts went searching, calling as they went through the island, "Hylas, Hylas, Hylas!" But only their own calls came back to them. The morning star came up, and Tiphys, the steersman, called to them from the *Argo*. And when they came to the ship Tiphys told them that they would have to go aboard and make ready to sail from that place.

They called to Heracles, and Heracles at last came down to the ship. They spoke to him, saying that they would have to sail away. Heracles would not go on board. "I will not leave this island," he said, "until I find young Hylas or learn what has happened to him."

Then Jason arose to give the command to depart. But before the words were said Telamon stood up and faced him. "Jason," he said angrily, "you do not bid Heracles come on board, and you would have the *Argo* leave without him. You would leave Heracles here so that he may not be with us on the quest where his glory might overshadow your glory, Jason."

Jason said no word, but he sat back on his bench with head bowed. And then, even as Telamon said these angry words, a strange figure rose up out of the waves of the sea.

It was the figure of a man, wrinkled and old, with seaweed in his beard and his hair. There was a majesty about him, and the Argonauts all knew that this was one of the immortals—he was Nereus, the ancient one of the sea.

"To Heracles, and to you, the rest of the Argonauts, I have a thing to say," said the ancient one, Nereus. "Know, first, that Hylas has been taken by the nymphs who love him and who think to win his love, and that he will stay forever with them in their cold and glimmering cave. For Hylas seek no more. And to you, Heracles, I will say this: Go aboard the *Argo* again; the ship will take you to where a great labor awaits you, and which, in accomplishing, you will work out the will of Zeus. You will know what this labor is when a spirit seizes on you." So the ancient one of the sea said, and he sank back beneath the waves.

Heracles went aboard the *Argo* once more, and he took his place on the bench, the new oar in his hand. Sad he was to think that young Hylas who used to sit at his knee would never be there again. The breeze filled the sail, the Argonauts pulled at the oars, and in sadness they watched the island where young Hylas had been lost to them recede from their view.

VII. King Phineus

SAID Tiphys, the steersman: "If we could enter the Sea of Pontus, we could make our way across that sea to Colchis in a short time. But the passage into the Sea of Pontus is most perilous, and few mortals dare even to make approach to it."

Said Jason, the chieftain of the host: "The dangers of the passage, Tiphys, we have spoken of, and it may be that we shall have to carry *Argo* overland to the Sea of Pontus. But you, Tiphys, have spoken of a wise king who is hereabouts, and who might help us to make the dangerous passage. Speak again to us, and tell us what the dangers of the passage are, and who the king is who may be able to help us to make these dangers less."

Then said Tiphys, the steersman of the *Argo*: "No ship sailed by mortals has as yet gone through the passage that brings this sea into the Sea of Pontus. In the way are the rocks that mariners call The Clashers. These rocks are not fixed as rocks should be, but they rush one against the other, dashing up the sea, and crushing whatever may be between. Yea, if *Argo* were of iron, and if she were between these rocks when they met, she would be crushed to bits. I have sailed as far as that passage, but seeing The Clashers strike together I turned back my ship, and journeyed as far as the Sea of Pontus overland.

"But I have been told of one who knows how a ship may be taken through the passage that The Clashers make so perilous. He who knows is a king hereabouts, Phineus, who has made himself as wise as the gods. To no one has

Phineus told how the passage may be made, but knowing
what high favor has been shown to us, the Argonauts, it
may be that he will tell us."

So Tiphys said, and Jason commanded him to steer the
Argo toward the city where ruled Phineus, the wise king.

To Salmydessus, then, where Phineus ruled, Tiphys
steered the *Argo*. They left Heracles with Tiphys aboard
to guard the ship, and, with the rest of the heroes, Jason
went through the streets of the city. They met many men,
but when they asked any of them how they might come to
the palace of King Phineus the men turned fearfully away.

They found their way to the king's palace. Jason spoke
to the servants and bade them tell the king of their coming. The servants, too, seemed fearful, and as Jason and
his comrades were wondering what there was about him
that made men fearful at his name, Phineus, the king,
came amongst them.

Were it not that he had a purple border to his robe no
one would have known him for the king, so miserable did
this man seem. He crept along, touching the walls, for the
eyes in his head were blind and withered. His body was
shrunken, and when he stood before them leaning on his
staff he was like to a lifeless thing. He turned his blinded
eyes upon them, looking from one to the other as if he
were searching for a face.

Then his sightless eyes rested upon Zetes and Calais,
the sons of Boreas, the North Wind. A change came into
his face as it turned upon them. One would think that he
saw the wonder that these two were endowed with—the
wings that grew upon their ankles. It was a while before he
turned his face from them; then he spoke to Jason and
said:

"You have come to have counsel with one who has the
wisdom of the gods. Others before you have come for
such counsel, but seeing the misery that is visible upon
me they went without asking for counsel. I would strive to
hold you here for a while. Stay, and have sight of the mis-

ery the gods visit upon those who would be as wise as they. And when you have seen the thing that is wont to befall me, it may be that help will come from you for me."

Then Phineus, the blind king, left them, and after a while the heroes were brought into a great hall, and they were invited to rest themselves there while a banquet was being prepared for them.

The hall was richly adorned, but it looked to the heroes as if it had known strange happenings; rich hangings were strewn upon the ground, an ivory chair was overturned, and the dais where the king sat had stains upon it. The servants who went through the hall making ready the banquet were white-faced and fearful.

The feast was laid on a great table, and the heroes were invited to sit down to it. The king did not come into the hall before they sat down, but a table with food was set before the dais. When the heroes had feasted, the king came into the hall. He sat at the table, blind, white-faced, and shrunken, and the Argonauts all turned their faces to him.

Said Phineus, the blind king: "You see, O heroes, how much my wisdom avails me. You see me blind and shrunken, who tried to make myself in wisdom equal to the gods. And yet you have not seen all. Watch now and see what feasts Phineus, the wise king, has to delight him."

He made a sign, and the white-faced and trembling servants brought food and set it upon the table that was before him. The king bent forward as if to eat, and they saw that his face was covered with the damp of fear. He took food from the dish and raised it to his mouth. As he did, the doors of the hall were flung open as if by a storm. Strange shapes flew into the hall and set themselves beside the king. And when the Argonauts looked upon them they saw that these were terrible and unsightly shapes.

They were things that had the wings and claws of birds and the heads of women. Black hair and gray feathers

They were things that had the wings and claws of birds
and the heads of women. . . . And as the king raised the food to his
mouth they flew at him and buffeted his head with their wings,
and snatched the food from his hands. *See page 41.*

were mixed upon them; they had red eyes, and streaks of blood were upon their breasts and wings. And as the king raised the food to his mouth they flew at him and buffeted his head with their wings, and snatched the food from his hands. Then they devoured or scattered what was upon the table, and all the time they screamed and laughed and mocked.

"Ah, now ye see," Phineus panted, "what it is to have wisdom equal to the wisdom of the gods. Now ye all see my misery. Never do I strive to put food to my lips but these foul things, the Harpies, the Snatchers, swoop down and scatter or devour what I would eat. Crumbs they leave me that my life may not altogether go from me, but these crumbs they make foul to my taste and my smell."

And one of the Harpies perched herself on the back of the king's throne and looked upon the heroes with red eyes. "Hah," she screamed, "you bring armed men into your feasting hall, thinking to scare us away. Never, Phineus, can you scare us from you! Always you will have us, the Snatchers, beside you when you would still your ache of hunger. What can these men do against us who are winged and who can travel through the ways of the air?"

So said the unsightly Harpy, and the heroes drew together, made fearful by these awful shapes. All drew back except Zetes and Calais, the sons of the North Wind. They laid their hands upon their swords. The wings on their shoulders spread out and the wings at their heels trembled. Phineus, the king, leaned forward and panted: "By the wisdom I have I know that there are two amongst you who can save me. O make haste to help me, ye who can help me, and I will give the counsel that you Argonauts have come to me for, and besides I will load down your ship with treasure and costly stuffs. Oh, make haste, ye who can help me!"

Hearing the king speak like this, the Harpies gathered together and gnashed with their teeth, and chattered to one another. Then, seeing Zetes and Calais with their hands upon their swords, they rose up on their wings and flew through the wide doors of the hall. The king cried out to Zetes and Calais. But the sons of the North Wind had already risen with their wings, and they were after the Harpies, their bright swords in their hands.

On flew the Harpies, screeching and gnashing their teeth in anger and dismay, for now they felt that they might be driven from Salmydessus, where they had had such royal feasts. They rose high in the air and flew out toward the sea. But high as the Harpies rose, the sons of the North Wind rose higher. The Harpies cried pitiful cries as they flew on, but Zetes and Calais felt no pity for them, for they knew that these dread Snatchers, with the stains of blood upon their breasts and wings, had shown pity neither to Phineus nor to any other.

On they flew until they came to the island that is called the Floating Island. There the Harpies sank down with wearied wings. Zetes and Calais were upon them now, and they would have cut them to pieces with their bright swords, if the messenger of Zeus, Iris, with the golden wings, had not come between.

"Forbear to slay the Harpies, sons of Boreas," cried Iris warningly, "forbear to slay the Harpies that are the hounds of Zeus. Let them cower here and hide themselves, and I, who come from Zeus, will swear the oath that the gods most dread, that they will never again come to Salmydessus to trouble Phineus, the king."

The heroes yielded to the words of Iris. She took the oath that the gods most dread—the oath by the Water of Styx—that never again would the Harpies show themselves to Phineus. Then Zetes and Calais turned back toward the city of Salmydessus. The island that they drove the Harpies to had been called the Floating Island, but thereafter it was called the Island of Turning. It was evening when they turned back, and all night long the Argonauts and King Phineus sat in the hall of the palace and awaited the return of Zetes and Calais, the sons of the North Wind.

VIII. King Phineus's Counsel; the Landing in Lemnos

THEY came into King Phineus's hall, their bright swords in their hands. The Argonauts crowded around them and King Phineus raised his head and stretched out his thin hands to them. And Zetes and Calais told their comrades and told the king how they had driven the Harpies down to the Floating Island, and how Iris, the messenger of Zeus, had sworn the great oath that was by the Water of Styx that never again would the Snatchers show themselves in the palace.

Then a great golden cup brimming with wine was brought to the king. He stood holding it in his trembling hands, fearful even then that the Harpies would tear the cup out of his hands. He drank—long and deeply he drank—and the dread shapes of the Snatchers did not appear. Down amongst the heroes he came and he took into his the hands of Zetes and Calais, the sons of the North Wind.

"O heroes greater than any kings," he said, "ye have delivered me from the terrible curse that the gods had sent upon me. I thank ye, and I thank ye all, heroes of the quest. And the thanks of Phineus will much avail you all."

Clasping the hands of Zetes and Calais he led the heroes through hall after hall of his palace and down into his treasure chamber. There he bestowed upon the banishers of the Harpies crowns and arm rings of gold and richly colored garments and brazen chests in which to store the treasure that he gave. And to Jason he gave an ivory-hilted and golden-cased sword, and on each of the voyagers he bestowed a rich gift, not forgetting the heroes who had remained on the *Argo,* Heracles and Tiphys.

They went back to the great hall, and a feast was spread for the king and for the Argonauts. They ate from rich dishes and they drank from flowing wine cups. Phineus ate and drank as the heroes did, and no dread shapes came before him to snatch from him nor to buffet him. But as Jason looked upon the man who had striven to equal the gods in wisdom, and noted his blinded eyes and shrunken face, he resolved never to harbor in his heart such presumption as Phineus had harbored.

When the feast was finished the king spoke to Jason, telling him how the *Argo* might be guided through the Symplegades, the dread passage into the Sea of Pontus. He told them to bring their ship near to the Clashing Rocks. And one who had the keenest sight amongst them was to stand at the prow of the ship holding a pigeon in his hands. As the rocks came together he was to loose the pigeon. If it found a space to fly through they would know that the *Argo* could make the passage, and they were to steer straight toward where the pigeon had flown. But if it fluttered down to the sea, or flew back to them, or became lost in the clouds of spray, they were to know that the *Argo* might not make that passage. Then the heroes would have to take their ship overland to where they might reach the Sea of Pontus.

That day they bade farewell to Phineus, and with the treasures he had bestowed upon them they went down to the *Argo*. To Heracles and Tiphys they gave the presents that the king had sent them. In the morning they drew the *Argo* out of the harbor of Salmydessus, and set sail again.

But not until long afterward did they come to the Symplegades, the passage that was to be their great trial. For they landed first in a country that was full of woods, where they were welcomed by a king who had heard of the voyagers and of their quest. There they stayed and hunted for many days in the woods. And there a great loss befell the Argonauts, for Tiphys, as he went through the woods, was bitten by a snake and died. He who had braved so many seas and so many storms lost his life away from the ship. The Argonauts made a tomb for him on the shore of that land—a great pile of stones, in which they fixed upright his steering oar. Then they set sail again, and Nauplius was made the steersman of the ship.

The course was not so clear to Nauplius as it had been to Tiphys. The steersman did not find his bearings, and for many days and nights the *Argo* was driven on a backward course. They came to an island that they knew to be that Island of Lemnos that they had passed on the first days of the voyage, and they resolved to rest there for a while, and then to press on for the passage into the Sea of Pontus.

They brought the *Argo* near the shore. They blew trumpets and set the loudest voiced of the heroes to call out to those upon the island. But no answer came to them, and all day the *Argo* lay close to the island.

There were hidden people watching them, people with bows in their hands and arrows laid along the bowstrings. And the people who thus threatened the unknowing Argonauts were women and young girls.

There were no men upon the Island of Lemnos. Years before a curse had fallen upon the people of that island, putting strife between the men and the women. And the women had mastered the men and had driven them away from Lemnos. Since then some of the women had grown old, and the girls who were children when their fathers and brothers had been banished were now of an age with Atalanta, the maiden who went with the Argonauts.

They chased the wild beasts of the island, and they tilled the fields, and they kept in good repair the houses that were built before the banishing of the men. The older women served those who were younger, and they had a queen, a girl whose name was Hypsipyle.

The women who watched with bows in their hands would have shot their arrows at the Argonauts if Hypsipyle's nurse, Polyxo, had not stayed them. She forbade them to shoot at the strangers until she had brought to them the queen's commands.

She hastened to the palace and she found the young

queen weaving at a loom. She told her about the ship and the strangers on board the ship, and she asked the queen what word she should bring to the guardian maidens.

"Before you give a command, Hypsipyle," said Polyxo, the nurse, "consider these words of mine. We, the elder women, are becoming ancient now; in a few years we will not be able to serve you, the younger women, and in a few years more we will have gone into the grave and our places will know us no more. And you, the younger women, will be becoming strengthless, and no more will be you able to hunt in the woods nor to till the fields, and a hard old age will be before you.

"The ship that is beside our shore may have come at a good time. Those on board are goodly heroes. Let them land in Lemnos, and stay if they will. Let them wed with the younger women so that there may be husbands and wives, helpers and helpmeets, again in Lemnos."

Hypsipyle, the queen, let the shuttle fall from her hands and stayed for a while looking full into Polyxo's face. Had her nurse heard her say something like this out of her dreams, she wondered? She bade the nurse tell the guardian maidens to let the heroes land in safety, and that she herself would put the crown of King Thoas, her father, upon her head, and go down to the shore to welcome them.

And now the Argonauts saw people along the shore and they caught sight of women's dresses. The loudest voiced amongst them shouted again, and they heard an answer given in a woman's voice. They drew up the *Argo* upon the shore, and they set foot upon the land of Lemnos.

Jason stepped forth at the head of his comrades, and he was met by Hypsipyle, her father's crown upon her head, at the head of her maidens. They greeted each other, and Hypsipyle bade the heroes come with them to their town that was called Myrine and to the palace that was there.

Wonderingly the Argonauts went, looking on women's forms and faces and seeing no men. They came to the palace and went within. Hypsipyle mounted the stone throne that was King Thoas's and the four maidens who were her guards stood each side of her. She spoke to the heroes in greeting and bade them stay in peace for as long as they would. She told them of the curse that had fallen upon the people of Lemnos, and of how the menfolk had been banished. Jason, then, told the queen what voyage he and his companions were upon and what quest they were making. Then in friendship the Argonauts and the women of Lemnos stayed together—all the Argonauts except Heracles, and he, grieving still for Hylas, stayed aboard the *Argo*.

IX. The Lemnian Maidens

AND now the Argonauts were no longer on a ship that was being dashed on by the sea and beaten upon by the winds. They had houses to live in; they had honey-tasting things to eat, and when they went through the island each man might have with him one of the maidens of Lemnos. It was a change that was welcome to the wearied voyagers.

They helped the women in the work of the fields; they hunted the beasts with them, and over and over again they were surprised at how skillfully the women had ordered all affairs. Everything in Lemnos was strange to the Argonauts, and they stayed day after day, thinking each day a fresh adventure.

Sometimes they would leave the fields and the chase, and this hero or that hero, with her who was his friend amongst the Lemnian maidens, would go far into that strange land and look upon lakes that were all covered with golden and silver water lilies, or would gather the blue flowers from creepers that grew around dark trees, or would hide themselves so that they might listen to the quick-moving birds that sang in the thickets. Perhaps on their way homeward they would see the *Argo* in the harbor, and they would think of Heracles who was aboard, and they would call to him. But the ship and the voyage they had been on now seemed far away to them, and the Quest of the Golden Fleece seemed to them a story they had heard and that they had thought of, but that they could never think on again with all that fervor.

When Jason looked on Hypsipyle he saw one who seemed to him to be only childlike in size. Greatly was he amazed at the words that poured forth from her as she stood at the stone throne of King Thoas—he was amazed as one is amazed at the rush of rich notes that comes from the throat of a little bird; all that she said was made lightninglike by her eyes—her eyes that were not clear and quiet like the eyes of the maidens he had seen in Iolcus, but that were dark and burning. Her mouth was heavy and this heavy mouth gave a shadow to her face that but for it was all bright and lovely.

Hypsipyle spoke two languages—one, the language of the mothers of the women of Lemnos, which was rough and harsh, a speech to be flung out to slaves, and the other the language of Greece, which their fathers had spoken, and which Hypsipyle spoke in a way that made it sound like strange music. She spoke and walked and did all things in a queenlike way, and Jason could see that, for all her youth and childlike size, Hypsipyle was one who was a ruler.

From the moment she took his hand it seemed that she could not bear to be away from him. Where he walked, she walked too; where he sat she sat before him, looking at him with her great eyes while she laughed or sang.

Like the perfume of strange flowers, like the savor of strange fruit was Hypsipyle to Jason. Hours and hours he would spend sitting beside her or watching her while she arrayed herself in white or in brightly colored garments. Not to the chase and not into the fields did Jason go, nor did he ever go with the others into the Lemnian land; all

. . . all day he sat in the palace with her, watching her,
or listening to her singing. . . *See page 50.*

day he sat in the palace with her, watching her, or listening to her singing, or to the long, fierce speeches that she used to make to her nurse or to the four maidens who attended her.

In the evening they would gather in the hall of the palace, the Argonauts and the Lemnian maidens who were their comrades. There were dances, and always Jason and Hypsipyle danced together. All the Lemnian maidens sang beautifully, but none of them had any stories to tell.

And when the Argonauts would have stories told the Lemnian maidens would forbid any tale that was about a god or a hero; only stories that were about the goddesses or about some maiden would they let be told.

Orpheus, who knew the histories of the gods, would have told them many stories, but the only story of his that they would come from the dance to listen to was a story of the goddesses, of Demeter and her daughter Persephone.

DEMETER AND PERSEPHONE

I

Once when Demeter was going through the world, giving men grain to be sown in their fields, she heard a cry that came to her from across high mountains and that mounted up to her from the sea. Demeter's heart shook when she heard that cry, for she knew that it came to her from her daughter, from her only child, young Persephone.

She stayed not to bless the fields in which the grain was being sown, but she hurried, hurried away, to Sicily and to the fields of Enna, where she had left Persephone. All Enna she searched, and all Sicily, but she found no trace of Persephone, nor of the maidens whom Persephone had been playing with. From all whom she met she begged for tidings, but although some had seen maidens gathering flowers and playing together, no one could tell Demeter why her child had cried out nor where she had since gone to.

There were some who could have told her. One was Cyane, a water nymph. But Cyane, before Demeter came to her, had been changed into a spring of water. And now, not being able to speak and tell Demeter where her child had gone to and who had carried her away, she showed in the water the girdle of Persephone that she had caught in her hands. And Demeter, finding the girdle of her child in the spring, knew that she had been carried off by violence. She lighted a torch at Ætna's burning mountain, and for nine days and nine nights she went searching for her through the darkened places of the earth.

Then, upon a high and a dark hill, the Goddess Demeter came face to face with Hecate, the Moon. Hecate, too, had heard the cry of Persephone; she had sorrow for Demeter's sorrow: she spoke to her as the two stood upon that dark, high hill, and told her that she should go to Helios for tidings—to bright Helios, the watcher for the gods, and beg Helios to tell her who it was who had carried off by violence her child Persephone.

Demeter came to Helios. He was standing before his shining steeds, before the impatient steeds that draw the sun through the course of the heavens. Demeter stood in the way of those impatient steeds; she begged of Helios who sees all things upon the earth to tell her who it was had carried off by violence Persephone, her child.

And Helios, who may make no concealment, said: "Queenly Demeter, know that the king of the Underworld, dark Aidoneus, has carried off Persephone to make her his queen in the realm that I never shine upon." He spoke, and as he did, his horses shook their manes and breathed out fire, impatient to be gone. Helios sprang into his chariot and went flashing away.

Demeter, knowing that one of the gods had carried off Persephone against her will, and knowing that what was done had been done by the will of Zeus, would go no more into the assemblies of the gods. She quenched the torch that she had held in her hands for nine days and nine nights; she put off her robe of goddess, and she went wandering over the earth, uncomforted for the loss of her child. And no longer did she appear as a gracious goddess to men; no longer did she give them grain; no longer did she bless their fields. None of the things that it had pleased her once to do would Demeter do any longer.

II

Persephone had been playing with the nymphs who are the daughters of Ocean—Phæno, Ianthe, Melita, Ianeira, Acaste—in the lovely fields of Enna. They went to gather flowers—irises and crocuses, lilies, narcissus, hyacinths and roseblooms—that grow in those fields. As they went, gathering flowers in their baskets, they had sight of Pergus, the pool that the white swans come to sing in.

Beside a deep chasm that had been made in the earth a wonder flower was growing—in color it was like the crocus, but it sent forth a perfume that was like the perfume of a hundred flowers. And Persephone thought as she went toward it that having gathered that flower she would have something much more wonderful than her companions had.

She did not know that Aidoneus, the lord of the Underworld, had caused that flower to grow there so that she might be drawn by it to the chasm that he had made.

As Persephone stooped to pluck the wonder flower, Aidoneus, in his chariot of iron, dashed up through the chasm, and grasping the maiden by the waist, set her beside him. Only Cyane, the nymph, tried to save Persephone, and it was then that she caught the girdle in her hands.

The maiden cried out, first because her flowers had been spilled, and then because she was being reft away. She cried out to her mother, and her cry went over high mountains and sounded up from the sea. The daughters of Ocean, affrighted, fled and sank down into the depths of the sea.

In his great chariot of iron that was drawn by black steeds Aidoneus rushed down through the chasm he had made. Into the Underworld he went, and he dashed across the River Styx, and he brought his chariot up beside his throne. And on his dark throne he seated Persephone, the fainting daughter of Demeter.

III

No more did the Goddess Demeter give grain to men; no more did she bless their fields: weeds grew where grain had been growing, and men feared that in a while they would famish for lack of bread.

She wandered through the world, her thought all upon her child, Persephone, who had been taken from her. Once she sat by a well by a wayside, thinking upon the child that she might not come to and who might not come to her.

She saw four maidens come near; their grace and their youth reminded her of her child. They stepped lightly along, carrying bronze pitchers in their hands, for they were coming to the Well of the Maiden beside which Demeter sat.

The maidens thought when they looked upon her that the goddess was some ancient woman who had a sorrow in her heart. Seeing that she was so noble and so sorrowful looking, the maidens, as they drew the clear water into their pitchers, spoke kindly to her.

"Why do you stay away from the town, old mother?" one of the maidens said. "Why do you not come to the houses? We think that you look as if you were shelterless and alone, and we should like to tell you that there are many houses in the town where you would be welcomed."

Demeter's heart went out to the maidens, because they looked so young and fair and simple and spoke out of such kind hearts. She said to them: "Where can I go, dear children? My people are far away, and there are none in all the world who would care to be near me."

Said one of the maidens: "There are princes in the land

who would welcome you in their houses if you would consent to nurse one of their young children. But why do I speak of other princes beside Celeus, our father? In his house you would indeed have a welcome. But lately a baby has been born to our mother, Metaneira, and she would greatly rejoice to have one as wise as you mind little Demophoön."

All the time that she watched them and listened to their voices Demeter felt that the grace and youth of the maidens made them like Persephone. She thought that it would ease her heart to be in the house where these maidens were, and she was not loath to have them go and ask of their mother to have her come to nurse the infant child.

Swiftly they ran back to their home, their hair streaming behind them like crocus flowers; kind and lovely girls whose names are well remembered—Callidice and Cleisidice, Demo and Callithoë. They went to their mother and they told her of the stranger-woman whose name was Doso. She would make a wise and a kind nurse for little Demophoön, they said. Their mother, Metaneira, rose up from the couch she was sitting on to welcome the stranger. But when she saw her at the doorway, awe came over her, so majestic she seemed.

Metaneira would have her seat herself on the couch but the goddess took the lowliest stool, saying in greeting: "May the gods give you all good, lady."

"Sorrow has set you wandering from your good home," said Metaneira to the goddess, "but now that you have come to this place you shall have all that this house can bestow if you will rear up to youth the infant Demophoön, child of many hopes and prayers."

The child was put into the arms of Demeter; she clasped him to her breast, and little Demophoön looked up into her face and smiled. Then Demeter's heart went out to the child and to all who were in the household.

He grew in strength and beauty in her charge. And little Demophoön was not nourished as other children are

But one night Metaneira looked out from the chamber where she lay, and she saw the nurse take little Demophoön and lay him in a place on the hearth with the burning brands all around him. *See page 58.*

nourished, but even as the gods in their childhood were nourished. Demeter fed him on ambrosia, breathing on him with her divine breath the while. And at night she laid him on the hearth, amongst the embers, with the fire all around him. This she did that she might make him immortal, and like to the gods.

But one night Metaneira looked out from the chamber where she lay, and she saw the nurse take little Demophoön and lay him in a place on the hearth with the burning brands all around him. Then Metaneira started up, and she sprang to the hearth, and she snatched the child from beside the burning brands. "Demophoön, my son," she cried, "what would this stranger-woman do to you, bringing bitter grief to me that ever I let her take you in her arms?"

Then said Demeter: "Foolish indeed are you mortals, and not able to foresee what is to come to you of good or of evil! Foolish indeed are you, Metaneira, for in your heedlessness you have cut off this child from an immortality like to the immortality of the gods themselves. For he had lain in my bosom and had become dear to me and I would have bestowed upon him the greatest gift that the Divine Ones can bestow, for I would have made him deathless and unaging. All this, now, has gone by. Honor he shall have indeed, but Demophoön will know age and death."

The seeming old age that was upon her had fallen from Demeter; beauty and stature were hers, and from her robe there came a heavenly fragrance. There came such light from her body that the chamber shone. Metaneira remained trembling and speechless, unmindful even to take up the child that had been laid upon the ground.

It was then that his sisters heard Demophoön wail; one ran from her chamber and took the child in her arms; another kindled again the fire upon the hearth, and the others made ready to bathe and care for the infant. All night they cared for him, holding him in their arms and at their breasts, but the child would not be comforted, because

But still she kept away from the assemblies of the gods.
Zeus sent a messenger to her, Iris with the golden wings,
bidding her to Olympus. *See page 60.*

the nurses who handled him now were less skillful than was the goddess-nurse.

And as for Demeter, she left the house of Celeus and went upon her way, lonely in her heart, and unappeased. And in the world that she wandered through, the plow went in vain through the ground; the furrow was sown without any avail, and the race of men saw themselves near perishing for lack of bread.

But again Demeter came near the Well of the Maiden. She thought of the daughters of Celeus as they came toward the well that day, the bronze pitchers in their hands, and with kind looks for the stranger—she thought of them as she sat by the well again. And then she thought of little Demophoön, the child she had held at her breast. No stir of living was in the land near their home, and only weeds grew in their fields. As she sat there and looked around her there came into Demeter's heart a pity for the people in whose house she had dwelt.

She rose up and she went to the house of Celeus. She found him beside his house measuring out a little grain. The goddess went to him and she told him that because of the love she bore his household she would bless his fields so that the seed he had sown in them would come to growth. Celeus rejoiced, and he called all the people together, and they raised a temple to Demeter. She went through the fields and blessed them, and the seed that they had sown began to grow. And the goddess for a while dwelt amongst that people, in her temple at Eleusis.

IV

But still she kept away from the assemblies of the gods. Zeus sent a messenger to her, Iris with the golden wings, bidding her to Olympus. Demeter would not join the Olympians. Then, one after the other, the gods and goddesses of Olympus came to her; none were able to make her cease from grieving for Persephone, or to go again into the company of the immortal gods.

And so it came about that Zeus was compelled to send

a messenger down to the Underworld to bring Persephone back to the mother who grieved so much for the
loss of her. Hermes was the messenger whom Zeus sent.
Through the darkened places of the earth Hermes went,
and he came to that dark throne where the lord Aidoneus
sat, with Persephone beside him. Then Hermes spoke to
the lord of the Underworld, saying that Zeus commanded
that Persephone should come forth from the Underworld
that her mother might look upon her.

Then Persephone, hearing the words of Zeus that might
not be gainsaid, uttered the only cry that had left her lips
since she had sent out that cry that had reached her
mother's heart. And Aidoneus, hearing the command of
Zeus that might not be denied, bowed his dark, majestic
head.

She might go to the Upperworld and rest herself in the
arms of her mother, he said. And then he cried out: "Ah,
Persephone, strive to feel kindliness in your heart toward
me who carried you off by violence and against your will.
I can give to you one of the great kingdoms that the
Olympians rule over. And I, who am brother to Zeus, am
no unfitting husband for you, Demeter's child."

So Aidoneus, the dark lord of the Underworld said, and
he made ready the iron chariot with its deathless horses
that Persephone might go up from his kingdom.

Beside the single tree in his domain Aidoneus stayed
the chariot. A single fruit grew on that tree, a bright pomegranate fruit. Persephone stood up in the chariot and
plucked the fruit from the tree. Then did Aidoneus prevail
upon her to divide the fruit, and, having divided it, Persephone ate seven of the pomegranate seeds.

It was Hermes who took the whip and the reins of the
chariot. He drove on, and neither the sea nor the water-
courses, nor the glens nor the mountain peaks stayed the
deathless horses of Aidoneus, and soon the chariot was
brought near to where Demeter awaited the coming of her
daughter.

And when, from a hilltop, Demeter saw the chariot ap-

A single fruit grew on that tree, a bright pomegranate fruit.
Persephone stood up in the chariot and plucked the fruit
from the tree. *See page 61.*

proaching, she flew like a wild bird to clasp her child. Persephone, when she saw her mother's dear eyes, sprang out of the chariot and fell upon her neck and embraced her. Long and long Demeter held her dear child in her arms, gazing, gazing upon her. Suddenly her mind misgave her. With a great fear at her heart she cried out: "Dearest, has any food passed your lips in all the time you have been in the Underworld?"

She had not tasted food in all the time she was there, Persephone said. And then, suddenly, she remembered the pomegranate that Aidoneus had asked her to divide. When she told that she had eaten seven seeds from it Demeter wept, and her tears fell upon Persephone's face.

"Ah, my dearest," she cried, "if you had not eaten the pomegranate seeds you could have stayed with me, and always we should have been together. But now that you have eaten food in it, the Underworld has a claim upon you. You may not stay always with me here. Again you will have to go back and dwell in the dark places under the earth and sit upon Aidoneus's throne. But not always you will be there. When the flowers bloom upon the earth you shall come up from the realm of darkness, and in great joy we shall go through the world together, Demeter and Persephone."

And so it has been since Persephone came back to her mother after having eaten of the pomegranate seeds. For two seasons of the year she stays with Demeter, and for one season she stays in the Underworld with her dark lord. While she is with her mother there is springtime upon the earth. Demeter blesses the furrows, her heart being glad because her daughter is with her once more. The furrows become heavy with grain, and soon the whole wide earth has grain and fruit, leaves and flowers. When the furrows are reaped, when the grain has been gathered, when the dark season comes, Persephone goes from her mother, and going down into the dark places, she sits beside her mighty lord Aidoneus and upon his throne. Not sorrowful is she there; she sits with head unbowed, for she knows herself to be a mighty queen. She has joy, too, knowing of the seasons when she may walk with Demeter, her mother, on the wide places of the earth, through fields of flowers and fruit and ripening grain.

Such was the story that Orpheus told—Orpheus who knew the histories of the gods.

A day came when the heroes, on their way back from a journey they had made with the Lemnian maidens, called out to Heracles upon the *Argo*. Then Heracles, standing on the prow of the ship, shouted angrily to them. Terrible did he seem to the Lemnian maidens, and they ran off, drawing the heroes with them. Heracles shouted to his comrades again, saying that if they did not come aboard the *Argo* and make ready for the voyage to Colchis, he would go ashore and carry them to the ship, and force them again to take the oars in their hands. Not all of what Heracles said did the Argonauts hear.

That evening the men were silent in Hypsipyle's hall, and it was Atalanta, the maiden, who told the evening's story.

ATALANTA'S RACE

There are two Atalantas, she said; she herself, the Huntress, and another who is noted for her speed of foot and her delight in the race—the daughter of Schœneus, King of Bœotia, Atalanta of the Swift Foot.

So proud was she of her swiftness that she made a vow to the gods that none would be her husband except the youth who won past her in the race. Youth after youth came and raced against her, but Atalanta, who grew fleeter and fleeter of foot, left each one of them far behind her. The youths who came to the race were so many and the clamor they made after defeat was so great, that her father made a law that, as he thought, would lessen their number. The law that he made was that the youth who came to race against Atalanta and who lost the race should lose his life into the bargain. After that the youths who had care for their lives stayed away from Bœotia.

Once there came a youth from a far part of Greece into the country that Atalanta's father ruled over. Hippomenes was his name. He did not know of the race, but having come into the city and seeing the crowd of people, he went with them to the course. He looked upon the youths who were girded for the race, and he heard the folk say amongst themselves, "Poor youths, as mighty and as high-spirited as they look, by sunset the life will be out of each of them, for Atalanta will run past them as she ran past the others." Then Hippomenes spoke to the folk in wonder, and they told him of Atalanta's race and of what would befall the youths who were defeated in it. "Unlucky youths," cried Hippomenes, "how foolish they are to try to win a bride at the price of their lives."

Then, with pity in his heart, he watched the youths prepare for the race. Atalanta had not yet taken her place, and he was fearful of looking upon her. "She is a witch," he said to himself, "she must be a witch to draw so many youths to their deaths, and she, no doubt, will show in her face and figure the witch's spirit."

But even as he said this, Hippomenes saw Atalanta. She stood with the youths before they crouched for the first dart in the race. He saw that she was a girl of a light and a lovely form. Then they crouched for the race; then the trumpets rang out, and the youths and the maiden darted like swallows over the sand of the course.

On came Atalanta, far, far ahead of the youths who had started with her. Over her bare shoulders her hair streamed, blown backward by the wind that met her flight. Her fair neck shone, and her little feet were like flying doves. It seemed to Hippomenes as he watched her that there was fire in her lovely body. On and on she went as swift as the arrow that the Scythian shoots from his bow. And as he watched the race he was not sorry that the youths were being left behind. Rather would he have been enraged if one came near overtaking her, for now his heart was set upon winning her for his bride, and he cursed himself for not having entered the race.

She passed the last goal mark and she was given the victor's wreath of flowers. Hippomenes stood and watched her and he did not see the youths who had started with her—they had thrown themselves on the ground in their despair.

Then wild, as though he were one of the doomed youths, Hippomenes made his way through the throng and came before the black-bearded King of Bœotia. The king's brows were knit, for even then he was pronouncing doom upon the youths who had been left behind in the race. He looked upon Hippomenes, another youth who would make the trial, and the frown became heavier upon his face.

But Hippomenes saw only Atalanta. She came beside her father; the wreath was upon her head of gold, and her eyes were wide and tender. She turned her face to him, and then she knew by the wildness that was in his look that he had come to enter the race with her. Then the flush that was on her face died away, and she shook her head as if she were imploring him to go from that place.

The dark-bearded king bent his brows upon him and said, "Speak, O youth, speak and tell us what brings you here."

Then cried Hippomenes as if his whole life were bursting out with his words: "Why does this maiden, your daughter, seek an easy renown by conquering weakly youths in the race? She has not striven yet. Here stand I, one of the blood of Poseidon, the god of the sea. Should I be defeated by her in the race, then, indeed, might Atalanta have something to boast of."

Atalanta stepped forward and said: "Do not speak of it, youth. Indeed I think that it is some god, envious of your beauty and your strength, who sent you here to strive with me and to meet your doom. Ah, think of the youths who have striven with me even now! Think of the hard doom that is about to fall upon them! You venture your life in the race, but indeed I am not worthy of the price. Go hence, O stranger youth, go hence and live happily, for indeed I think that there is some maiden who loves you well."

"Nay, maiden," said Hippomenes, "I will enter the race and I will venture my life on the chance of winning you for my bride. What good will my life and my spirit be to me if they cannot win this race for me?"

She drew away from him then and looked upon him no more, but bent down to fasten the sandals upon her feet. And the black-bearded king looked upon Hippomenes and said, "Face, then, this race to-morrow. You will be the only one who will enter it. But bethink thee of the doom that awaits thee at the end of it." The king said no more, and Hippomenes went from him and from Atalanta, and he came again to the place where the race had been run.

He looked across the sandy course with its goal marks, and in his mind he saw again Atalanta's swift race. He would not meet doom at the hands of the king's soldiers, he knew, for his spirit would leave him with the greatness of the effort he would make to reach the goal before her. And he thought it would be well to die in that effort and on that sandy place that was so far from his own land.

Even as he looked across the sandy course now deserted by the throng, he saw one move across it, coming toward him with feet that did not seem to touch the ground. She was a woman of wonderful presence. As Hippomenes looked upon her he knew that she was Aphrodite, the goddess of beauty and of love.

"Hippomenes," said the immortal goddess, "the gods are mindful of you who are sprung from one of the gods, and I am mindful of you because of your own worth. I have come to help you in your race with Atalanta, for I would not have you slain, nor would I have that maiden go unwed. Give your greatest strength and your greatest swiftness to the race, and behold! here are wonders that will prevent the fleet-footed Atalanta from putting all her spirit into the race."

And then the immortal goddess held out to Hippomenes a branch that had upon it three apples of shining gold.

"In Cyprus," said the goddess, "where I have come from, there is a tree on which these golden apples grow. Only I may pluck them. I have brought them to you, Hippomenes. Keep them in your girdle, and in the race you will find out what to do with them, I think."

So Aphrodite said, and then she vanished, leaving a fragrance in the air and the three shining apples in the hands of Hippomenes. Long he looked upon their brightness. They were beside him that night, and when he arose in the dawn he put them in his girdle. Then, before the throng, he went to the place of the race.

When he showed himself beside Atalanta all around the course were silent, for they all admired Hippomenes for his beauty and for the spirit that was in his face; they were silent out of compassion, for they knew the doom that befell the youths who raced with Atalanta.

And now Schœneus, the black-bearded king, stood up, and he spoke to the throng, saying, "Hear me all, both young and old: this youth, Hippomenes, seeks to win the race from my daughter, winning her for his bride. Now, if he be victorious and escape death I will give him my dear child, Atalanta, and many fleet horses besides as gifts from me, and in honor he shall go back to his native land. But if he fail in the race, then he will have to share the doom that has been meted out to the other youths who raced with Atalanta hoping to win her for a bride."

Then Hippomenes and Atalanta crouched for the start. The trumpets were sounded and they darted off.

Side by side with Atalanta Hippomenes went. Her flying hair touched his breast, and it seemed to him that they were skimming the sandy course as if they were swallows. But then Atalanta began to draw away from him. He saw her ahead of him, and then he began to hear the words of cheer that came from the throng—"Bend to the race, Hippomenes! Go on, go on! Use your strength to the utmost." He bent himself to the race, but further and further from him Atalanta drew.

Then it seemed to him that she checked her swiftness a

little to look back at him. He gained on her a little. And then his hand touched the apples that were in his girdle. As it touched them it came into his mind what to do with the apples.

He was not far from her now, but already her swiftness was drawing her further and further away. He took one of the apples into his hand and tossed it into the air so that it fell on the track before her.

Atalanta saw the shining apple. She checked her speed and stooped in the race to pick it up. And as she stooped Hippomenes darted past her, and went flying toward the goal that now was within his sight.

But soon she was beside him again. He looked, and he saw that the goal marks were far, far ahead of him. Atalanta with the flying hair passed him, and drew away and away from him. He had not speed to gain upon her now, he thought, so he put his strength into his hand and he flung the second of the shining apples. The apple rolled before her and rolled off the course. Atalanta turned off the course, stooped and picked up the apple.

Then did Hippomenes draw all his spirit into his breast as he raced on. He was now nearer to the goal than she was. But he knew that she was behind him, going lightly where he went heavily. And then she was beside him, and then she went past him. She paused in her speed for a moment and she looked back on him.

As he raced on, his chest seemed weighted down and his throat was crackling dry. The goal marks were far away still, but Atalanta was nearing them. He took the last of the golden apples into his hand. Perhaps she was now so far that the strength of his throw would not be great enough to bring the apple before her.

But with all the strength he could put into his hand he flung the apple. It struck the course before her feet and then went bounding wide. Atalanta swerved in her race and followed where the apple went. Hippomenes marveled that he had been able to fling it so far. He saw Atalanta stoop to pick up the apple, and he bounded on. And then, although his strength was failing, he saw the goal marks near him. He set his feet between them and then fell down on the ground.

The attendants raised him up and put the victor's wreath upon his head. The concourse of people shouted with joy to see him victor. But he looked around for Atalanta and he saw her standing there with the golden apples in her hands. "He has won," he heard her say, "and I have not to hate myself for bringing a doom upon him. Gladly, gladly do I give up the race, and glad am I that it is this youth who has won the victory from me."

She took his hand and brought him before the king. Then Schœneus, in the sight of all the rejoicing people, gave Atalanta to Hippomenes for his bride, and he bestowed upon him also a great gift of horses. With his dear and hard-won bride, Hippomenes went to his own country, and the apples that she brought with her, the golden apples of Aphrodite, were reverenced by the people.

X. The Departure from Lemnos

A DAY came when Heracles left the *Argo* and went on the Lemnian land. He gathered the heroes about him, and they, seeing Heracles come amongst them, clamored to go to hunt the wild bulls that were inland from the sea.

So, for once, the heroes left the Lemnian maidens who were their friends. Jason, too, left Hypsipyle in the palace and went with Heracles. And as they went, Heracles spoke to each of the heroes, saying that they were forgetting the Fleece of Gold that they had sailed to gain. Jason blushed to think that he had almost let go out of his mind the quest that had brought him from Iolcus. And then he thought upon Hypsipyle and of how her little hand would stay in his, and his own hand became loose upon the spear so that it nearly fell from him. How could he, he thought, leave Hypsipyle and this land of Lemnos behind?

He heard the clear voice of Atalanta as she, too, spoke to the Argonauts. What Heracles said was brave and wise, said Atalanta. Forgetfulness would cover their names if they stayed longer in Lemnos—forgetfulness and shame, and they would come to despise themselves. Leave Lemnos, she cried, and draw *Argo* into the sea, and depart for Colchis.

All day the Argonauts stayed by themselves, hunting the bulls. On their way back from the chase they were met by Lemnian maidens who carried wreaths of flowers for them. Very silent were the heroes as the maidens greeted them. Heracles went with Jason to the palace, and Hypsipyle, seeing the mighty stranger coming, seated herself, not on the couch where she was wont to sit looking into the face of Jason, but on the stone throne of King Thoas, her father. And seated on that throne she spoke to Jason and to Heracles as a queen might speak.

In the hall that night the heroes and the Lemnian maidens who were with them were quiet. A story was told; Castor began it and Polydeuces ended it. And the story that Helen's brothers told was:

THE GOLDEN MAID

Epimetheus the Titan had a brother who was the wisest of all beings—Prometheus called the Foreseer. But Epimetheus himself was slow-witted and scatter-brained. His wise brother once sent him a message bidding him beware of the gifts that Zeus might send him. Epimetheus heard, but he did not heed the warning, and thereby he brought upon the race of men troubles and cares.

Prometheus, the wise Titan, had saved men from a great trouble that Zeus would have brought upon them. Also he had given them the gift of fire. Zeus was the more wroth with men now because fire, stolen from him, had been given them; he was wroth with the race of Titans, too, and he pondered in his heart how he might injure men, and how he might use Epimetheus, the mindless Titan, to further his plan.

While he pondered there was a hush on high Olympus, the mountain of the gods. Then Zeus called upon the artisan of the gods, lame Hephæstus, and he commanded him to make a being out of clay that would have the likeness of a lovely maiden. With joy and pride Hephæstus worked at the task that had been given him, and he fashioned a being that had the likeness of a lovely maiden, and he brought the thing of his making before the gods and the goddesses.

All strove to add a grace or a beauty to the work of Hephœstus. Zeus granted that the maiden should see and feel. Athene dressed her in garments that were as lovely as flowers. Aphrodite, the goddess of love, put a charm on her lips and in her eyes. The Graces put necklaces around her neck and set a golden crown upon her head. The Hours brought her a girdle of spring flowers. Then the herald of the gods gave her speech that was sweet and flowing. All the gods and goddesses had given gifts to her, and for that reason the maiden of Hephæstus's making was called Pandora, the All-endowed.

She was lovely, the gods knew; not beautiful as they themselves are, who have a beauty that awakens reverence rather than love, but lovely, as flowers and bright waters and earthly maidens are lovely. Zeus smiled to himself when he looked upon her, and he called to Hermes who knew all the ways of the earth, and he put her into the charge of Hermes. Also he gave Hermes a great jar to take along; this jar was Pandora's dower.

Epimetheus lived in a deep-down valley. Now one day, as he was sitting on a fallen pillar in the ruined place that was now forsaken by the rest of the Titans, he saw a pair coming toward him. One had wings, and he knew him to be Hermes, the messenger of the gods. The other was a maiden. Epimetheus marveled at the crown upon her head and at her lovely garments. There was a glint of gold

Epimetheus lived in a deep-down valley. Now one day, as he was
sitting on a fallen pillar in the ruined place that was now forsaken
by the rest of the Titans, he saw a pair coming toward him.
One had wings, and he knew him to be Hermes, the messenger
of the gods. The other was a maiden. *See page 72.*

all around her. He rose from where he sat upon the broken pillar and he stood to watch the pair. Hermes, he saw, was carrying by its handle a great jar.

In wonder and delight he looked upon the maiden. Epimetheus had seen no lovely thing for ages. Wonderful indeed was this Golden Maid, and as she came nearer the charm that was on her lips and in her eyes came to the Earth-born One, and he smiled with more and more delight.

Hermes came and stood before him. He also smiled, but his smile had something baleful in it. He put the hands of the Golden Maid into the great soft hand of the Titan, and he said, "O Epimetheus, Father Zeus would be reconciled with thee, and as a sign of his good will he sends thee this lovely goddess to be thy companion."

Oh, very foolish was Epimetheus the Earth-born One! As he looked upon the Golden Maid who was sent by Zeus he lost memory of the wars that Zeus had made upon the Titans and the Elder Gods; he lost memory of his brother chained by Zeus to the rock; he lost memory of the warning that his brother, the wisest of all beings, had sent him. He took the hands of Pandora, and he thought of nothing at all in all the world but her. Very far away seemed the voice of Hermes saying, "This jar, too, is from Olympus; it has in it Pandora's dower."

The jar stood forgotten for long, and green plants grew over it while Epimetheus walked in the garden with the Golden Maid, or watched her while she gazed on herself in the stream, or searched in the untended places for the fruits that the Elder Gods would eat, when they feasted with the Titans in the old days, before Zeus had come to his power. And lost to Epimetheus was the memory of his brother now suffering upon the rock because of the gift he had given to men.

And Pandora, knowing nothing except the brightness of the sunshine and the lovely shapes and colors of things and the sweet taste of the fruits that Epimetheus brought to her, could have stayed forever in that garden.

But every day Epimetheus would think that the men and women of the world should be able to talk to him about this maiden with the wonderful radiance of gold, and with the lovely garments, and the marvelous crown. And one day he took Pandora by the hand, and he brought her out of that deep-lying valley, and toward the homes of men. He did not forget the jar that Hermes had left with her. All things that belonged to the Golden Maid were precious, and Epimetheus took the jar along.

The race of men at the time were simple and content. Their days were passed in toil, but now, since Prometheus had given them fire, they had good fruits of their toil. They had well-shaped tools to dig the earth and to build houses. Their homes were warmed with fire, and fire burned upon the altars that were upon their ways.

Greatly they reverenced Prometheus, who had given them fire, and greatly they reverenced the race of the Titans. So when Epimetheus came amongst them, tall as a man walking with stilts, they welcomed him and brought him and the Golden Maid to their hearths. And Epimetheus showed Pandora the wonderful element that his brother had given to men, and she rejoiced to see the fire, clapping her hands with delight. The jar that Epimetheus brought he left in an open place.

In carrying it up the rough ways out of the valley Epimetheus may have knocked the jar about, for the lid that had been tight upon it now fitted very loosely. But no one gave heed to the jar as it stood in the open space where Epimetheus had left it.

At first the men and women looked upon the beauty of Pandora, upon her lovely dresses, and her golden crown and her girdle of flowers, with wonder and delight. Epimetheus would have every one admire and praise her. The men would leave off working in the fields, or hammering on iron, or building houses, and the women would leave off spinning or weaving, and come at his call, and stand about and admire the Golden Maid. But as time

went by a change came upon the women: one woman
would weep, and another would look angry, and a third
would go back sullenly to her work when Pandora was admired or praised.

Once the women were gathered together, and one who
was the wisest amongst them said: "Once we did not think
about ourselves, and we were content. But now we think
about ourselves, and we say to ourselves that we are
harsh and ill-favored indeed compared to the Golden
Maid that the Titan is so enchanted with. And we hate to
see our own men praise and admire her, and often, in our
hearts, we would destroy her if we could."

"That is true," the women said. And then a young woman
cried out in a most yearnful voice, "O tell us, you who are
wise, how can we make ourselves as beautiful as Pandora!"

Then said that woman who was thought to be wise,
"This Golden Maid is lovely to look upon because she has
lovely apparel and all the means of keeping herself lovely.
The gods have given her the ways, and so her skin remains fair, and her hair keeps its gold, and her lips are
ever red and her eyes shining. And I think that the means
that she has of keeping lovely are all in that jar that
Epimetheus brought with her."

When the woman who was thought to be wise said this,
those around her were silent for a while. But then one
arose and another arose, and they stood and whispered
together, one saying to the other that they should go to the
place where the jar had been left by Epimetheus, and that
they should take out of it the salves and the charms and
the washes that would leave them as beautiful as Pandora.

So the women went to that place. On their way they
stopped at a pool and they bent over to see themselves
mirrored in it, and they saw themselves with dusty and
unkempt hair, with large and knotted hands, with troubled
eyes, and with anxious mouths. They frowned as they
looked upon their images, and they said in harsh voices
that in a while they would have ways of making themselves as lovely as the Golden Maid.

As the hands of the women grasped it to take off the lid the jar
was cast down, and the things that were inside spilled
themselves forth. *See page 78.*

And as they went on they saw Pandora. She was playing in a flowering field, while Epimetheus, high as a man upon stilts, went gathering the blossoms of the bushes for her. They went on, and they came at last to the place where Epimetheus had left the jar that held Pandora's dower.

A great stone jar it was; there was no bird, nor flower, nor branch painted upon it. It stood high as a woman's shoulder. And as the women looked on it they thought that there were things enough in it to keep them beautiful for all the days of their lives. But each one thought that she should not be the last to get her hands into it.

Once the lid had been fixed tightly down on the jar. But the lid was shifted a little now. As the hands of the women grasped it to take off the lid the jar was cast down, and the things that were inside spilled themselves forth.

They were black and gray and red; they were crawling and flying things. And, as the women looked, the things spread themselves abroad or fastened themselves upon them.

The jar, like Pandora herself, had been made and filled out of the ill will of Zeus. And it had been filled, not with salves and charms and washes, as the women had thought, but with Cares and Troubles. Before the women came to it one Trouble had already come forth from the jar—Self-thought that was upon the top of the heap. It was Self-thought that had afflicted the women, making them troubled about their own looks, and envious of the graces of the Golden Maid.

And now the others spread themselves out—Sickness and War and Strife between friends. They spread themselves abroad and entered the houses, while Epimetheus, the mindless Titan, gathered flowers for Pandora, the Golden Maid.

Lest she should weary of her play he called to her. He would take her into the houses of men. As they drew near to the houses they saw a woman seated on the ground, weeping; her husband had suddenly become hard to her and had shut the door on her face. They came upon a child crying because of a pain that he could not understand. And then they found two men struggling, their strife being on account of a possession that they had both held peaceably before.

In every house they went to Epimetheus would say, "I am the brother of Prometheus, who gave you the gift of fire." But instead of giving them a welcome the men would say, "We know nothing about your relation to Prometheus. We see you as a foolish man upon stilts."

Epimetheus was troubled by the hard looks and the cold words of the men who once had reverenced him. He turned from the houses and went away. In a quiet place he sat down, and for a while he lost sight of Pandora. And then it seemed to him that he heard the voice of his wise and suffering brother saying, "Do not accept any gift that Zeus may send you."

He rose up and he hurried away from that place, leaving Pandora playing by herself. There came into his scattered mind Regret and Fear. As he went on he stumbled. He fell from the edge of a cliff, and the sea washed away the body of the mindless brother of Prometheus.

Not everything had been spilled out of the jar that had been brought with Pandora into the world of men. A beautiful, living thing was in that jar also. This was Hope. And this beautiful, living thing had got caught under the rim of the jar and had not come forth with the others. One day a weeping woman found Hope under the rim of Pandora's jar and brought this living thing into the house of men. And now because of Hope they could see an end to their troubles. And the men and women roused themselves in the midst of their afflictions and they looked toward gladness. Hope, that had been caught under the rim of the jar, stayed behind the thresholds of their houses.

As for Pandora, the Golden Maid, she played on, knowing only the brightness of the sunshine and the lovely shapes of things. Beautiful would she have seemed to any being who saw her, but now she had strayed away from the houses of men and Epimetheus was not there to look upon her. Then Hephæstus, the lame artisan of the gods, left down his tools and went to seek her. He found Pandora, and he took her back to Olympus. And in his brazen house she stays, though sometimes at the will of Zeus she goes down into the world of men.

When Polydeuces had ended the story that Castor had begun, Heracles cried out: "For the Argonauts, too, there has been a Golden Maid—nay, not one, but a Golden Maid for each. Out of the jar that has been with her ye have taken forgetfulness of your honor. As for me, I go back to the *Argo* lest one of these Golden Maids should hold me back from the labors that make great a man."

So Heracles said, and he went from Hypsipyle's hall. The heroes looked at each other, and they stood up, and shame that they had stayed so long away from the quest came over each of them. The maidens took their hands; the heroes unloosed those soft hands and turned away from them.

Hypsipyle left the throne of King Thoas and stood before Jason. There was a storm in all her body; her mouth was shaken, and a whole life's trouble was in her great eyes. Before she spoke Jason cried out: "What Heracles said is true, O Argonauts! On the Quest of the Golden Fleece our lives and our honors depend. To Colchis—to Colchis must we go!"

He stood upright in the hall, and his comrades gathered around him. The Lemnian maidens would have held out their arms and would have made their partings long delayed, but that a strange cry came to them through the night. Well did the Argonauts know that cry—it was the cry of the ship, of *Argo* herself. They knew that they must go to her now or stay from the voyage for ever. And the maidens knew that there was something in the cry of the ship that might not be gainsaid, and they put their hands before their faces, and they said no other word.

Then said Hypsipyle, the queen, "I, too, am a ruler, Jason, and I know that there are great commands that we have to obey. Go, then, to the *Argo*. Ah, neither I nor the women of Lemnos will stay your going now. But to-

When the other Lemnian women slept she put her head upon
her nurse's knees and wept; bitterly Hypsipyle wept, but softly,
for she would not have the others hear her weeping. *See page 82*.

morrow speak to us from the deck of the ship and bid us farewell. Do not go from us in the night, Jason."

Jason and the Argonauts went from Hypsipyle's hall. The maidens who were left behind wept together. All but Hypsipyle. She sat on the throne of King Thoas and she had Polyxo, her nurse, tell her of the ways of Jason's voyage as he had told of them, and of all that he would have to pass through. When the other Lemnian women slept she put her head upon her nurse's knees and wept; bitterly Hypsipyle wept, but softly, for she would not have the others hear her weeping.

By the coming of the morning's light the Argonauts had made all ready for their sailing. They were standing on the deck when the light came, and they saw the Lemnian women come to the shore. Each looked at her friend aboard the *Argo,* and spoke, and went away. And last, Hypsipyle, the queen, came. "Farewell, Hypsipyle," Jason said to her, and she, in her strange way of speaking, said:

"What you told us I have remembered—how you will come to the dangerous passage that leads into the Sea of Pontus, and how by the flight of a pigeon you will know whether or not you may go that way. O Jason, let the dove you fly when you come to that dangerous place be Hypsipyle's."

She showed a pigeon held in her hands. She loosed it, and the pigeon alighted on the ship, and stayed there on pink feet, a white-feathered pigeon. Jason took up the pigeon and held it in his hands, and the *Argo* drew swiftly away from the Lemnian land.

XI. The Passage of the Symplegades

THEY came near Salmydessus, where Phineus, the wise king, ruled, and they sailed past it; they sighted the pile of stones, with the oar upright upon it that they had raised on the seashore over the body of Tiphys, the skillful steersman whom they had lost; they sailed on until they heard a sound that grew more and more thunderous, and then the heroes said to each other, "Now we come to the Symplegades and the dread passage into the Sea of Pontus."

It was then that Jason cried out: "Ah, when Pelias spoke of this quest to me, why did I not turn my head away and refuse to be drawn into it? Since we came near the dread passage that is before us I have passed every night in groans. As for you who have come with me, you may take your ease, for you need care only for your own lives. But I have to care for you all, and to strive to win for you all a safe return to Greece. Ah, greatly am I afflicted now, knowing to what a great peril I have brought you!"

So Jason said, thinking to make trial of the heroes. They, on their part, were not dismayed, but shouted back cheerful words to him. Then he said: "O friends of mine, by your spirit my spirit is quickened. Now if I knew that I was being borne down into the black gulfs of Hades, I should fear nothing, knowing that you are constant and faithful of heart."

As he said this they came into water that seethed all around the ship. Then into the hands of Euphemus, a youth of Iolcus, who was the keenest-eyed amongst the Argonauts, Jason put the pigeon that Hypsipyle had given him. He bade him stand by the prow of the *Argo,* ready to loose the pigeon as the ship came nigh that dreadful gate of rock.

They saw the spray being dashed around in showers; they saw the sea spread itself out in foam; they saw the high, black rocks rush together, sounding thunderously as they met. The caves in the high rocks rumbled as the sea surged into them, and the foam of the dashing waves spurted high up the rocks.

Jason shouted to each man to grip hard on the oars. The *Argo* dashed on as the rocks rushed toward each other again. Then there was such noise that no man's voice could be heard above it.

As the rocks met, Euphemus loosed the pigeon. With his keen eyes he watched her fly through the spray. Would she, not finding an opening to fly through, turn back? He watched, and meanwhile the Argonauts gripped hard on the oars to save the ship from being dashed on the rocks. The pigeon fluttered as though she would sink down and let the spray drown her. And then Euphemus saw her raise herself and fly forward. Toward the place where she had flown he pointed. The rowers gave a loud cry, and Jason called upon them to pull with might and main.

The rocks were parting asunder, and to the right and left broad Pontus was seen by the heroes. Then suddenly a huge wave rose before them, and at the sight of it they all uttered a cry and bent their heads. It seemed to them that it would dash down on the whole ship's length and over- whelm them all. But Nauplius was quick to ease the ship, and the wave rolled away beneath the keel, and at the stern it raised the *Argo* and dashed her away from the rocks.

They felt the sun as it streamed upon them through the sundered rocks. They strained at the oars until the oars bent like bows in their hands. The ship sprang forward. Surely they were now in the wide Sea of Pontus!

The Argonauts shouted. They saw the rocks behind them with the sea fowl screaming upon them. Surely they were in the Sea of Pontus—the sea that had never been entered before through the Rocks Wandering. The rocks no longer dashed together; each remained fixed in its place, for it was the will of the gods that these rocks should no more clash together after a mortal's ship had passed between them.

They were now in the Sea of Pontus, the sea into which flowed the river that Colchis was upon—the River Phasis. And now above Jason's head the bird of peaceful days, the Halcyon, fluttered, and the Argonauts knew that this was a sign from the gods that the voyage would not any more be troublous.

XII. The Mountain Caucasus

THEY rested in the harbor of Thynias, the desert island, and sailing from there they came to the land of the Mariandyni, a people who were constantly at war with the Bebrycians; there the hero Polydeuces was welcomed as a god. Twelve days afterward they passed the mouth of the River Callichorus; then they came to the mouth of that river that flows through the land of the Amazons, the River Thermodon. Fourteen days from that place brought them to the island that is filled with the birds of Ares, the god of war. These birds dropped upon the heroes heavy, pointed feathers that would have pierced them as arrows if they had not covered themselves with their shields; then by shouting, and by striking their shields with their spears, they raised such a clamor as drove the birds away.

They sailed on, borne by a gentle breeze, until a gulf of the sea opened before them, and lo! a mountain that they knew bore some mighty name. Orpheus, looking on its peak and its crags, said, "Lo, now! We, the Argonauts, are looking upon the mountain that is named Caucasus!"

When he declared the name the heroes all stood up and looked on the mountain with awe. And in awe they cried out a name, and that name was "Prometheus!"

For upon that mountain the Titan god was held, his limbs bound upon the hard rocks by fetters of bronze. Even as the Argonauts looked toward the mountain a great shadow fell upon their ship, and looking up they saw a monstrous bird flying. The beat of the bird's wings filled out the sail and drove the *Argo* swiftly onward. "It is the bird sent by Zeus," Orpheus said. "It is the vulture that every day devours the liver of the Titan god." They cowered down on the ship as they heard that word—all the Argonauts save Heracles; he stood upright and looked out toward where the bird was flying. Then, as the bird came near to the mountain, the Argonauts heard a great cry of anguish go up from the rocks.

"It is Prometheus crying out as the bird of Zeus flies down upon him," they said to one another. Again they cowered down on the ship, all save Heracles, who stayed looking toward where the great vulture had flown.

The night came and the Argonauts sailed on in silence, thinking in awe of the Titan god and of the doom that Zeus had inflicted upon him. Then, as they sailed on under the stars, Orpheus told them of Prometheus, of his gift to men, and of the fearful punishment that had been meted out to him by Zeus.

PROMETHEUS

The gods more than once made a race of men: the first was a Golden Race. Very close to the gods who dwell on Olympus was this Golden Race; they lived justly although there were no laws to compel them. In the time of the Golden Race the earth knew only one season, and that season was everlasting Spring. The men and women of the Golden Race lived through a span of life that was far beyond that of the men and women of our day, and when they died it was as though sleep had become everlasting with them. They had all good things, and that without labor, for the earth without any forcing bestowed fruits and crops upon them. They had peace all through their lives, this Golden Race, and after they had passed away their spirits remained above the earth, inspiring the men of the race that came after them to do great and gracious things and to act justly and kindly to one another.

After the Golden Race had passed away, the gods made for the earth a second race—a Silver Race. Less noble in spirit and in body was this Silver Race, and the seasons that visited them were less gracious. In the time of the Silver Race the gods made the seasons—Summer and Spring, and Autumn and Winter. They knew parching heat, and the bitter winds of winter, and snow and rain and hail. It was the men of the Silver Race who first built houses for shelter. They lived through a span of life that was longer than our span, but it was not long enough to give wisdom to them. Children were brought up at their mothers' sides for a hundred years, playing at childish things. And when they came to years beyond a hundred they quarreled with one another, and wronged one another, and did not know enough to give reverence to the immortal gods. Then, by the will of Zeus, the Silver Race passed away as the Golden Race had passed away. Their spirits stay in the Underworld, and they are called by men the blessed spirits of the Underworld.

And then there was made the third race—the Race of Bronze. They were a race great of stature, terrible and strong. Their armor was of bronze, their swords were of bronze, their implements were of bronze, and of bronze, too, they made their houses. No great span of life was theirs, for with the weapons that they took in their terrible hands they slew one another. Thus they passed away, and went down under the earth to Hades, leaving no name that men might know them by.

Then the gods created a fourth race—our own: a Race of Iron. We have not the justice that was amongst the men of the Golden Race, nor the simpleness that was amongst the men of the Silver Race, nor the stature nor the great strength that the men of the Bronze Race possessed. We are of iron that we may endure. It is our doom that we must never cease from labor and that we must very quickly grow old.

But miserable as we are to-day, there was a time when the lot of men was more miserable. With poor implements they had to labor on a hard ground. There was less justice and kindliness amongst men in those days than there is now.

Once it came into the mind of Zeus that he would destroy the fourth race and leave the earth to the nymphs and the satyrs. He would destroy it by a great flood. But Prometheus, the Titan god who had given aid to Zeus against the other Titans—Prometheus, who was called the Foreseer—could not consent to the race of men being destroyed utterly, and he considered a way of saving some of them. To a man and a woman, Deucalion and Pyrrha, just and gentle people, he brought word of the plan of Zeus, and he showed them how to make a ship that would bear them through what was about to be sent upon the earth.

Then Zeus shut up in their cave all the winds but the wind that brings rain and clouds. He bade this wind, the South Wind, sweep over the earth, flooding it with rain. He called upon Poseidon and bade him to let the sea pour in upon the land. And Poseidon commanded the rivers to put forth all their strength, and sweep dykes away, and overflow their banks.

The clouds and the sea and the rivers poured upon the earth. The flood rose higher and higher, and in the places where the pretty lambs had played the ugly sea calves now gambolled; men in their boats drew fishes out of the tops of elm trees, and the water nymphs were amazed to come on men's cities under the waves.

Soon even the men and women who had boats were overwhelmed by the rise of water—all perished then except Deucalion and Pyrrha, his wife; them the waves had not overwhelmed, for they were in a ship that Prometheus had shown them how to build. The flood went down at last, and Deucalion and Pyrrha climbed up to a high and a dry ground. Zeus saw that two of the race of men had been left alive. But he saw that these two were just and kindly, and had a right reverence for the gods. He spared them, and he saw their children again peopling the earth.

Prometheus, who had saved them, looked on the men and women of the earth with compassion. Their labor was hard, and they wrought much to gain little. They were chilled at night in their houses, and the winds that blew in the daytime made the old men and women bend double like a wheel. Prometheus thought to himself that if men and women had the element that only the gods knew of— the element of fire—they could make for themselves implements for labor; they could build houses that would

keep out the chilling winds, and they could warm themselves at the blaze.

But the gods had not willed that men should have fire,
and to go against the will of the gods would be impious.
Prometheus went against the will of the gods. He stole fire
from the altar of Zeus, and he hid it in a hollow fennel
stalk, and he brought it to men.

Then men were able to hammer iron into tools, and cut
down forests with axes, and sow grain where the forests
had been. Then were they able to make houses that the
storms could not overthrow, and they were able to warm
themselves at hearth fires. They had rest from their labor
at times. They built cities; they became beings who no
longer had heads and backs bent but were able to raise
their faces even to the gods.

And Zeus spared the race of men who had now the sacred element of fire. But he knew that Prometheus had
stolen this fire even from his own altar and had given it to
men. And he thought on how he might punish the great
Titan god for his impiety.

He brought back from the Underworld the giants that
he had put there to guard the Titans that had been hurled
down to Tartarus. He brought back Gyes, Cottus, and Briareus, and he commanded them to lay hands upon
Prometheus and to fasten him with fetters to the highest,
blackest crag upon Caucasus. And Briareus, Cottus, and
Gyes seized upon the Titan god, and carried him to Caucasus, and fettered him with fetters of bronze to the highest, blackest crag—with fetters of bronze that may not be
broken. There they have left the Titan stretched, under
the sky, with the cold winds blowing upon him, and with
the sun streaming down on him. And that his punishment
might exceed all other punishments Zeus had sent a vulture to prey upon him—a vulture that tears at his liver
each day.

And yet Prometheus does not cry out that he has re-
pented of his gift to man; although the winds blow upon
him, and the sun streams upon him, and the vulture tears

at his liver, Prometheus will not cry out his repentance to heaven. And Zeus may not utterly destroy him. For Prometheus the Foreseer knows a secret that Zeus would fain have him disclose. He knows that even as Zeus overthrew his father and made himself the ruler in his stead, so, too, another will overthrow Zeus. And one day Zeus will have to have the fetters broken from around the limbs of Prometheus, and will have to bring from the rock and the vulture, and into the Council of the Olympians, the unyielding Titan god.

When the light of the morning came the *Argo* was very near to the Mountain Caucasus. The voyagers looked in awe upon its black crags. They saw the great vulture circling over a high rock, and from beneath where the vulture circled they heard a weary cry. Then Heracles, who all night had stood by the mast, cried out to the Argonauts to bring the ship near to a landing place.

But Jason would not have them go near; fear of the wrath of Zeus was strong upon him; rather, he bade the Argonauts put all their strength into their rowing, and draw far off from that forbidden mountain. Heracles, not heeding what Jason ordered, declared that it was his purpose to make his way up to the black crag, and, with his shield and his sword in his hands, slay the vulture that preyed upon the liver of Prometheus.

Then Orpheus in a clear voice spoke to the Argonauts. "Surely some spirit possesses Heracles," he said. "Despite all we do or say he will make his way to where Prometheus is fettered to the rock. Do not gainsay him in this! Remember what Nereus, the ancient one of the sea, declared! Did Nereus not say that a great labor awaited Heracles, and that in the doing of it he should work out the will of Zeus? Stay him not! How just it would be if he who is the son of Zeus freed from his torments the muchenduring Titan god!"

So Orpheus said in his clear, commanding voice. They drew near to the Mountain Caucasus. Then Heracles, grip-

And that his punishment might exceed all other punishments Zeus
had sent a vulture to prey upon him—a vulture that tears
at his liver each day. *See page 89.*

ping the sword and shield that were the gifts of the gods, sprang out on the landing place. The Argonauts shouted farewell to him. But he, filled as he was with an overmastering spirit, did not heed their words.

A strong breeze drove them onward; darkness came down, and the *Argo* went on through the night. With the morning light those who were sleeping were awakened by the cry of Nauplius—"Lo! The Phasis, and the utmost bourne of the sea!" They sprang up, and looked with many strange feelings upon the broad river they had come to.

Here was the Phasis emptying itself into the Sea of Pontus! Up that river was Colchis and the city of King Æetes, the end of their voyage, the place where was kept the Golden Fleece! Quickly they let down the sail; they lowered the mast and they laid it along the deck; strongly they grasped the oars; they swung the *Argo* around, and they entered the broad stream of the Phasis.

Up the river they went with the Mountain Caucasus on their left hand, and on their right the groves and gardens of Aea, King Æetes's city. As they went up the stream, Jason poured from a golden cup an offering to the gods. And to the dead heroes of that country the Argonauts prayed for good fortune to their enterprise.

It was Jason's counsel that they should not at once appear before King Æetes, but visit him after they had seen the strength of his city. They drew their ship into a shaded backwater, and there they stayed while day grew and faded around them.

Night came, and the heroes slept upon the deck of *Argo*. Many things came back to them in their dreams or through their half-sleep: they thought of the Lemnian maidens they had parted from; of the Clashing Rocks they had passed between; of the look in the eyes of Heracles as he raised his face to the high, black peak of Caucasus. They slept, and they thought they saw before them THE GOLDEN FLEECE; darkness surrounded it; it seemed to the dreaming Argonauts that the darkness was the magic power that King Æetes possessed.

PART TWO
The Return to Greece

I. King Æetes

THEY had come into a country that was the strangest of all countries, and amongst a people that were the strangest of all peoples. They were in the land, this people said, before the moon had come into the sky. And it is true that when the great king of Egypt had come so far, finding in all other places men living on the high hills and eating the acorns that grew on the oaks there, he found in Colchis the city of Aea with a wall around it and with pillars on which writings were graven. That was when Egypt was called the Morning Land.

And many of the magicians of Egypt who had come with King Sesostris stayed in that city of Aea, and they taught people spells that could stay the moon in her going and coming, in her rising and setting. Priests of the Moon ruled the city of Aea until King Æetes came.

Æetes had no need of their magic, for Helios, the bright Sun, was his father, as he thought. Also, Hephæstus, the artisan of the gods, was his friend, and Hephæstus made for him many wonderful things to be his protection. Medea, too, his wise daughter, knew the secrets taught by those who could sway the moon.

But Æetes once was made afraid by a dream that he had: he dreamt that a ship had come up the Phasis, and then, sailing on a mist, had rammed his palace that was standing there in all its strength and beauty until it had fallen down. On the morning of the night that he had had this dream Æetes called Medea, his wise daughter, and he

93

bade her go to the temple of Hecate, the Moon, and search out spells that might destroy those who came against his city.

That morning the Argonauts, who had passed the night in the backwater of the river, had two youths come to them. They were in a broken ship, and they had one oar only. When Jason, after giving them food and fresh garments, questioned them, he found out that these youths were of the city of Aea, and that they were none others than the sons of Phrixus—of Phrixus who had come there with the Golden Ram.

And the youths, Phrontis and Melas, were as amazed as was Jason when they found out whose ship they had come aboard. For Jason was the grandson of Cretheus, and Cretheus was the brother of Athamas, their grandfather. They had ventured from Aea, where they had been reared, thinking to reach the country of Athamas and lay claim to his possessions. But they had been wrecked at a place not far from the mouth of the Phasis, and with great pain and struggle they had made their way back.

They were fearful of Aea and of their uncle King Æetes, and they would gladly go with Jason and the Argonauts back to Greece. They would help Jason, they said, to persuade Æetes to give the Golden Fleece peaceably to them. Their mother was the daughter of Æetes—Chalciope, whom the king had given in marriage to Phrixus, his guest.

A council of the Argonauts was held, and it was agreed that Jason should go with two comrades to King Æetes, Phrontis and Melas going also. They were to ask the king to give them the Golden Fleece and to offer him a recompense. Jason took Peleus and Telamon with him.

As they came to the city a mist fell, and Jason and his comrades with the sons of Phrixus went through the city without being seen. They came before the palace of King Æetes. Then Phrontis and Melas were some way behind. The mist lifted, and before the heroes was the wonder of the palace in the bright light of the morning.

Vines with broad leaves and heavy clusters of fruit grew from column to column, the columns holding a gallery up. And under the vines were the four fountains that Hephæstus had made for King Æetes. They gushed out into golden, silver, bronze, and iron basins. And one fountain gushed out clear water, and another gushed out milk; another gushed out wine; and another oil. On each side of the courtyard were the palace buildings; in one King Æetes lived with Apsyrtus, his son, and in the other Chalciope and Medea lived with their handmaidens.

Medea was passing from her father's house. The mist lifted suddenly and she saw three strangers in the palace courtyard. One had a crimson mantle on; his shoulders were such as to make him seem a man that a whole world could not overthrow, and his eyes had all the sun's light in them.

Amazed, Medea stood looking upon Jason, wondering at his bright hair and gleaming eyes and at the lightness and strength of the hand that he had raised. And then a dove flew toward her: it was being chased by a hawk, and Medea saw the hawk's eyes and beak. As the dove lighted upon her shoulder she threw her veil around it, and the hawk dashed itself against a column. And as Medea, trembling, leaned against the column she heard a cry from her sister, who was within.

For now Phrontis and Melas had come up, and Chalciope who was spinning by the door saw them and cried out. All the servants rushed out. Seeing Chalciope's sons there they, too, uttered loud cries, and made such commotion that Apsyrtus and then King Æetes came out of the palace.

Jason saw King Æetes. He was old and white, but he had great green eyes, and the strength of a leopard was in all he did. And Jason looked upon Apsyrtus too; the son of Æetes looked like a Phœnician merchant, black of beard and with rings in his ears, with a hooked nose and a gleam of copper in his face.

Phrontis and Melas went from their mother's embrace and made reverence to King Æetes. Then they spoke of the heroes who were with them, of Jason and his two comrades. Æetes bade all enter the palace; baths were made ready for them, and a banquet was prepared.

After the banquet, when they all sat together, Æetes, addressing the eldest of Chalciope's sons, said:

"Sons of Phrixus, of that man whom I honored above all men who came to my halls, speak now and tell me how it is that you have come back to Aea so soon, and who they are, these men who come with you?"

Æetes, as he spoke, looked sharply upon Phrontis and Melas, for he suspected them of having returned to Aea, bringing these armed men with them, with an evil intent. Phrontis looked at the King, and said:

"Æetes, our ship was driven upon the Island of Ares, where it was almost broken upon the rocks. That was on a murky night, and in the morning the birds of Ares shot their sharp feathers upon us. We pulled away from that place, and thereafter we were driven by the winds back to the mouth of the Phasis. There we met with these heroes who were friendly to us. Who they are, what they have come to your city for, I shall now tell you.

"A certain king, longing to drive one of these heroes from his land, and hoping that the race of Cretheus might perish utterly, led him to enter a most perilous adventure. He came here upon a ship that was made by the command of Hera, the wife of Zeus, a ship more wonderful than mortals ever sailed in before. With him there came the mightiest of the heroes of Greece. He is Jason, the grandson of Cretheus, and he has come to beg that you will grant him freely the famous Fleece of Gold that Phrixus brought to Aea.

"But not without recompense to you would he take the Fleece. Already he has heard of your bitter foes, the Sauromatæ. He with his comrades would subdue them for you. And if you would ask of the names and the lineage of the heroes who are with Jason I shall tell you. This is

Peleus and this is Telamon; they are brothers, and they are sons of Æacus, who was of the seed of Zeus. And all the other heroes who have come with them are of the seed of the gods."

So Phrontis said, but the King was not placated by what he said. He thought that the sons of Chalciope had returned to Aea bringing these warriors with them so that they might wrest the kingship from him, or, failing that, plunder the city. Æetes's heart was filled with wrath as he looked upon them, and his eyes shone as a leopard's eyes.

"Begone from my sight," he cried, "robbers that ye are! Tricksters! If you had not eaten at my table, assuredly I should have had your tongues cut out for speaking falsehoods about the blessed gods, saying that this one and that of your companions was of their divine race."

Telamon and Peleus strode forward with angry hearts; they would have laid their hands upon King Æetes only Jason held them back. And then speaking to the king in a quiet voice, Jason said:

"Bear with us, King Æetes, I pray you. We have not come with such evil intent as you think. Ah, it was the evil command of an evil king that sent me forth with these companions of mine across dangerous gulfs of the sea, and to face your wrath and the armed men you can bring against us. We are ready to make great recompense for the friendliness you may show to us. We will subdue for you the Sauromatæ, or any other people that you would lord it over."

But Æetes was not made friendly by Jason's words. His heart was divided as to whether he should summon his armed men and have them slain upon the spot, or whether he should put them into danger by the trial he would make of them. At last he thought that it would be better to put them to the trial that he had in mind, slaying them afterward if need be. And then he spoke to Jason, saying:

"Strangers to Colchis, it may be true what my nephews

have said. It may be that ye are truly of the seed of the immortals. And it may be that I shall give you the Golden Fleece to bear away after I have made trial of you."

As he spoke Medea, brought there by his messenger so that she might observe the strangers, came into the chamber. She entered softly and she stood away from her father and the four who were speaking with him. Jason looked upon her, and even although his mind was filled with the thought of bending King Æetes to his will, he saw what manner of maiden she was, and what beauty and what strength was hers.

She had a dark face that was made very strange by her crown of golden hair. Her eyes, like her father's, were wide and full of light, and her lips were so full and red that they made her mouth like an opening rose. But her brows were always knit as if there was some secret anger within her.

"With brave men I have no quarrel," said Æetes. "I will make a trial of your bravery, and if your bravery wins through the trial, be very sure that you will have the Golden Fleece to bring back in triumph to Iolcus.

"But the trial that I would make of you is hard for a great hero even. Know that on the plain of Ares yonder I have two fire-breathing bulls with feet of brass. These bulls were once conquered by me; I yoked them to a plow of adamant, and with them I plowed the field of Ares for four plow-gates. Then I sowed the furrows, not with the seed that Demeter gives, but with teeth of a dragon. And from the dragon's teeth that I sowed in the field of Ares armed men sprang up. I slew them with my spear as they rose around me to slay me. If you can accomplish this that I accomplished in days gone by I shall submit to you and give you the Golden Fleece. But if you cannot accomplish what I once accomplished you shall go from my city empty-handed, for it is not right that a brave man should yield aught to one who cannot show himself as brave."

So Æetes said. Then Jason, utterly confounded, cast his eyes upon the ground. He raised them to speak to the king, and as he did he found the strange eyes of Medea

upon him. With all the courage that was in him he spoke:
"I will dare this contest, monstrous as it is. I will face this doom. I have come far, and there is nothing else for me to do but to yoke your fire-breathing bulls to the plow of adamant, and plow the furrows in the field of Ares, and struggle with the Earth-born Men." As he said this he saw the eyes of Medea grow wide as with fear.

Then Æetes said, "Go back to your ship and make ready for the trial." Jason, with Peleus and Telamon, left the chamber, and the king smiled grimly as he saw them go. Phrontis and Melas went to where their mother was. But Medea stayed, and Æetes looked upon her with his great leopard's eyes. "My daughter, my wise Medea," he said, "go, put spells upon the Moon, that Hecate may weaken that man in his hour of trial." Medea turned away from her father's eyes, and went to her chamber.

II. Medea the Sorceress

SHE turned away from her father's eyes and she went into her own chamber. For a long time she stood there with her hands clasped together. She heard the voice of Chalciope lamenting because Æetes had taken a hatred to her sons and might strive to destroy them. She heard the voice of her sister lamenting, but Medea thought that the cause that her sister had for grieving was small compared with the cause that she herself had.

She thought on the moment when she had seen Jason for the first time—in the courtyard as the mist lifted and the dove flew to her; she thought of him as he lifted those bright eyes of his; then she thought of his voice as he spoke after her father had imposed the dreadful trial upon him. She would have liked then to have cried out to him, "O youth, if others rejoice at the doom that you go to, I do not rejoice."

Still her sister lamented. But how great was her own grief compared to her sister's! For Chalciope could try to help her sons and could lament for the danger they were in and no one would blame her. But she might not strive to help Jason nor might she lament for the danger he was in. How terrible it would be for a maiden to help a stranger against her father's design! How terrible it would be for a woman of Colchis to help a stranger against the will of the king! How terrible it would be for a daughter to plot against King Æetes in his own palace!

And then Medea hated Aea, her city. She hated the furious people who came together in the assembly, and she hated the brazen bulls that Hephæstus had given her father. And then she thought that there was nothing in Aea except the furious people and the fire-breathing bulls. O how pitiful it was that the strange hero and his friends should have come to such a place for the sake of the Golden Fleece that was watched over by the sleepless serpent in the grove of Ares!

Still Chalciope lamented. Would Chalciope come to her and ask her, Medea, to help her sons? If she should come she might speak of the strangers, too, and of the danger they were in. Medea went to her couch and lay down upon it. She longed for her sister to come to her or to call to her.

But Chalciope stayed in her own chamber. Medea, lying upon her couch, listened to her sister's laments. At last she went near where Chalciope was. Then shame that she should think so much about the stranger came over her. She stood there without moving; she turned to go back to the couch, and then trembled so much that she could not stir. As she stood between her couch and her sister's chamber she heard the voice of Chalciope calling to her.

She went into the chamber where her sister stood. Chalciope flung her arms around her. "Swear," said she to Medea, "swear by Hecate, the Moon, that you will never speak of something I am going to ask you." Medea swore that she would never speak of it.

Chalciope spoke of the danger her sons were in. She asked Medea to devise a way by which they could escape with the stranger from Aea. "In Aea and in Colchis," she said, "there will be no safety for my sons henceforth." And to save Phrontis and Melas, she said, Medea would have to save the strangers also. Surely she knew of a charm that would save the stranger from the brazen bulls in the contest on the morrow!

So Chalciope came to the very thing that was in Medea's mind. Her heart bounded with joy and she embraced her. "Chalciope," she said, "I declare that I am your sister, indeed—aye, and your daughter, too, for did you not care for me when I was an infant? I will strive to save your sons. I will strive to save the strangers who came with your sons. Send one to the strangers—send him to the leader of the strangers, and tell him that I would see him at daybreak in the temple of Hecate."

When Medea said this Chalciope embraced her again. She was amazed to see how Medea's tears were flowing. "Chalciope," she said, "no one will know the dangers that I shall go through to save them."

Swiftly then Chalciope went from the chamber. But Medea stayed there with her head bowed and the blush of shame on her face. She thought that already she had deceived her sister, making her think that it was Phrontis and Melas and not Jason that was in her mind to save. And she thought on how she would have to plot against her father and against her own people, and all for the sake of a stranger who would sail away without thought of her, without the image of her in his mind.

Jason, with Peleus and Telamon, went back to the *Argo*. His comrades asked how he had fared, and when he spoke to them of the fire-breathing bulls with feet of brass, of the dragon's teeth that had to be sown, and of the Earth-born Men that had to be overcome, the Argonauts were greatly cast down, for this task, they thought, was one that could not be accomplished. He who stood before the fire-breathing bulls would perish on the moment. But they knew that one amongst them must strive to accomplish the task. And if Jason held back, Peleus, Telamon, Theseus, Castor, Polydeuces, or any one of the others would undertake it.

But Jason would not hold back. On the morrow, he said, he would strive to yoke the fire-breathing, brazen-footed bulls to the plow of adamant. If he perished the Argonauts should then do what they thought was best—make other trials to gain the Golden Fleece, or turn their ship and sail back to Greece.

While they were speaking, Phrontis, Chalciope's son, came to the ship. The Argonauts welcomed him, and in a while he began to speak of his mother's sister and of the help she could give. They grew eager as he spoke of her, all except rough Arcas, who stood wrapped in his bear's skin. "Shame on us," rough Arcas cried, "shame on us if we have come here to crave the help of girls! Speak no more of this! Let us, the Argonauts, go with swords into the city of Aea, and slay this king, and carry off the Fleece of Gold."

Some of the Argonauts murmured approval of what Arcas said. But Orpheus silenced him and them, for in his prophetic mind Orpheus saw something of the help that Medea would give them. It would be well, Orpheus said, to take help from this wise maiden; Jason should go to her in the temple of Hecate. The Argonauts agreed to this; they listened to what Phrontis told them about the brazen bulls, and the night wore on.

When darkness came upon the earth; when, at sea, sailors looked to the Bear and the stars of Orion; when, in the city, there was no longer the sound of barking dogs nor of men's voices, Medea went from the palace. She came to a path; she followed it until it brought her into the part of the grove that was all black with the shadow that oak trees made.

She raised up her hands and she called upon Hecate,

the Moon. As she did, there was a blaze as from torches all around, and she saw horrible serpents stretching themselves toward her from the branches of the trees. Medea shrank back in fear. But again she called upon Hecate. And now there was a howling as from the hounds of Hades all around her. Fearful, indeed, Medea grew as the howling came near her; almost she turned to flee. But she raised her hands again and called upon Hecate. Then the nymphs who haunted the marsh and the river shrieked, and at those shrieks Medea crouched down in fear.

She called upon Hecate, the Moon, again. She saw the moon rise above the treetops, and then the hissing and shrieking and howling died away. Holding up a goblet in her hand Medea poured out a libation of honey to Hecate, the Moon.

And then she went to where the moon made a brightness upon the ground. There she saw a flower that rose above the other flowers—a flower that grew from two joined stalks, and that was of the color of a crocus. Medea cut the stalks with a brazen knife, and as she did there came a deep groan out of the earth.

This was the Promethean flower. It had come out of the earth first when the vulture that tore at Prometheus's liver had let fall to earth a drop of his blood. With a Caspian shell that she had brought with her Medea gathered the dark juice of this flower—the juice that went to make her most potent charm. All night she went through the grove gathering the juice of secret herbs; then she mingled them in a phial that she put away in her girdle.

She went from that grove and along the river. When the sun shed its first rays upon snowy Caucasus she stood outside the temple of Hecate. She waited, but she had not long to wait, for, like the bright star Sirius rising out of Ocean, soon she saw Jason coming toward her. She made a sign to him, and he came and stood beside her in the portals of the temple.

They would have stood face to face if Medea did not

have her head bent. A blush had come upon her face, and
Jason seeing it, and seeing how her head was bent, knew
how grievous it was to her to meet and speak to a
stranger in this way. He took her hand and he spoke to her
reverently, as one would speak to a priestess.

"Lady," he said, "I implore you by Hecate and by Zeus
who helps all strangers and suppliants to be kind to me
and to the men who have come to your country with me.
Without your help I cannot hope to prevail in the grievous
trial that has been laid upon me. If you will help us,
Medea, your name will be renowned throughout all
Greece. And I have hopes that you will help us, for your
face and form show you to be one who can be kind and
gracious."

The blush of shame had gone from Medea's face and a
softer blush came over her as Jason spoke. She looked
upon him and she knew that she could hardly live if the
breath of the brazen bulls withered his life or if the Earth-
born Men slew him. She took the charm from out her girdle; ungrudgingly she put it into Jason's hands. And as
she gave him the charm that she had gained with such
danger, the fear and trouble that was around her heart
melted as the dew melts from around the rose when it is
warmed by the first light of the morning.

Then they spoke standing close together in the portal
of the temple. She told him how he should anoint his body
all over with the charm; it would give him, she said,
boundless and untiring strength, and make him so that
the breath of the bulls could not wither him nor the horns
of the bulls pierce him. She told him also to sprinkle his
shield and his sword with the charm.

And then they spoke of the dragon's teeth and of the
Earth-born Men who would spring from them. Medea told
Jason that when they arose out of the earth he was to cast
a great stone amongst them. The Earth-born Men would
struggle about the stone, and they would slay each other
in the contest.

Her dark and delicate face was beautiful. Jason looked

upon her, and it came into his mind that in Colchis there was something else of worth besides the Golden Fleece. And he thought that after he had won the Fleece there would be peace between the Argonauts and King Æetes, and that he and Medea might sit together in the king's hall. But when he spoke of being joined in friendship with her father, Medea cried:

"Think not of treaties nor of covenants. In Greece such are regarded, but not here. Ah, do not think that the king, my father, will keep any peace with you! When you have won the Fleece you must hasten away. You must not tarry in Aea."

She said this and her cheeks were wet with tears to think that he should go so soon, that he would go so far, and that she would never look upon him again. She bent her head again and she said: "Tell me about your own land; about the place of your father, the place where you will live when you win back from Colchis."

Then Jason told her of Ioclus; he told her how it was circled by mountains not so lofty as her Caucasus; he told her of the pasture lands of Iolcus with their flocks of sheep; he told her of the Mountain Pelion where he had been reared by Chiron, the ancient centaur; he told her of his father who lingered out his life in waiting for his return.

Medea said: "When you go back to Iolcus do not forget me, Medea. I shall remember you, Jason, even in my father's despite. And it will be my hope that some rumor of you will come to me like some messenger-bird. If you forget me may some blast of wind sweep me away to Iolcus, and may I sit in your hall an unknown and an unexpected guest!"

Then they parted; Medea went swiftly back to the palace, and Jason, turning to the river, went to where the *Argo* was moored.

The heroes embraced and questioned him; he told them of Medea's counsel and he showed them the charm she had given him. That savage man Arcas scoffed at

Medea's counsel and Medea's charm, saying that the Argonauts had become poor-spirited indeed when they had to depend upon a girl's help.

Jason bathed in the river; then he anointed himself with the charm; he sprinkled his spear and shield and sword with it. He came to Arcas who sat upon his bench, still nursing his anger, and he held the spear toward him.

Arcas took up his heavy sword and he hewed at the butt of the spear. The edge of the sword turned. The blade leaped back in his hand as if it had been struck against an anvil. And Jason, feeling within him a boundless and tireless strength, laughed aloud.

III. The Winning of the Golden Fleece

THEY took the ship out of the backwater and they brought her to a wharf in the city. At a place that was called "The Ram's Couch" they fastened the *Argo*. Then they marched to the field of Ares, where the king and the Colchian people were.

Jason, carrying his shield and spear, went before the king. From the king's hand he took the gleaming helmet that held the dragon's teeth. This he put into the hands of Theseus, who went with him. Then with the spear and shield in his hands, with his sword girt across his shoulders, and with his mantle stripped off, Jason looked across the field of Ares.

He saw the plow that he was to yoke to the bulls; he saw the yoke of bronze near it; he saw the tracks of the bulls' hooves. He followed the tracks until he came to the lair of the fire-breathing bulls. Out of that lair, which was underground, smoke and fire belched.

He set his feet firmly upon the ground and he held his shield before him. He awaited the onset of the bulls. They came clanging up with loud bellowing, breathing out fire.

They lowered their heads, and with mighty, iron-tipped horns they came to gore and trample him.

Medea's charm had made him strong; Medea's charm had made his shield impregnable. The rush of the bulls did not overthrow him. His comrades shouted to see him standing firmly there, and in wonder the Colchians gazed upon him. All round him, as from a furnace, there came smoke and fire.

The bulls roared mightily. Grasping the horns of the bull that was upon his right hand, Jason dragged him until he had brought him beside the yoke of bronze. Striking the brazen knees of the bull suddenly with his foot he forced him down. Then he smote the other bull as it rushed upon him, and it too he forced down upon its knees.

Castor and Polydeuces held the yoke to him. Jason bound it upon the necks of the bulls. He fastened the plow to the yoke. Then he took his shield and set it upon his back, and grasping the handles of the plow he started to make the furrow.

With his long spear he drove the bulls before him as with a goad. Terribly they raged, furiously they breathed out fire. Beside Jason Theseus went holding the helmet that held the dragon's teeth. The hard ground was torn up by the plow of adamant, and the clods groaned as they were cast up. Jason flung the teeth between the open sods, often turning his head in fear that the deadly crop of the Earth-born Men were rising behind him.

By the time that a third of the day was finished the field of Ares had been plowed and sown. As yet the furrows were free of the Earth-born Men. Jason went down to the river and filled his helmet full of water and drank deeply. And his knees that were stiffened with the plowing he bent until they were made supple again.

He saw the field rising into mounds. It seemed that there were graves all over the field of Ares. Then he saw spears and shields and helmets rising up out of the earth. Then armed warriors sprang up, a fierce battle cry upon their lips.

Jason remembered the counsel of Medea. He raised a boulder that four men could hardly raise and with arms hardened by the plowing he cast it. The Colchians shouted to see such a stone cast by the hands of one man. Right into the middle of the Earth-born Men the stone came. They leaped upon it like hounds, striking at one another as they came together. Shield crashed on shield, spear rang upon spear as they struck at each other. The Earth-born Men, as fast as they arose, went down before the weapons in the hands of their brethren.

Jason rushed upon them, his sword in his hand. He slew some that had risen out of the earth only as far as the shoulders; he slew others whose feet were still in the earth; he slew others who were ready to spring upon him. Soon all the Earth-born Men were slain, and the furrows ran with their dark blood as channels run with water in springtime.

The Argonauts shouted loudly for Jason's victory. King Æetes rose from his seat that was beside the river and he went back to the city. The Colchians followed him. Day faded, and Jason's contest was ended.

But it was not the will of Æetes that the strangers should be let depart peaceably with the Golden Fleece that Jason had won. In the assembly place, with his son Apsyrtus beside him, and with the furious Colchians all around him, the king stood: on his breast was the gleaming corselet that Ares had given him, and on his head was that golden helmet with its four plumes that made him look as if he were truly the son of Helios, the Sun. Lightnings flashed from his great eyes; he spoke fiercely to the Colchians, holding in his hand his bronze-topped spear.

He would have them attack the strangers and burn the *Argo*. He would have the sons of Phrixus slain for bringing them to Aea. There was a prophecy, he declared, that would have him be watchful of the treachery of his own offspring: this prophecy was being fulfilled by the children of Chalciope; he feared, too, that his daughter,

Medea, had aided the strangers. So the king spoke, and the Colchians, hating all strangers, shouted around him.

Word of what her father had said was brought to Medea. She knew that she would have to go to the Argonauts and bid them flee hastily from Aea. They would not go, she knew, without the Golden Fleece; then she, Medea, would have to show them how to gain the Fleece.

Then she could never again go back to her father's palace, she could never again sit in this chamber and talk to her handmaidens, and be with Chalciope, her sister. Forever afterward she would be dependent on the kindness of strangers. Medea wept when she thought of all this. And then she cut off a tress of her hair and she left it in her chamber as a farewell from one who was going afar. Into the chamber where Chalciope was she whispered farewell.

The palace doors were all heavily bolted, but Medea did not have to pull back the bolts. As she chanted her Magic Song the bolts softly drew back, the doors softly opened. Swiftly she went along the ways that led to the river. She came to where fires were blazing and she knew that the Argonauts were there.

She called to them, and Phrontis, Chalciope's son, heard the cry and knew the voice. To Jason he spoke, and Jason quickly went to where Medea stood.

She clasped Jason's hand and she drew him with her. "The Golden Fleece," she said, "the time has come when you must pluck the Golden Fleece off the oak in the grove of Ares." When she said these words all Jason's being became taut like the string of a bow.

It was then the hour when huntsmen cast sleep from their eyes—huntsmen who never sleep away the end of the night, but who are ever ready to be up and away with their hounds before the beams of the sun efface the track and the scent of the quarry. Along a path that went from the river Medea drew Jason. They entered a grove. Then Jason saw something that was like a cloud filled with the light of the rising sun. It hung from a great oak tree. In awe he stood and looked upon it, knowing that at last he looked upon THE GOLDEN FLEECE.

His hand let slip Medea's hand and he went to seize the Fleece. As he did he heard a dreadful hiss. And then he saw the guardian of the Golden Fleece. Coiled all around the tree, with outstretched neck and keen and sleepless eyes, was a deadly serpent. Its hiss ran all through the grove and the birds that were wakening up squawked in terror.

Like rings of smoke that rise one above the other, the coils of the serpent went around the tree—coils covered by hard and gleaming scales. It uncoiled, stretched itself, and lifted its head to strike. Then Medea dropped on her knees before it, and began to chant her Magic Song.

As she sang, the coils around the tree grew slack. Like a dark, noiseless wave the serpent sank down on the ground. But still its jaws were open, and those dreadful jaws threatened Jason. Medea, with a newly cut spray of juniper dipped in a mystic brew, touched its deadly eyes. And still she chanted her Magic Song. The serpent's jaws closed; its eyes became deadened; far through the grove its length was stretched out.

Then Jason took the Golden Fleece. As he raised his hands to it, its brightness was such as to make a flame on his face. Medea called to him. He strove to gather it all up in his arms; Medea was beside him, and they went swiftly on.

They came to the river and down to the place where the *Argo* was moored. The heroes who were aboard started up, astonished to see the Fleece that shone as with the lightning of Zeus. Over Medea Jason cast it, and he lifted her aboard the *Argo*.

"O friends," he cried, "the quest on which we dared the gulfs of the sea and the wrath of kings is accomplished, thanks to the help of this maiden. Now may we return to Greece; now have we the hope of looking upon our fathers and our friends once more. And in all honor will we bring this maiden with us, Medea, the daughter of King Æetes."

Like rings of smoke that rise one above the other, the coils
of the serpent went around the tree—coils covered by hard
and gleaming scales. It uncoiled, stretched itself, and lifted its head
to strike. Then Medea dropped on her knees before it, and began
to chant her Magic Song. *See page 110.*

Then he drew his sword and cut the hawsers of the ship, calling upon the heroes to drive the *Argo* on. There was a din and a strain and a splash of oars, and away from Aea the *Argo* dashed. Beside the mast Medea stood; the Golden Fleece had fallen at her feet, and her head and face were covered by her silver veil.

IV. The Slaying of Apsyrtus

THAT silver veil was to be splashed with a brother's blood, and the Argonauts, because of that calamity, were for a long time to be held back from a return to their native land.

Now as they went down the river they saw that dangers were coming swiftly upon them. The chariots of the Colchians were upon the banks. Jason saw King Æetes in his chariot, a blazing torch lighting his corselet and his helmet. Swiftly the *Argo* went, but there were ships behind her, and they went swiftly too.

They came into the Sea of Pontus, and Phrontis, the son of Phrixus, gave counsel to them. "Do not strive to make the passage of the Symplegades," he said. "All who live around the Sea of Pontus are friendly to King Æetes; they will be warned by him, and they will be ready to slay us and take the *Argo*. Let us journey up the River Ister, and by that way we can come to the Thrinacian Sea that is close to your land."

The Argonauts thought well of what Phrontis said; into the waters of the Ister the ship was brought. Many of the Colchian ships passed by the mouth of the river, and went seeking the *Argo* toward the passage of the Symplegades.

But the Argonauts were on a way that was dangerous for them. For Apsyrtus had not gone toward the Symplegades seeking the *Argo*. He had led his soldiers overland to the River Ister at a place that was at a distance above its mouth. There were islands in the river at that place, and the soldiers of Apsyrtus landed on the islands, while Apsyrtus went to the kings of the people around and claimed their support.

The *Argo* came and the heroes found themselves cut off. They could not make their way between the islands that were filled with the Colchian soldiers, nor along the banks that were lined with men friendly to King Æetes. *Argo* was stayed. Apsyrtus sent for the chiefs; he had men enough to overwhelm them, but he shrank from a fight with the heroes, and he thought that he might gain all he wanted from them without a struggle.

Theseus and Peleus went to him. Apsyrtus would have them give up the Golden Fleece; he would have them give up Medea and the sons of Phrixus also.

Theseus and Peleus appealed to the judgment of the kings who supported Apsyrtus. Æetes, they said, had no more claim on the Golden Fleece. He had promised it to Jason as a reward for tasks that he had imposed. The tasks had been accomplished and the Fleece, no matter in what way it was taken from the grove of Ares, was theirs. So Theseus and Peleus said, and the kings who supported Apsyrtus gave judgment for the Argonauts.

But Medea would have to be given to her brother. If that were done the *Argo* would be let go on her course, Apsyrtus said, and the Golden Fleece would be left with them. Apsyrtus said, too, that he would not take Medea back to the wrath of her father; if the Argonauts gave her up she would be let stay on the island of Artemis and under the guardianship of the goddess.

The chiefs brought Apsyrtus's words back. There was a council of the Argonauts, and they agreed that they should leave Medea on the island of Artemis.

But grief and wrath took hold of Medea when she heard of this resolve. Almost she would burn the *Argo*. She went to where Jason stood, and she spoke again of all she had done to save his life and win the Golden Fleece for the Argonauts. Jason made her look on the ships and the soldiers that were around them; he showed her how these could overwhelm the Argonauts and slay them all. With all the heroes slain, he said, Medea would come into the hands of Apsyrtus, who then could leave her on the island of Artemis or take her back to the wrath of her father.

But Medea would not consent to go nor could Jason's heart consent to let her go. Then these two made a plot to deceive Apsyrtus.

"I have not been of the council that agreed to give you up to him," Jason said. "After you have been left there I will take you off the island of Artemis secretly. The Colchians and the kings who support them, not knowing that you have been taken off and hidden on the *Argo,* will let us pass." This Medea and Jason planned to do, and it was an ill thing, for it was breaking the covenant that the chiefs had entered with Apsyrtus.

Medea then was left by the Argonauts on the island of Artemis. Now Apsyrtus had been commanded by his father to bring her back to Aea; he thought that when she had been left by the Argonauts he could force her to come with him. So he went over to the island. Jason, secretly leaving his companions, went to the island from the other side.

Before the temple of Artemis Jason and Apsyrtus came face to face. Both men, thinking they had been betrayed to their deaths, drew their swords. Then, before the vestibule of the temple and under the eyes of Medea, Jason and Apsyrtus fought. Jason's sword pierced the son of Æetes; as he fell Apsyrtus cried out bitter words against Medea, saying that it was on her account that he had come on his death. And as he fell the blood of her brother splashed Medea's silver veil.

Jason lifted Medea up and carried her to the *Argo*. They hid the maiden under the Fleece of Gold and they sailed past the ships of the Colchians. When darkness came they were far from the island of Artemis. It was then that they heard a loud wailing, and they knew that the Colchians had discovered that their prince had been slain.

Jason's sword pierced the son of Æetes; as he fell Apsyrtus cried out bitter words against Medea, saying that it was on her account that he had come on his death. *See page 114.*

The Colchians did not pursue them. Fearing the wrath of Æetes they made settlements in the lands of the kings who had supported Apsyrtus; they never went back to Aea; they called themselves Apsyrtians henceforward, naming themselves after the prince they had come with.

They had escaped the danger that had hemmed them in, but the Argonauts, as they sailed on, were not content; covenants had been broken, and blood had been shed in a bad cause. And as they went on through the darkness the voice of the ship was heard; at the sound of that voice fear and sorrow came upon the voyagers, for they felt that it had a prophecy of doom.

Castor and Polydeuces went to the front of the ship; holding up their hands, they prayed. Then they heard the words that the voice uttered: in the night as they went on the voice proclaimed the wrath of Zeus on account of the slaying of Apsyrtus.

What was their doom to be? It was that the Argonauts would have to wander forever over the gulfs of the sea unless Medea had herself cleansed of her brother's blood. There was one who could cleanse Medea—Circe, the daughter of Helios and Perse. The voice urged the heroes to pray to the immortal gods that the way to the island of Circe be shown to them.

V. Medea Comes to Circe

THEY sailed up the River Ister until they came to the Eridanus, that river across which no bird can fly. Leaving the Eridanus they entered the Rhodanus, a river that rises in the extreme north, where Night herself has her habitation. And voyaging up this river they came to the Stormy Lakes. A mist lay upon the lakes night and day; voyaging through them the Argonauts at last brought out their ship upon the Sea of Ausonia.

It was Zetes and Calais, the sons of the North Wind, who brought the *Argo* safely along this dangerous course. And to Zetes and Calais Iris, the messenger of the gods, appeared and revealed to them where Circe's island lay.

Deep blue water was all around that island, and on its height a marble house was to be seen. But a strange haze covered everything as with a veil. As the Argonauts came near they saw what looked to them like great dragonflies; they came down to the shore, and then the heroes saw that they were maidens in gleaming dresses.

The maidens waved their hands to the voyagers, calling them to come on the island. Strange beasts came up to where the maidens were and made whimpering cries.

The Argonauts would have drawn the ship close and would have sprung upon the island only that Medea cried out to them. She showed them the beasts that whimpered around the maidens, and then, as the Argonauts looked upon them, they saw that these were not beasts of the wild. There was something strange and fearful about them; the heroes gazed upon them with troubled eyes. They brought the ship near, but they stayed upon their benches, holding the oars in their hands.

Medea sprang to the island; she spoke to the maidens so that they shrank away; then the beasts came and whimpered around her. "Forbear to land here, O Argonauts," Medea cried, "for this is the island where men are changed into beasts." She called to Jason to come; only Jason would she have come upon the island.

They went swiftly toward the marble house, and the beasts followed them, looking up at Jason and Medea with pitiful human eyes. They went into the marble house of Circe, and as suppliants they seated themselves at the hearth.

Circe stood at her loom, weaving her many-colored threads. Swiftly she turned to the suppliants; she looked for something strange in them, for just before they came the walls of her house dripped with blood and the flame ran over and into her pot, burning up all the magic herbs

She went toward where they sat, Medea with her face hidden
by her hands, and Jason, with his head bent, holding with its point
in the ground the sword with which he had slain the son of Æetes.
See page 119.

she was brewing. She went toward where they sat, Medea with her face hidden by her hands, and Jason, with his head bent, holding with its point in the ground the sword with which he had slain the son of Æetes.

When Medea took her hands away from before her face, Circe knew that, like herself, this maiden was of the race of Helios. Medea spoke to her, telling her first of the voyage of the heroes and of their toils; telling her then of how she had given help to Jason against the will of Æetes, her father; telling her then, fearfully, of the slaying of Apsyrtus. She covered her face with her robe as she spoke of it. And then she told Circe she had come, warned by the judgment of Zeus, to ask of Circe, the daughter of Helios, to purify her from the stain of her brother's blood.

Like all the children of Helios, Circe had eyes that were wide and full of life, but she had stony lips—lips that were heavy and moveless. Bright golden hair hung smoothly along each of her sides. First she held a cup to them that was filled with pure water, and Jason and Medea drank from that cup.

Then Circe stayed by the hearth; she burnt cakes in the flame, and all the while she prayed to Zeus to be gentle with these suppliants. She brought both to the seashore. There she washed Medea's body and her garments with the spray of the sea.

Medea pleaded with Circe to tell her of the life she foresaw for her, but Circe would not speak of it. She told Medea that one day she would meet a woman who knew nothing about enchantments but who had much human wisdom. She was to ask of her what she was to do in her life or what she was to leave undone. And whatever this woman out of her wisdom told her, that Medea was to regard. Once more Circe offered them the cup filled with clear water, and when they had drunken of it she left them upon the seashore. As she went toward her marble house the strange beasts followed Circe, whimpering as they went. Jason and Medea went aboard the *Argo,* and the heroes drew away from Circe's island.

VI. In the Land of the Phæacians

WEARIED were the heroes now. They would have fain gone upon the island of Circe to rest there away from the oars and the sound of the sea. But the wisest of them, looking upon the beasts that were men transformed, held the *Argo* far off the shore. Then Jason and Medea came aboard, and with heavy hearts and wearied arms they turned to the open sea again.

No longer had they such high hearts as when they drove the *Argo* between the Clashers and into the Sea of Pontus. Now their heads drooped as they went on, and they sang such songs as slaves sing in their hopeless labor. Orpheus grew fearful for them now.

For Orpheus knew that they were drawing toward a danger. There was no other way for them, he knew, but past the Island Anthemœssa in the Tyrrhenian Sea where the Sirens were. Once they had been nymphs and had tended Persephone before she was carried off by Aidoneus to be his queen in the Underworld. Kind they had been, but now they were changed, and they cared only for the destruction of men.

All set around with rocks was the island where they were. As the *Argo* came near, the Sirens, ever on the watch to draw mariners to their destruction, saw them and came to the rocks and sang to them, holding each other's hands.

They sang all together their lulling song. That song made the wearied voyagers long to let their oars go with the waves, and drift, drift to where the Sirens were. Bending down to them the Sirens, with soft hands and white arms, would lift them to soft resting places. Then each of the Sirens sang a clear, piercing song that called to each of the voyagers. Each man thought that his own name was in that song. "O how well it is that you have come near," each one sang, "how well it is that you have come near where I have awaited you, having all delight prepared for you!"

Orpheus took up his lyre as the Sirens began to sing. He sang to the heroes of their own toils. He sang of them, how, gaunt and weary as they were, they were yet men, men who were the strength of Greece, men who had been fostered by the love and hope of their country. They were the winners of the Golden Fleece and their story would be told forever. And for the fame that they had won men would forego all rest and all delight. Why should they not toil, they who were born for great labors and to face dangers that other men might not face? Soon hands would be stretched out to them—the welcoming hands of the men and women of their own land.

So Orpheus sang, and his voice and the music of his lyre prevailed above the Sirens' voices. Men dropped their oars, but other men remained at their benches, and pulled steadily, if wearily, on. Only one of the Argonauts, Butes, a youth of Iolcus, threw himself into the water and swam toward the rocks from which the Sirens sang.

But an anguish that nearly parted their spirits from their bodies was upon them as they went wearily on. Toward the end of the day they beheld another island—an island that seemed very fair; they longed to land and rest themselves there and eat the fruits of the island. But Orpheus would not have them land. The island, he said, was Thrinacia. Upon that island the Cattle of the Sun pastured, and if one of the cattle perished through them their return home might not be won. They heard the lowing of the cattle through the mist, and a deep longing for the sight of their own fields, with a white house near, and flocks and herds at pasture, came over the heroes. They came near the Island of Thrinacia, and they saw the Cattle of the Sun feeding by the meadow streams; not one of them was black; all were white as milk, and the horns upon their heads were golden. They saw the two nymphs who herded the kine—Phæthusa and Lampetia, one with a staff of silver and the other with a staff of gold.

Driven by the breeze that came over the Thrinacian Sea the Argonauts came to the land of the Phæacians. It was a good land as they saw when they drew near; a land of orchards and fresh pastures, with a white and sun-lit city upon the height. Their spirits came back to them as they drew into the harbor; they made fast the hawsers, and they went upon the ways of the city.

And then they saw everywhere around them the dark faces of Colchian soldiers. These were the men of King Æetes, and they had come overland to the Phæacian city, hoping to cut off the Argonauts. Jason, when he saw the soldiers, shouted to those who had been left on the *Argo*, and they drew out of the harbor, fearful lest the Colchians should grapple with the ship and wrest from them the Fleece of Gold. Then Jason made an encampment upon the shore, and the captain of the Colchians went here and there, gathering together his men.

Medea left Jason's side and hastened through the city. To the palace of Alcinous, king of the Phæacians, she went. Within the palace she found Arete, the queen. And Arete was sitting by her hearth, spinning golden and silver threads.

Arete was young at that time, as young as Medea, and as yet no child had been born to her. But she had the clear eyes of one who understands, and who knows how to order things well. Stately, too, was Arete, for she had been reared in the house of a great king. Medea came to her, and fell upon her knees before her, and told her how she had fled from the house of her father, King Æetes.

She told Arete, too, how she had helped Jason to win the Golden Fleece, and she told her how through her her brother had been led to his death. As she told this part of her story she wept and prayed at the knees of the queen.

Arete was greatly moved by Medea's tears and prayers. She went to Alcinous in his garden, and she begged of him to save the Argonauts from the great force of the Colchians that had come to cut them off. "The Golden Fleece," said Arete, "has been won by the tasks that Jason performed. If the Colchians should take Medea, it would be to bring her back to Aea and to a bitter doom. And the maiden," said the queen, "has broken my heart by her prayers and tears."

King Alcinous said: "Æetes is strong, and although his kingdom is far from ours, he can bring war upon us." But still Arete pleaded with him to protect Medea from the Colchians. Alcinous went within; he raised up Medea from where she crouched on the floor of the palace, and he promised her that the Argonauts would be protected in his city.

Then the king mounted his chariot; Medea went with him, and they came down to the seashore where the heroes had made their encampment. The Argonauts and the Colchians were drawn up against each other, and the Colchians far outnumbered the wearied heroes.

Alcinous drove his chariot between the two armies. The Colchians prayed him to have the strangers make surrender to them. But the king drove his chariot to where the heroes stood, and he took the hand of each, and received them as his guests. Then the Colchians knew that they might not make war upon the heroes. They drew off. The next day they marched away.

It was a rich land that they had come to. Once Aristæus dwelt there, the king who discovered how to make bees store up their honey for men and how to make the good olive grow. Macris, his daughter, tended Dionysus, the son of Zeus, when Hermes brought him of the flame, and moistened his lips with honey. She tended him in a cave in the Phæacian land, and ever afterward the Phæacians were blessed with all good things.

Now as the heroes marched to the palace of King Alcinous the people came to meet them, bringing them sheep and calves and jars of wine and honey. The women brought them fresh garments; to Medea they gave fine linen and golden ornaments.

Amongst the Phæacians who loved music and games

and the telling of stories the heroes stayed for long. There were dances, and to the Phæacians who honored him as a god, Orpheus played upon his lyre. And every day, for the seven days that they stayed amongst them, the Phæacians brought rich presents to the heroes.

And Medea, looking into the clear eyes of Queen Arete, knew that she was the woman of whom Circe had prophesied, the woman who knew nothing of enchantments, but who had much human wisdom. She was to ask of her what she was to do in her life and what she was to leave undone. And what this woman told her Medea was to regard. Arete told her that she was to forget all the witcheries and enchantments that she knew, and that she was never to practice against the life of any one. This she told Medea upon the shore, before Jason lifted her aboard the *Argo*.

VII. They Come to the Desert Land

AND now with sail spread wide the *Argo* went on, and the heroes rested at the oars. The wind grew stronger. It became a great blast, and for nine days and nine nights the ship was driven fearfully along.

The blast drove them into the Gulf of Libya, from whence there is no return for ships. On each side of the gulf there are rocks and shoals, and the sea runs toward the limitless sand. On the top of a mighty tide the *Argo* was lifted, and she was flung high up on the desert sands.

A flood tide such as might not come again for long left the Argonauts on the empty Libyan land. And when they came forth and saw that vast level of sand stretching like a mist away into the distance, a deadly fear came over each of them. No spring of water could they descry; no path; no herdsman's cabin; over all that vast land there was silence and dead calm. And one said to the other: "What land is this? Whither have we come? Would that the tempest had overwhelmed us, or would that we had lost the ship and our lives between the Clashing Rocks at the time when we were making our way into the Sea of Pontus."

And the helmsman, looking before him, said with a breaking heart: "Out of this we may not come, even should the breeze blow from the land, for all around us are shoals and sharp rocks—rocks that we can see fretting the water, line upon line. Our ship would have been shattered far from the shore if the tide had not borne her far up on the sand. But now the tide rushes back toward the sea, leaving only foam on which no ship can sail to cover the sand. And so all hope of our return is cut off."

He spoke with tears flowing upon his cheeks, and all who had knowledge of ships agreed with what the helmsman had said. No dangers that they had been through were as terrible as this. Hopelessly, like lifeless specters, the heroes strayed about the endless strand.

They embraced each other and they said farewell as they laid down upon the sand that might blow upon them and overwhelm them in the night. They wrapped their heads in their cloaks, and, fasting, they laid themselves down.

Jason crouched beside the ship, so troubled that his life nearly went from him. He saw Medea huddled against a rock and with her hair streaming on the sand. He saw the men who, with all the bravery of their lives, had come with him, stretched on the desert sand, weary and without hope. He thought that they, the best of men, might die in this desert with their deeds all unknown; he thought that he might never win home with Medea, to make her his queen in Iolcus.

He lay against the side of the ship, his cloak wrapped around his head. And there death would have come to him and to the others if the nymphs of the desert had been unmindful of these brave men. They came to Jason. It was midday then, and the fierce rays of the sun were scorching all Libya. They drew off the cloak that wrapped his head; they stood near him, three nymphs girded around with goatskins.

"Why art thou so smitten with despair?" the nymphs said to Jason. "Why art thou smitten with despair, thou who hast wrought so much and hast won so much? Up! Arouse thy comrades! We are the solitary nymphs, the warders of the land of Libya, and we have come to show a way of escape to you, the Argonauts.

"Look around and watch for the time when Poseidon's great horse shall be unloosed. Then make ready to pay recompense to the mother that bore you all. What she did for you all, that you all must do for her; by doing it you will win back to the land of Greece." Jason heard them say these words and then he saw them no more; the nymphs vanished amongst the desert mounds.

Then Jason rose up. He did not know what to make out of what had been told him, but there was courage now and hope in his heart. He shouted; his voice was like the roar of a lion calling to his mate. At his shout his comrades roused themselves; all squalid with the dust of the desert the Argonauts stood around him.

"Listen, comrades, to me," Jason said, "while I speak of a strange thing that has befallen me. While I lay by the side of our ship three nymphs came before me. With light hands they drew away the cloak that wrapped my head. They declared themselves to be the solitary nymphs, the warders, of Libya. Very strange were the words they said to me. When Poseidon's great horse shall be unloosed, they said, we were to make the mother of us all a recompense, doing for her what she had done for us all. This the nymphs told me to say, but I cannot understand the meaning of their words."

There were some there who would not have given heed to Jason's words, deeming them words without meaning. But even as he spoke a wonder came before their eyes. Out of the far-off sea a great horse leaped. Vast he was of size and he had a golden mane. He shook the spray of the sea off his sides and mane. Past them he trampled and

Out of the far-off sea a great horse leaped. Vast he was of size and he had a golden mane. *See page 126.*

away toward the horizon, leaving great tracks in the sand.

Then Nestor spoke rejoicingly. "Behold the great horse! It is the horse that the desert nymphs spoke of, Poseidon's horse. Even now has the horse been unloosed, and now is the time to do what the nymphs bade us do.

"Who but *Argo* is the mother of us all? She has carried us. Now we must make her a recompense and carry her even as she carried us. With untiring shoulders we must bear *Argo* across this great desert.

"And whither shall we bear her? Whither but along the tracks that Poseidon's horse has left in the sand! Poseidon's horse will not go under the earth—once again he will plunge into the sea!"

So Nestor said and the Argonauts saw truth in his saying. Hope came to them again—the hope of leaving that desert and coming to the sea. Surely when they came to the sea again, and spread the sail and held the oars in their hands, their sacred ship would make swift course to their native land!

VIII. The Carrying of the *Argo*

WITH the terrible weight of the ship upon their shoulders the Argonauts made their way across the desert, following the tracks of Poseidon's golden-maned horse. Like a wounded serpent that drags with pain its length along, they went day after day across that limitless land.

A day came when they saw the great tracks of the horse no more. A wind had come up and had covered them with sand. With the mighty weight of the ship upon their shoulders, with the sun beating upon their heads, and with no marks on the desert to guide them, the heroes stood there, and it seemed to them that the blood must gush up and out of their hearts.

Then Zetes and Calais, sons of the North Wind, rose up upon
their wings to strive to get sight of the sea. Up, up, they soared.
See page 130.

Then Zetes and Calais, sons of the North Wind, rose up upon their wings to strive to get sight of the sea. Up, up, they soared. And then as a man sees, or thinks he sees, at the month's beginning, the moon through a bank of clouds, Zetes and Calais, looking over the measureless land, saw the gleam of water. They shouted to the Argonauts; they marked the way for them, and wearily, but with good hearts, the heroes went upon the way.

They came at last to the shore of what seemed to be a wide inland sea. They set *Argo* down from off their over-wearied shoulders and they let her keel take water once more.

All salt and brackish was that water; they dipped their hands into and tasted the salt. Orpheus was able to name the water they had come to; it was that lake that was called after Triton, the son of Nereus, the ancient one of the sea. They set up an altar and they made sacrifices in thanksgiving to the gods.

They had come to water at last, but now they had to seek for other water—for the sweet water that they could drink. All around them they looked, but they saw no sign of a spring. And then they felt a wind blow upon them—a wind that had in it not the dust of the desert but the fragrance of growing things. Toward where that wind blew from they went.

As they went on they saw a great shape against the sky; they saw mountainous shoulders bowed. Orpheus bade them halt and turn their faces with reverence toward that great shape: for this was Atlas the Titan, the brother of Prometheus, who stood there to hold up the sky on his shoulders.

Then they were near the place that the fragrance had blown from: there was a garden there; the only fence that ran around it was a lattice of silver. "Surely there are springs in the garden," the Argonauts said. "We will enter this fair garden now and slake our thirst."

Orpheus bade them walk reverently, for all around them, he said, was sacred ground. This garden was the

Garden of the Hesperides that was watched over by the Daughters of the Evening Land. The Argonauts looked through the silver lattice; they saw trees with lovely fruit, and they saw three maidens moving through the garden with watchful eyes. In this garden grew the tree that had the golden apples that Zeus gave to Hera as a wedding gift.

They saw the tree on which the golden apples grew. The maidens went to it and then looked watchfully all around them. They saw the faces of the Argonauts looking through the silver lattice and they cried out, one to the other, and they joined their hands around the tree.

But Orpheus called to them, and the maidens understood the divine speech of Orpheus. He made the Daughters of the Evening Land know that they who stood before the lattice were men who reverenced the gods, who would not strive to enter the forbidden garden. The maidens came toward them. Beautiful as the singing of Orpheus was their utterance, but what they said was a complaint and a lament.

Their lament was for the dragon Ladon, that dragon with a hundred heads that guarded sleeplessly the tree that had the golden apples. Now that dragon was slain. With arrows that had been dipped in the poison of the Hydra's blood their dragon, Ladon, had been slain.

The Daughters of the Evening Land sang of how a mortal had come into the garden that they watched over. He had a great bow, and with his arrow he slew the dragon that guarded the golden apples. The golden apples he had taken away; they had come back to the tree they had been plucked from, for no mortal might keep them in his possession. So the maidens sang—Hespere, Eretheis, and Ægle—and they complained that now, unhelped by the hundred-headed dragon, they had to keep guard over the tree.

The Argonauts knew of whom they told the tale—Heracles, their comrade. Would that Heracles were with them now!

The Hesperides told them of Heracles—of how the springs in the garden dried up because of his plucking the golden apples. He came out of the garden thirsting. Nowhere could he find a spring of water. To yonder great rock he went. He smote it with his foot and water came out in full flow. Then he, leaning on his hands and with his chest upon the ground, drank and drank from the water that flowed from the rifted rock.

The Argonauts looked to where the rock stood. They caught the sound of water. They carried Medea over. And then, company after company, all huddled together, they stooped down and drank their fill of the clear good water. With lips wet with the water they cried to each other, "Heracles! Although he is not with us, in very truth Heracles has saved his comrades from deadly thirst!"

They saw his footsteps printed upon the rocks, and they followed them until they led to the sand where no footsteps stay. Heracles! How glad his comrades would have been if they could have had sight of him then! But it was long ago—before he had sailed with them—that Heracles had been here.

Still hearing their complaint they turned back to the lattice, to where the Daughters of the Evening Land stood. The Daughters of the Evening Land bent their heads to listen to what the Argonauts told one another, and, seeing them bent to listen, Orpheus told a story about one who had gone across the Libyan desert, about one who was a hero like unto Heracles.

THE STORY OF PERSEUS

Beyond where Atlas stands there is a cave where the strange women, the ancient daughters of Phorcys, live. They have been gray from their birth. They have but one eye and one tooth between them, and they pass the eye and the tooth, one to the other, when they would see or eat. They are called the Graiai, these two sisters.

Up to the cave where they lived a youth once came. He was beardless, and the garb he wore was torn and travel-

stained, but he had shapeliness and beauty. In his leath-
ern belt there was an exceedingly bright sword; this
sword was not straight like the swords we carry, but it
was hooked like a sickle. The strange youth with the
bright, strange sword came very quickly and very silently
up to the cave where the Graiai lived and looked over a
high boulder into it.

One was sitting munching acorns with the single tooth.
The other had the eye in her hand. She was holding it to
her forehead and looking into the back of the cave. These
two ancient women, with their gray hair falling over them
like thick fleeces, and with faces that were only forehead
and cheeks and nose and mouth, were strange creatures
truly. Very silently the youth stood looking at them.

"Sister, sister," cried the one who was munching acorns,
"sister, turn your eye this way. I heard the stir of something."

The other turned, and with the eye placed against her
forehead looked out to the opening of the cave. The youth
drew back behind the boulder. "Sister, sister, there is
nothing there," said the one with the eye.

Then she said: "Sister, give me the tooth for I would eat
my acorns. Take the eye and keep watch."

The one who was eating held out the tooth, and the one
who was watching held out the eye. The youth darted into
the cave. Standing between the eyeless sisters, he took
with one hand the tooth and with the other the eye.

"Sister, sister, have you taken the eye?"

"I have not taken the eye. Have you taken the tooth?"

"I have not taken the tooth."

"Some one has taken the eye, and some one has taken
the tooth."

They stood together, and the youth watched their blink-
ing faces as they tried to discover who had come into the
cave, and who had taken the eye and the tooth.

Then they said, screaming together: "Who ever has
taken the eye and the tooth from the Graiai, the ancient
daughters of Phorcys, may Mother Night smother him."

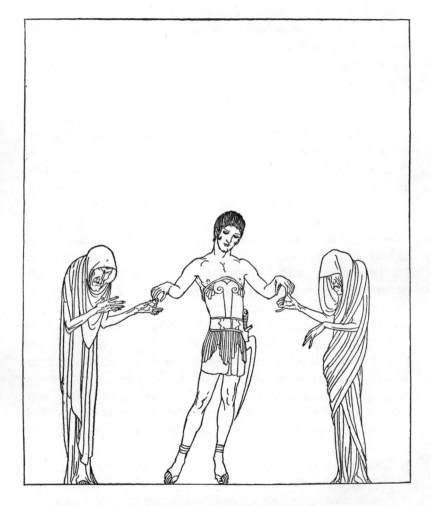

Standing between the eyeless sisters, he took with one hand
the tooth and with the other the eye. *See page 133.*

The youth spoke. "Ancient daughters of Phorcys," he said, "Graiai, I would not rob from you. I have come to your cave only to ask the way to a place."

"Ah, it is a mortal, a mortal," screamed the sisters. "Well, mortal, what would you have from the Graiai?"

"Ancient Graiai," said the youth, "I would have you tell me, for you alone know, where the nymphs dwell who guard the three magic treasures—the cap of darkness, the shoes of flight, and the magic pouch."

"We will not tell you, we will not tell you that," screamed the two ancient sisters.

"I will keep the eye and the tooth," said the youth, "and I will give them to one who will help me."

"Give me the eye and I will tell you," said one. "Give me the tooth and I will tell you," said the other. The youth put the eye in the hand of one and the tooth in the hand of the other, but he held their skinny hands in his strong hands until they should tell him where the nymphs dwelt who guarded the magic treasures. The Gray Ones told him. Then the youth with the bright sword left the cave. As he went out he saw on the ground a shield of bronze, and he took it with him.

To the other side of where Atlas stands he went. There he came upon the nymphs in their valley. They had long dwelt there, hidden from gods and men, and they were startled to see a stranger youth come into their hidden valley. They fled away. Then the youth sat on the ground, his head bent like a man who is very sorrowful.

The youngest and the fairest of the nymphs came to him at last. "Why have you come, and why do you sit here in such great trouble, youth?" said she. And then she said: "What is this strange sickle-sword that you wear? Who told you the way to our dwelling place? What name have you?"

"I have come here," said the youth, and he took the bronze shield upon his knees and began to polish it, "I have come here because I want you, the nymphs who guard them, to give to me the cap of darkness and the shoes of flight and the magic pouch. I must gain these things; without them I must go to my death. Why I must gain them you will know from my story."

When he said that he had come for the three magic treasures that they guarded, the kind nymph was more startled than she and her sisters had been startled by the appearance of the strange youth in their hidden valley. She turned away from him. But she looked again and she saw that he was beautiful and brave looking. He had spoken of his death. The nymph stood looking at him pitifully, and the youth, with the bronze shield laid beside his knees and the strange hooked sword lying across it, told her his story.

"I am Perseus," he said, "and my grandfather, men say, is king in Argos. His name is Acrisius. Before I was born a prophecy was made to him that the son of Danaë, his daughter, would slay him. Acrisius was frightened by the prophecy, and when I was born he put my mother and myself into a chest, and he sent us adrift upon the waves of the sea.

"I did not know what a terrible peril I was in, for I was an infant newly born. My mother was so hopeless that she came near to death. But the wind and the waves did not destroy us: they brought us to a shore; a shepherd found the chest, and he opened it and brought my mother and myself out of it alive. The land we had come to was Seriphus. The shepherd who found the chest and who rescued my mother and myself was the brother of the king. His name was Dictys.

"In the shepherd's wattled house my mother stayed with me, a little infant, and in that house I grew from babyhood to childhood, and from childhood to boyhood. He was a kind man, this shepherd Dictys. His brother Polydectes had put him away from the palace, but Dictys did not grieve for that, for he was happy minding his sheep upon the hillside, and he was happy in his little hut of wattles and clay.

"Polydectes, the king, was seldom spoken to about his brother, and it was years before he knew of the mother and child who had been brought to live in Dictys's hut. But at last he heard of us, for strange things began to be said about my mother—how she was beautiful, and how she looked like one who had been favored by the gods. Then one day when he was hunting, Polydectes the king came to the hut of Dictys the shepherd.

"He saw Danaë, my mother, there. By her looks he knew that she was a king's daughter and one who had been favored by the gods. He wanted her for his wife. But my mother hated this harsh and overbearing king, and she would not wed with him. Often he came storming around the shepherd's hut, and at last my mother had to take refuge from him in a temple. There she became the priestess of the goddess.

"I was taken to the palace of Polydectes, and there I was brought up. The king still stormed around where my mother was, more and more bent on making her marry him. If she had not been in the temple where she was under the protection of the goddess he would have wed her against her will.

"But I was growing up now, and I was able to give some protection to my mother. My arm was a strong one, and Polydectes knew that if he wronged my mother in any way, I had the will and the power to be deadly to him. One day I heard him say before his princes and his lords that he would wed, and would wed one who was not Danaë, I was overjoyed to hear him say this. He asked the lords and the princes to come to the wedding feast; they declared they would, and they told him of the presents they would bring.

"Then King Polydectes turned to me and he asked me to come to the wedding feast. I said I would come. And then, because I was young and full of the boast of youth, and because the king was now ceasing to be a terror to me, I said that I would bring to his wedding feast the head of the Gorgon.

"The king smiled when he heard me say this, but he smiled not as a good man smiles when he hears the boast of youth. He smiled, and he turned to the princes and lords, and he said: 'Perseus will come, and he will bring a greater gift than any of you, for he will bring the head of her whose gaze turns living creatures into stone.'

"When I heard the king speak so grimly about my boast the fearfulness of the thing I had spoken of doing came over me. I thought for an instant that the Gorgon's head appeared before me, and that I was then and there turned into stone.

"The day of the wedding feast came. I came and I brought no gift. I stood with my head hanging for shame. Then the princes and the lords came forward, and they showed the great gifts of horses that they had brought. I thought that the king would forget about me and about my boast. And then I heard him call my name. 'Perseus,' he said, 'Perseus, bring before us now the Gorgon's head that, as you told us, you would bring for the wedding gift.'

"The princes and lords and people looked toward me, and I was filled with a deeper shame. I had to say that I had failed to bring a present. Then that harsh and over-bearing king shouted at me. 'Go forth,' he said, 'go forth and fetch the present that you spoke of. If you do not bring it remain for ever out of my country, for in Seriphus we will have no empty boasters.' The lords and the princes applauded what the king said; the people were sad for me and sad for my mother, but they might not do anything to help me, so just and so due to me did the words of the king seem. There was no help for it, and I had to go from the country of Seriphus, leaving my mother at the mercy of Polydectes.

"I bade good-by to my sorrowful mother and I went from Seriphus—from that land that I might not return to without the Gorgon's head. I traveled far from that country. One day I sat down in a lonely place and prayed to the gods that my strength might be equal to the will that now moved in me— the will to take the Gorgon's head, and take from my name the shame of a broken promise, and win back to Seriphus to save my mother from the harshness of the king.

"When I looked up I saw one standing before me. He was a youth, too, but I knew by the way he moved, and I knew by the brightness of his face and eyes, that he was of the immortals. I raised my hands in homage to him, and he came near me. 'Perseus,' he said, 'if you have the courage to strive, the way to win the Gorgon's head will be shown you.' I said that I had the courage to strive, and he knew that I was making no boast.

"He gave me this bright sickle-sword that I carry. He told me by what ways I might come near enough to the Gorgons without being turned into stone by their gaze. He told me how I might slay the one of the three Gorgons who was not immortal, and how, having slain her, I might take her head and flee without being torn to pieces by her sister Gorgons.

"Then I knew that I should have to come on the Gorgons from the air. I knew that having slain the one that could be slain I should have to fly with the speed of the wind. And I knew that that speed even would not save me—I should have to be hidden in my flight. To win the head and save myself I would need three magic things—the shoes of flight and the magic pouch, and the dogskin cap of Hades that makes its wearer invisible.

"The youth said: 'The magic pouch and the shoes of flight and the dogskin cap of Hades are in the keeping of the nymphs whose dwelling place no mortal knows. I may not tell you where their dwelling place is. But from the Gray Ones, from the ancient daughters of Phorcys who live in a cave near where Atlas stands, you may learn where their dwelling place is.'

"Thereupon he told me how I might come to the Graiai, and how I might get them to tell me where you, the nymphs, had your dwelling. The one who spoke to me was Hermes, whose dwelling is on Olympus. By this sickle-sword that he gave me you will know that I speak the truth."

Perseus ceased speaking, and she who was the youngest and fairest of the nymphs came nearer to him. She knew that he spoke truthfully, and besides she had pity for the youth. "But we are the keepers of the magic treasures," she said, "and some one whose need is greater even than yours may some time require them from us. But will you swear that you will bring the magic treasures back to us when you have slain the Gorgon and have taken her head?"

Perseus declared that he would bring the magic treasures back to the nymphs and leave them once more in their keeping. Then the nymph who had compassion for him called to the others. They spoke together while Perseus stayed far away from them, polishing his shield of bronze. At last the nymph who had listened to him came back, the others following her. They brought to Perseus and they put into his hands the things they had guarded— the cap made from dogskin that had been brought up out of Hades, a pair of winged shoes, and a long pouch that he could hang across his shoulder.

And so with the shoes of flight and the cap of darkness and the magic pouch, Perseus went to seek the Gorgons. The sickle-sword that Hermes gave him was at his side, and on his arm he held the bronze shield that was now well polished.

He went through the air, taking a way that the nymphs had shown him. He came to Oceanus that was the rim around the world. He saw forms that were of living creatures all in stone, and he knew that he was near the place where the Gorgons had their lair.

Then, looking upon the surface of his polished shield, he saw the Gorgons below him. Two were covered with hard serpent scales; they had tusks that were long and were like the tusks of boars, and they had hands of gleaming brass and wings of shining gold. Still looking upon the shining surface of his shield Perseus went down and down. He saw the third sister—she who was not immortal. She had a woman's face and form, and her countenance was beautiful, although there was something deadly in its fairness. The two scaled and winged sisters were asleep, but the third, Medusa, was awake, and she was tearing with her hands a lizard that had come near her.

Upon her head was a tangle of serpents all with heads raised as though they were hissing. Still looking into the mirror of his shield Perseus came down and over Medusa. He turned his head away from her. Then, with a sweep of the sickle-sword he took her head off. There was no scream from the Gorgon, but the serpents upon her head hissed loudly.

Still with his face turned from it he lifted up the head by its tangle of serpents. He put it into the magic pouch. He rose up in the air. But now the Gorgon sisters were awake. They had heard the hiss of Medusa's serpents, and now they looked upon her headless body. They rose up on their golden wings, and their brazen hands were stretched out to tear the one who had slain Medusa. As they flew after him they screamed aloud.

Although he flew like the wind the Gorgon sisters would have overtaken him if he had been plain to their eyes. But the dogskin cap of Hades saved him, for the Gorgon sisters did not know whether he was above or below them, behind or before them. On Perseus went, flying toward where Atlas stood. He flew over this place, over Libya. Drops of blood from Medusa's head fell down upon the desert. They were changed and became the deadly serpents that are on these sands and around these rocks. On and on Perseus flew toward Atlas and toward the hidden valley where the nymphs who were again to guard the magic treasures had their dwelling place. But before he came to the nymphs Perseus had another adventure.

In Ethopia, which is at the other side of Libya, there ruled a king whose name was Cepheus. This king had permitted his queen to boast that she was more beautiful than the nymphs of the sea. In punishment for the queen's impiety and for the king's folly Poseidon sent a monster out of the sea to waste that country. Every year the monster came, destroying more and more of the country of Ethopia. Then the king asked of an oracle what he should do to save his land and his people. The oracle spoke of a dreadful thing that he would have to do—he would have to sacrifice his daughter, the beautiful Princess Andromeda.

The king was forced by his savage people to take the maiden Andromeda and chain her to a rock on the seashore, leaving her there for the monster to devour her, satisfying himself with that prey.

Perseus, flying near, heard the maiden's laments. He saw her lovely body bound with chains to the rock. He came near her, taking the cap of darkness off his head. She saw him, and she bent her head in shame, for she thought that he would think that it was for some dreadful fault of her own that she had been left chained in that place.

Her father had stayed near. Perseus saw him, and called to him, and bade him tell why the maiden was chained to the rock. The king told Perseus of the sacrifice that he had been forced to make. Then Perseus came near the maiden, and he saw how she looked at him with pleading eyes.

Then Perseus made her father promise that he would give Andromeda to him for his wife if he should slay the sea monster. Gladly Cepheus promised this. Then Perseus once again drew his sickle-sword; by the rock to which Andromeda was still chained he waited for sight of the sea monster.

It came rolling in from the open sea, a shapeless and unsightly thing. With the shoes of flight upon his feet Perseus rose above it. The monster saw his shadow upon the water, and savagely it went to attack the shadow. Perseus swooped down as an eagle swoops down; with his sickle-sword he attacked it, and he struck the hook through the monster's shoulder. Terribly it reared up from the sea. Perseus rose over it, escaping its wide-opened mouth with its treble rows of fangs. Again he swooped and struck at it. Its hide was covered all over with hard scales and with the shells of sea things, but Perseus's sword struck through it. It reared up again, spouting water mixed with blood. On a rock near the rock that Andromeda was chained to Perseus alighted. The monster, seeing him, bellowed and rushed swiftly through the water to overwhelm him. As it reared up he plunged the sword again and again into its body. Down into the water the monster sank, and water mixed with blood was spouted up from the depths into which it sank.

Then was Andromeda loosed from her chains. Perseus, the conqueror, lifted up the fainting maiden and carried her back to the king's palace. And Cepheus there renewed his promise to give her in marriage to her deliverer.

Perseus went on his way. He came to the hidden valley where the nymphs had their dwelling place, and he restored to them the three magic treasures that they had given him—the cap of darkness, the shoes of flight, and the magic pouch. And these treasures are still there, and the hero who can win his way to the nymphs may have them as Perseus had them.

Again he returned to the place where he had found Andromeda chained. With face averted he drew forth the Gorgon's head from where he had hidden it between the rocks. He made a bag for it out of the horny skin of the monster he had slain. Then, carrying his tremendous trophy, he went to the palace of King Cepheus to claim his bride.

Now before her father had thought of sacrificing her to the sea monster he had offered Andromeda in marriage to a prince of Ethopia—to a prince whose name was Phineus. Phineus did not strive to save Andromeda. But, hearing that she had been delivered from the monster, he came to take her for his wife; he came to Cepheus's palace, and he brought with him a thousand armed men.

The palace of Cepheus was filled with armed men when Perseus entered it. He saw Andromeda on a raised place in the hall. She was pale as when she was chained to the rock, and when she saw him in the palace she uttered a cry of gladness.

Cepheus, the craven king, would have let him who had come with the armed bands take the maiden. Perseus came beside Andromeda and he made his claim. Phineus spoke insolently to him, and then he urged one of his captains to strike Perseus down. Many sprang forward to attack him. Out of the bag Perseus drew Medusa's head. He held it before those who were bringing strife into the hall. They were turned to stone. One of Cepheus's men wished to defend Perseus: he struck at the captain who had come near; his sword made a clanging sound as it struck this one who had looked upon Medusa's head.

Perseus went from the land of Ethopia taking fair Andromeda with him. They went into Greece, for he had thought of going to Argos, to the country that his grandfather ruled over. At this very time Acrisius got tidings of Danaë and her son, and he knew that they had not perished on the waves of the sea. Fearful of the prophecy that told he would be slain by his grandson and fearing that he would come to Argos to seek him, Acrisius fled out of his country.

He came into Thessaly. Perseus and Andromeda were there. Now, one day the old king was brought to games that were being celebrated in honor of a dead hero. He was leaning on his staff, watching a youth throw a metal disk, when something in that youth's appearance made him want to watch him more closely. About him there was something of a being of the upper air; it made Acrisius think of a brazen tower and of a daughter whom he had shut up there.

He moved so that he might come nearer to the disk-thrower. But as he left where he had been standing he came into the line of the thrown disk. It struck the old man on the temple. He fell down dead, and as he fell the people cried out his name—"Acrisius, King Acrisius!" Then Perseus knew whom the disk, thrown by his hand, had slain.

And because he had slain the king by chance Perseus would not go to Argos, nor take over the kingdom that his grandfather had reigned over. With Andromeda he went to Seriphus where his mother was. And in Seriphus there still reigned Polydectes, who had put upon him the terrible task of winning the Gorgon's head.

He came to Seriphus and he left Andromeda in the hut of Dictys the shepherd. No one knew him; he heard his name spoken of as that of a youth who had gone on a foolish quest and who would never again be heard of. To the temple where his mother was a priestess he came. Guards were placed all around it. He heard his mother's voice and it was raised in lament: "Walled up here and given over to hunger I shall be made go to Polydectes's house and become his wife. O ye gods, have ye no pity for Danaë, the mother of Perseus?"

Perseus cried aloud, and his mother heard his voice and her moans ceased. He turned around and he went to the palace of Polydectes, the king.

The king received him with mockeries. "I will let you stay in Seriphus for a day," he said, "because I would have you at a marriage feast. I have vowed that Danaë, taken from the temple where she sulks, will be my wife by tomorrow's sunset."

So Polydectes said, and the lords and princes who were around him mocked at Perseus and flattered the king. Perseus went from them then. The next day he came back to the palace. But in his hands now there was a dread thing—the bag made from the hide of the sea monster that had in it the Gorgon's head.

He saw his mother. She was brought in white and fainting, thinking that she would now have to wed the harsh and overbearing king. Then she saw her son, and hope came into her face.

The king seeing Perseus, said: "Step forward, O

. . . Perseus drew out the Gorgon's head. Holding it by the snaky locks he stood before the company. *See page 147.*

youngling, and see your mother wed to a mighty man. Step forward to witness a marriage, and then depart, for it is not right that a youth that makes promises and does not keep them should stay in a land that I rule over. Step forward now, you with the empty hands."

But not with empty hands did Perseus step forward. He shouted out: "I have brought something to you at last, O king—a present to you and your mocking friends. But you, O my mother, and you, O my friends, avert your faces from what I have brought." Saying this Perseus drew out the Gorgon's head. Holding it by the snaky locks he stood before the company. His mother and his friends averted their faces. But Polydectes and his insolent friends looked full upon what Perseus showed. "This youth would strive to frighten us with some conjuror's trick," they said. They said no more, for they became as stones, and as stone images they still stand in that hall in Seriphus.

He went to the shepherd's hut, and he brought Dictys from it with Andromeda. Dictys he made king in Polydectes's stead. Then with Danaë and Andromeda, his mother and his wife, he went from Seriphus.

He did not go to Argos, the country that his grandfather had ruled over, although the people there wanted Perseus to come to them, and be king over them. He took the kingdom of Tiryns in exchange for that of Argos, and there he lived with Andromeda, his lovely wife out of Ethopia. They had a son named Perses who became the parent of the Persian people.

The sickle-sword that had slain the Gorgon went back to Hermes, and Hermes took Medusa's head also. That head Hermes's divine sister set upon her shield—Medusa's head upon the shield of Pallas Athene. O may Pallas Athene guard us all, and bring us out of this land of sands and stone where are the deadly serpents that have come from the drops of blood that fell from the Gorgon's head!

They turned away from the Garden of the Daughters of the Evening Land. The Argonauts turned from where the giant shape of Atlas stood against the sky and they went toward the Tritonian Lake. But not all of them reached the *Argo*. On his way back to the ship, Nauplius, the helmsman, met his death.

A sluggish serpent was in his way—it was not a serpent that would strike at one who turned from it. Nauplius trod upon it, and the serpent lifted its head up and bit his foot. They raised him on their shoulders and they hurried back with him. But his limbs became numb, and when they laid him down on the shore of the lake he stayed moveless. Soon he grew cold. They dug a grave for Nauplius beside the lake, and in that desert land they set up his helmsman's oar in the middle of his tomb of heaped stones.

And now like a snake that goes writhing this way and that way and that cannot find the cleft in the rock that leads to its lair, the *Argo* went hither and thither striving to find an outlet from that lake. No outlet could they find and the way of their homegoing seemed lost to them again. Then Orpheus prayed to the son of Nereus, to Triton, whose name was on that lake, to aid them.

Then Triton appeared. He stretched out his hand and showed them the outlet to the sea. And Triton spoke in friendly wise to the heroes, bidding them go upon their way in joy. "And as for labor," he said, "let there be no grieving because of that, for limbs that have youthful vigor should still toil."

They took up the oars and they pulled toward the sea, and Triton, the friendly immortal, helped them on. He laid hold upon *Argo*'s keel and he guided her through the water. The Argonauts saw him beneath the water; his body, from his head down to his waist, was fair and great and like to the body of one of the other immortals. But below his body was like a great fish's, forking this way and that. He moved with fins that were like the horns of the new moon. Triton helped *Argo* along until they came into the open sea. Then he plunged down into the abyss. The heroes shouted their thanks to him. Then they looked at each other and embraced each other with joy, for the sea that touched upon the land of Greece was open before them.

IX. Near to Iolcus Again

THE sun sank; then that star came that bids the shepherd bring his flock to the fold, that brings the wearied plowman to his rest. But no rest did that star bring to the Argonauts. The breeze that filled the sail died down; they furled the sail and lowered the mast; then, once again, they pulled at the oars. All night they rowed, and all day, and again when the next day came on. Then they saw the island that is halfway to Greece—the great and fair island of Crete.

It was Theseus who first saw Crete—Theseus who was to come to Crete upon another ship. They drew the *Argo* near the great island; they wanted water, and they were fain to rest there.

Minos, the great king, ruled over Crete. He left the guarding of the island to one of the race of bronze, to Talos, who had lived on after the rest of the bronze men had been destroyed. Thrice a day would Talos stride around the island; his brazen feet were tireless.

Now Talos saw the *Argo* drawing near. He took up great rocks and he hurled them at the heroes, and very quickly they had to draw their ship out of range.

They were wearied and their thirst was consuming them. But still that bronze man stood there ready to sink their ship with the great rocks that he took up in his hands. Medea stood forward upon the ship, ready to use her spells against the man of bronze.

In body and limbs he was made of bronze and in these he was invulnerable. But beneath a sinew in his ankle there was a vein that ran up to his neck and that was covered by a thin skin. If that vein were broken Talos would perish.

Medea did not know about this vein when she stood forward upon the ship to use her spells against him. Upon a cliff of Crete, all gleaming, stood that huge man of bronze. Then, as she was ready to fling her spells against him, Medea thought upon the words that Arete, the wise queen, had given her—that she was not to use spells and not to practice against the life of any one.

But she knew that there was no impiety in using spells and practicing against Talos, for Zeus had already doomed all his race. She stood upon the ship, and with her Magic Song she enchanted him. He whirled round and round. He struck his ankle against a jutting stone. The vein broke, and that which was the blood of the bronze man flowed out of him like molten lead. He stood towering upon the cliff. Like a pine upon a mountaintop that the woodman had left half hewn through and that a mighty wind pitches against, Talos stood upon his tireless feet, swaying to and fro. Then, emptied of all his strength, Minos's man of bronze fell into the Cretan Sea.

The heroes landed. That night they lay upon the land of Crete and rested and refreshed themselves. When dawn came they drew water from a spring, and once more they went on board the *Argo*.

A day came when the helmsman said, "To-morrow we shall see the shore of Thessaly, and by sunset we shall be in the harbor of Pagasæ. Soon, O voyagers, we shall be back in the city from which we went to gain the Golden Fleece."

Then Jason brought Medea to the front of the ship so that they might watch together for Thessaly, the homeland. The Mountain Pelion came into sight. Jason exulted as he looked upon that mountain; again he told Medea about Chiron, the ancient centaur, and about the days of his youth in the forests of Pelion.

The *Argo* went on; the sun sank, and darkness came on. Never was there darkness such as there was on that night. They called that night afterward the Pall of Darkness. To

Like a pine upon a mountaintop . . . Talos stood upon his tireless feet,
swaying to and fro. Then, emptied of all his strength, Minos's man
of bronze fell into the Cretan Sea. *See page 150.*

the heroes upon the *Argo* it seemed as if black chaos had come over the world again; they knew not whether they were adrift upon the sea or upon the River of Hades. No star pierced the darkness nor no beam from the moon.

After a night that seemed many nights the dawn came. In the sunrise they saw the land of Thessaly with its mountain, its forests, and its fields. They hailed each other as if they had met after a long parting. They raised the mast and unfurled the sail.

But not toward Pagasæ did they go. For now the voice of *Argo* came to them, shaking their hearts: Jason and Orpheus, Castor and Polydeuces, Zetes and Calais, Peleus and Telamon, Theseus, Admetus, Nestor, and Atalanta, heard the cry of their ship. And the voice of *Argo* warned them not to go into the harbor of Pagasæ.

As they stood upon the ship, looking toward Iolcus, sorrow came over all the heroes, such sorrow as made their hearts nearly break. For long they stood there in utter numbness.

Then Admetus spoke—Admetus who was the happiest of all those who went in quest of the Golden Fleece. "Although we may not go into the harbor of Pagasæ, nor into the city of Iolcus," Admetus said, "still we have come to the land of Greece. There are other harbors and other cities that we may go into. And in all the places that we go to we will be honored, for we have gone through toils and dangers, and we have brought to Greece the famous Fleece of Gold."

So Admetus said, and their spirits came back again to the heroes—came back to all of them save Jason. The rest had other cities to go to, and fathers and mothers and friends to greet them in other places, but for Jason there was only Iolcus.

Medea took his hand, and sorrow for him overcame her. For Medea could divine what had happened in Iolcus and why it was that the heroes might not go there.

It was to Corinth that the *Argo* went. Creon, the king of

Corinth, welcomed them and gave great honor to the heroes who had faced such labors and such dangers to bring the world's wonder to Greece.

The Argonauts stayed together until they went to Calydon, to hunt the boar that ravaged Prince Meleagrus's country. After that they separated, each one going to his own land. Jason came back to Corinth where Medea stayed. And in Corinth he had tidings of the happenings in Iolcus.

King Pelias now ruled more fearfully in Iolcus, having brought down from the mountains more and fiercer soldiers. And Æson, Jason's father, and Alcimide, his mother, were now dead, having been slain by King Pelias.

This Jason heard from men who came into Corinth from Thessaly. And because of the great army that Pelias had gathered there, Jason might not yet go into Iolcus, either to exact a vengeance, or to show the people THE GOLDEN FLEECE that he had gone so far to gain.

PART THREE
The Heroes of the Quest

I. Atalanta the Huntress

I

THEY came once more together, the heroes of the quest, to hunt a boar in Calydon—Jason and Peleus came, Telamon, Theseus, and rough Arcas, Nestor and Helen's brothers Polydeuces and Castor. And, most noted of all, there came the Arcadian huntress maid, Atalanta.

Beautiful they all thought her when they knew her aboard the *Argo*. But even more beautiful Atalanta seemed to the heroes when she came amongst them in her hunting gear. Her lovely hair hung in two bands across her shoulders, and over her breast hung an ivory quiver filled with arrows. They said that her face with its wide and steady eyes was maidenly for a boy's, and boyish for a maiden's face. Swiftly she moved with her head held high, and there was not one amongst the heroes who did not say, "Oh, happy would that man be whom Atalanta the unwedded would take for her husband!"

All the heroes said it, but the one who said it most feelingly was the prince of Calydon, young Meleagrus. He more than the other heroes felt the wonder of Atalanta's beauty.

Now the boar they had come to hunt was a monster boar. It had come into Calydon and it was laying waste the fields and orchards and destroying the people's cattle and horses. That boar had been sent into Calydon by an angry divinity. For when Œneus, the king of the country, was making sacrifice to the gods in thanksgiving for a bounteous harvest, he had neglected to make sacrifice to the

155

goddess of the wild things, Artemis. In her anger Artemis had sent the monster boar to lay waste Œneus's realm.

It was a monster boar indeed—one as huge as a bull, with tusks as great as an elephant's; the bristles on its back stood up like spear points, and the hot breath of the creature withered the growth on the ground. The boar tore up the corn in the fields and trampled down the vines with their clusters and heavy bunches of grapes; also it rushed against the cattle and destroyed them in the fields. And no hounds the huntsmen were able to bring could stand before it. And so it came to pass that men had to leave their farms and take refuge behind the walls of the city because of the ravages of the boar. It was then that the rulers of Calydon sent for the heroes of the quest to join with them in hunting the monster.

Calydon itself sent Prince Meleagrus and his two uncles, Plexippus and Toxeus. They were brothers to Meleagrus's mother, Althæa. Now Althæa was a woman who had sight to see mysterious things, but who had also a wayward and passionate heart. Once, after her son Meleagrus was born, she saw the three Fates sitting by her hearth. They were spinning the threads of her son's life, and as they spun they sang to each other, "An equal span of life we give to the newborn child, and to the billet of wood that now rests above the blaze of the fire." Hearing what the Fates sang and understanding it Althæa had sprung up from her bed, had seized the billet of wood, and had taken it out of the fire before the flames had burnt into it.

That billet of wood lay in her chest, hidden away. And Meleagrus nor any one else save Althæa knew of it, nor knew that the prince's life would last only for the space it would be kept from the burning. On the day of the hunting he appeared as the strongest and bravest of the youths of Calydon. And he knew not, poor Meleagrus, that the love for Atalanta that had sprung into his heart was to bring to the fire the billet of wood on which his life depended.

II

As Atalanta went, the bow in her hands, Prince Meleagrus pressed behind her. Then came Jason and Peleus, Telamon, Theseus and Nestor. Behind them came Meleagrus's dark-browed uncles, Plexippus and Toxeus. They came to a forest that covered the side of a mountain. Huntsmen had assembled here with hounds held in leashes and with nets to hold the rushing quarry. And when they had all gathered together they went through the forest on the track of the monster boar.

It was easy to track the boar, for it had left a broad trail through the forest. The heroes and the huntsmen pressed on. They came to a marshy covert where the boar had its lair. There was a thickness of osiers and willows and tall bullrushes, making a place that it was hard for the hunters to go through.

They roused the boar with the blare of horns and it came rushing out. Foam was on its tusks, and its eyes had in them the blaze of fire. On the boar came, breaking down the thicket in its rush. But the heroes stood steadily with the points of their spears toward the monster.

The hounds were loosed from their leashes and they dashed toward the boar. The boar slashed them with its tusks and trampled them into the ground. Jason flung his spear. The spear went wide of the mark. Another, Arcas, cast his, but the wood, not the point of the spear, struck the boar, rousing it further. Then its eyes flamed, and like a great stone shot from a catapult the boar rushed on the huntsmen who were stationed to the right. In that rush it flung two youths prone upon the ground.

Then might Nestor have missed his going to Troy and his part in that story, for the boar swerved around and was upon him in an instant. Using his spear as a leaping pole he vaulted upward and caught the branches of a tree as the monster dashed the spear down in its rush. In rage the beast tore at the trunk of the tree. The heroes might have been scattered at this moment, for Telamon had fallen, tripped by the roots of a tree, and Peleus had had to throw himself upon him to pull him out of the way of danger, if Polydeuces and Castor had not dashed up to their aid. They came riding upon high white horses, spears in their hands. The brothers cast their spears, but neither spear struck the monster boar.

Then the boar turned and was for drawing back into the thicket. They might have lost it then, for its retreat was impenetrable. But before it got clear away Atalanta put an arrow to the string, drew the bow to her shoulder, and let the arrow fly. It struck the boar, and a patch of blood was seen upon its bristles. Prince Meleagrus shouted out, "O first to strike the monster! Honor indeed shall you receive for this, Arcadian maid."

His uncles were made wroth by this speech, as was another, the Arcadian, rough Arcas. Arcas dashed forward, holding in his hands a two-headed axe. "Heroes and huntsmen," he cried, "you shall see how a man's strokes surpass a girl's." He faced the boar, standing on tiptoe with his axe raised for the stroke. Meleagrus's uncles shouted to encourage him. But the boar's tusks tore him before Arcas's axe fell, and the Arcadian was trampled upon the ground.

The boar, roused again by Atalanta's arrow, turned on the hunters. Jason hurled a spear again. It swerved and struck a hound and pinned it to the ground. Then, speaking the name of Atalanta, Meleagrus sprang before the heroes and the huntsmen.

He had two spears in his hands. The first missed and stuck quivering in the ground. But the second went right through the back of the monster boar. It whirled round and round, spouting out blood and foam. Meleagrus pressed on, and drove his hunting knife through the shoulders of the monster.

His uncles, Plexippus and Toxeus, were the first to come to where the monster boar was lying outstretched. "It is well, the deed you have done, boy," said one; "it is well that none of the strangers to our country slew the boar. Now will the head and tusks of the monster adorn our hall, and men will know that the arms of our house can well protect this land."

But one word only did Meleagrus say, and that word was the name, "Atalanta." The maiden came and Meleagrus, his spear upon the head, said, "Take, O fair Arcadian, the spoil of the chase. All know that it was you who inflicted the first wound upon the boar."

Plexippus and Toxeus tried to push him away, as if Meleagrus was still a boy under their tutoring. He shouted to them to stand off, and then he hacked out the terrible tusks and held them toward Atalanta.

She would have taken them, for she, who had never looked lovingly upon a youth, was moved by the beauty and the generosity of Prince Meleagrus. She would have taken from him the spoil of the chase. But as she held out her arms Meleagrus's uncles struck them with the poles of their spears. Heavy marks were made on the maiden's white arms. Madness then possessed Meleagrus, and he took up his spear and thrust it, first into the body of Plexippus and then into the body of Toxeus. His thrusts were terrible, for he was filled with the fierceness of the hunt, and his uncles fell down in death.

Then a great horror came over all the heroes. They raised up the bodies of Plexippus and Toxeus and carried them on their spears away from the place of the hunting and toward the temple of the gods. Meleagrus crouched down upon the ground in horror of what he had done. Atalanta stood beside him, her hand upon his head.

III

Althæa was in the temple making sacrifice to the gods. She saw men come in carrying across their spears the bodies of two men. She looked and she saw that the dead men were her two brothers, Plexippus and Toxeus.

Then she beat her breast and she filled the temple with the cries of her lamentation. "Who has slain my brothers? Who has slain my brothers?" she kept crying out.

Then she was told that her son Meleagrus had slain her brothers. She had no tears to shed then, and in a hard voice she asked, "Why did my son slay Plexippus and Toxeus, his uncles?"

The one who was wroth with Atalanta, Arcas the Arcadian, came to her and told her that her brothers had been slain because of a quarrel about the girl Atalanta.

"My brothers have been slain because a girl bewitched my son; then accursed be that son of mine," Althæa cried. She took off the gold-fringed robe of a priestess, and she put on a black robe of mourning.

Her brothers, the only sons of her father, had been slain, and for the sake of a girl. The image of Atalanta came before her, and she felt she could punish dreadfully her son. But her son was not there to punish; he was far away, and the girl for whose sake he had killed Plexippus and Toxeus was with him.

The rage she had went back into her heart and made her truly mad. "I gave Meleagrus life when I might have let it go from him with the burning billet of wood," she cried, "and now he has taken the lives of my brothers." And then her thought went to the billet of wood that was hidden in the chest.

Back to her house she went, and when she went within she saw a fire of pine knots burning upon the hearth. As she looked upon their burning a scorching pain went through her. But she went from the hearth, nevertheless, and into the inner room. There stood the chest that she had not opened for years. She opened it now, and out of it she took the billet of wood that had on it the mark of the burning.

She brought it to the hearth fire. Four times she went to throw it into the fire, and four times she stayed her hand. The fire was before her, but it was in her too. She saw the images of her brothers lying dead, and, saying that he who had slain them should lose his life, she threw the billet of wood into the fire of pine knots.

Straightway it caught fire and began to burn. And Althæa cried, "Let him die, my son, and let naught remain;

let all perish with my brothers, even the kingdom that Œneus, my husband, founded."

Then she turned away and remained stiffly standing by the hearth, the life withered up within her. Her daughters came and tried to draw her away, but they could not—her two daughters, Gorge and Deianira.

Meleagrus was crouching upon the ground with Atalanta watching beside him. Now he stood up, and taking her hand he said, "Let me go with you to the temple of the gods where I shall strive to make atonement for the deed I have done to-day."

She went with him. But even as they came to the street of the city a sharp and a burning pain seized upon Meleagrus. More and more burning it grew, and weaker and weaker he became. He could not have moved further if it had not been for the aid of Atalanta. Jason and Peleus lifted him across the threshold and carried him into the temple of the gods.

They laid him down with his head upon Atalanta's lap. The pain within him grew fiercer and fiercer, but at last it died down as the burning billet of wood sank down into the ashes. The heroes of the quest stood around, all overcome with woe. In the street they heard the lamentations for Plexippus and Toxeus, for Prince Meleagrus, and for the passing of the kingdom founded by Œneus. Atalanta left the temple, and attended by the two brothers on the white horses, Polydeuces and Castor, she went back to Arcady.

II. Peleus and His Bride from the Sea

I

PRINCE Peleus came on his ship to a bay on the coast of Thessaly. His painted ship lay between two great rocks, and from its poop he saw a sight that enchanted him. Out from the sea, riding on a dolphin, came a lovely maiden. And by the radiance of her face and limbs Peleus knew her for one of the immortal goddesses.

Now Peleus had borne himself so nobly in all things that he had won the favor of the gods themselves. Zeus, who is highest amongst the gods, had made this promise to Peleus: he would honor him as no one amongst the sons of men had been honored before, for he would give him an immortal goddess to be his bride.

She who came out of the sea went into a cave that was overgrown with vines and roses. Peleus looked into the cave and he saw her sleeping upon skins of the beasts of the sea. His heart was enchanted by the sight, and he knew that his life would be broken if he did not see this goddess day after day. So he went back to his ship and he prayed: "O Zeus, now I claim the promise that you once made to me. Let it be that this goddess come with me, or else plunge my ship and me beneath the waves of the sea."

And when Peleus said this he looked over the land and the water for a sign from Zeus.

Even then the goddess sleeping in the cave had dreams such as had never before entered that peaceful resting place of hers. She dreamt that she was drawn away from the deep and the wide sea. She dreamt that she was brought to a place that was strange and unfree to her. And as she lay in the cave, sleeping, tears that might never come into the eyes of an immortal lay around her heart.

But Peleus, standing on his painted ship, saw a rainbow touch upon the sea. He knew by that sign that Iris, the messenger of Zeus, had come down through the air. Then a strange sight came before his eyes. Out of the sea rose the head of a man; wrinkled and bearded it was, and the eyes were very old. Peleus knew that he who was there before him was Nereus, the ancient one of the sea.

Said old Nereus: "Thou hast prayed to Zeus, and I am here to speak an answer to thy prayer. She whom you have looked upon is Thetis, the goddess of the sea. Very loath will she be to take Zeus's command and wed with thee. It is her desire to remain in the sea, unwedded, and she has refused marriage even with one of the immortal gods."

Then said Peleus, "Zeus promised me an immortal bride. If Thetis may not be mine I cannot wed any other, goddess or mortal maiden."

"Then thou thyself wilt have to master Thetis," said Nereus, the wise one of the sea. "If she is mastered by thee, she cannot go back to the sea. She will strive with all her strength and all her wit to escape from thee; but thou must hold her no matter what she does, and no matter how she shows herself. When thou hast seen her again as thou didst see her at first, thou wilt know that thou hast mastered her." And when he had said this to Peleus, Nereus, the ancient one of the sea, went under the waves.

II

With his hero's heart beating more than ever it had beaten yet, Peleus went into the cave. Kneeling beside her he looked down upon the goddess. The dress she wore was like green and silver mail. Her face and limbs were pearly, but through them came the radiance that belongs to the immortals.

He touched the hair of the goddess of the sea, the yellow hair that was so long that it might cover her all over. As he touched her hair she started up, wakening suddenly out of her sleep. His hands touched her hands and held them. Now he knew that if he should loose his hold upon her she would escape from him into the depths of the sea, and that thereafter no command from the immortals would bring her to him.

She changed into a white bird that strove to bear itself away. Peleus held to its wings and struggled with the bird. She changed and became a tree. Around the trunk of the tree Peleus clung. She changed once more, and this time her form became terrible: a spotted leopard she was now, with burning eyes; but Peleus held to the neck of the

fierce-appearing leopard and was not affrighted by the
burning eyes. Then she changed and became as he had
seen her first—a lovely maiden, with the brow of a goddess, and with long yellow hair.

But now there was no radiance in her face or in her
limbs. She looked past Peleus, who held her, and out to
the wide sea. "Who is he," she cried, "who has been given
this mastery over me?"

Then said the hero: "I am Peleus, and Zeus has given me
the mastery over thee. Wilt thou come with me, Thetis?
Thou art my bride, given me by him who is highest
amongst the gods, and if thou wilt come with me, thou
wilt always be loved and reverenced by me."

"Unwillingly I leave the sea," she cried, "unwillingly I go
with thee, Peleus."

But life in the sea was not for her any more now that she
was mastered. She went to Peleus's ship and she went to
Phthia, his country. And when the hero and the sea goddess were wedded the immortal gods and goddesses
came to their hall and brought the bride and the bride-
groom wondrous gifts. The three sisters who are called
the Fates came also. These wise and ancient women said
that the son born of the marriage of Peleus and Thetis
would be a man greater than Peleus himself.

III

Now although a son was born to her, and although this
son had something of the radiance of the immortals about
him, Thetis remained forlorn and estranged. Nothing that
her husband did was pleasing to her. Prince Peleus was in
fear that the wildness of the sea would break out in her,
and that some great harm would be wrought in his house.

One night he wakened suddenly. He saw the fire upon
his hearth and he saw a figure standing by the fire. It was
Thetis, his wife. The fire was blazing around something
that she held in her hands. And while she stood there she
was singing to herself a strange-sounding song.

And then he saw what Thetis held in her hands and

what the fire was blazing around; it was the child, Achilles.

Prince Peleus sprang from the bed and caught Thetis around the waist and lifted her and the child away from the blazing fire. He put them both upon the bed, and he took from her the child that she held by the heel. His heart was wild within him, for the thought that wildness had come over his wife, and that she was bent upon destroying their child. But Thetis looked on him from under those goddess brows of hers and she said to him: "By the divine power that I still possess I would have made the child invulnerable; but the heel by which I held him has not been endued by the fire and in that place some day he may be stricken. All that the fire covered is invulnerable, and no weapon that strikes there can destroy his life. His heel I cannot now make invulnerable, for now the divine power is gone out of me."

When she said this Thetis looked full upon her husband, and never had she seemed so unforgiving as she was then. All the divine radiance that had remained with her was gone from her now, and she seemed a white-faced and bitter-thinking woman. And when Peleus saw that such a great bitterness faced him he fled from his house.

He traveled far from his own land, and first he went to the help of Heracles, who was then in the midst of his mighty labors. Heracles was building a wall around a city. Peleus labored, helping him to raise the wall for King Laomedon. Then, one night, as he walked by the wall he had helped to build, he heard voices speaking out of the earth. And one voice said: "Why has Peleus striven so hard to raise a wall that his son shall fight hard to overthrow?" No voice replied. The wall was built, and Peleus departed. The city around which the wall was built was the great city of Troy.

In whatever place he went Peleus was followed by the hatred of the people of the sea, and above all by the hatred of the nymph who is called Psamathe. Far, far from his own country he went, and at last he came to a coun-

try of bright valleys that was ruled over by a kindly king—
by Ceyx, who was called the Son of the Morning Star.

Bright of face and kindly and peaceable in all his ways
was this king, and kindly and peaceable was the land that
he ruled over. And when Prince Peleus went to him to beg
for his protection, and to beg for unfurrowed fields where
he might graze his cattle, Ceyx raised him up from where
he knelt. "Peaceable and plentiful is the land," he said,
"and all who come here may have peace and a chance to
earn their food. Live where you will, O stranger, and take
the unfurrowed fields by the seashore for pasture for your
cattle."

Peace came into Peleus's heart as he looked into the un-
troubled face of Ceyx, and as he looked over the bright
valleys of the land he had come into. He brought his cattle to the unfurrowed fields by the seashore and he left
herdsmen there to tend them. And as he walked along
these bright valleys he thought upon his wife and upon
his son Achilles, and there were gentle feelings in his
breast. But then he thought upon the enmity of Psamathe,
the woman of the sea, and great trouble came over him
again. He felt he could not stay in the palace of the kindly
king. He went where his herdsmen camped and he lived
with them. But the sea was very near and its sound tormented him, and as the days went by, Peleus, wild looking
and shaggy, became more and more unlike the hero whom
once the gods themselves had honored.

One day as he was standing near the palace having
speech with the king, a herdsman ran to him and cried
out: "Peleus, Peleus, a dread thing has happened in the
unfurrowed fields." And when he had got his breath the
herdsman told of the thing that had happened.

They had brought the herd down to the sea. Suddenly,
from the marshes where the sea and land came together,
a monstrous beast rushed out upon the herd; like a wolf
this beast was, but with mouth and jaws that were more
terrible than a wolf's even. The beast seized upon the cattle. Yet it was not hunger that made it fierce, for the beasts

that it killed it tore, but did not devour. It rushed on and on, killing and tearing more and more of the herd. "Soon," said the herdsman, "it will have destroyed all in the herd, and then it will not spare to destroy the other flocks and herds that are in the land."

Peleus was stricken to hear that his herd was being destroyed, but more stricken to know that the land of a friendly king would be ravaged, and ravaged on his account. For he knew that the terrible beast that had come from where the sea and the land joined had been sent by Psamathe. He went up on the tower that stood near the king's palace. He was able to look out on the sea and able to look over all the land. And looking across the bright valleys he saw the dread beast. He saw it rush through his own mangled cattle and fall upon the herds of the kindly king.

He looked toward the sea and he prayed to Psamathe to spare the land that he had come to. But, even as he prayed, he knew that Psamathe would not harken to him. Then he made a prayer to Thetis, to his wife who had seemed so unforgiving. He prayed her to deal with Psamathe so that the land of Ceyx would not be altogether destroyed.

As he looked from the tower he saw the king come forth with arms in his hands for the slaying of the terrible beast. Peleus felt fear for the life of the kindly king. Down from the tower he came, and taking up his spear he went with Ceyx.

Soon, in one of the brightest of the valleys, they came upon the beast; they came between it and a herd of silken-coated cattle. Seeing the men it rushed toward them with blood and foam upon its jaws. Then Peleus knew that the spears they carried would be of little use against the raging beast. His only thought was to struggle with it so that the king might be able to save himself.

Again he lifted up his hands and prayed to Thetis to draw away Psamathe's enmity. The beast rushed toward them; but suddenly it stopped. The bristles upon its body seemed to stiffen. The gaping jaws became fixed. The hounds that were with them dashed upon the beast, but then fell back with yelps of disappointment. And when Peleus and Ceyx came to where it stood they found that the monstrous beast had been turned into stone.

And a stone it remains in that bright valley, a wonder to all the men of Ceyx's land. The country was spared the ravages of the beast. And the heart of Peleus was uplifted to think that Thetis had harkened to his prayer and had prevailed upon Psamathe to forego her enmity. Not altogether unforgiving was his wife to him.

That day he went from the land of the bright valleys, from the land ruled over by the kindly Ceyx, and he came back to rugged Phthia, his own country. When he came near his hall he saw two at the doorway awaiting him. Thetis stood there, and the child Achilles was by her side. The radiance of the immortals was in her face no longer, but there was a glow there, a glow of welcome for the hero Peleus. And thus Peleus, long tormented by the enmity of the sea-born ones, came back to the wife he had won from the sea.

III. Theseus and the Minotaur

I

THEREAFTER Theseus made up his mind to go in search of his father, the unknown king, and Medea, the wise woman, counseled him to go to Athens. After the hunt in Calydon he set forth. On his way he fought with and slew two robbers who harassed countries and treated people unjustly.

The first was Sinnias. He was a robber who slew men cruelly by tying them to strong branches of trees and letting the branches fly apart. On him Theseus had no mercy. The second was a robber also, Procrustes: he had a great iron bed on which he made his captives lie; if they were too long for that bed he chopped pieces off them, and if they were too short he stretched out their bodies with terrible racks. On him, likewise, Theseus had no mercy; he slew Procrustes and gave liberty to his captives.

The King of Athens at the time was named Ægeus. He was father of Theseus, but neither Theseus nor he knew that this was so. Æthra was his mother, and she was the daughter of the King of Trœzen. Before Theseus was born his father left a great sword under a stone, telling Æthra that the boy was to have the sword when he was able to move that stone away.

King Ægeus was old and fearful now: there were wars and troubles in the city; besides, there was in his palace an evil woman, a witch, to whom the king listened. This woman heard that a proud and fearless young man had come into Athens, and she at once thought to destroy him.

So the witch spoke to the fearful king, and she made him believe that this stranger had come into Athens to make league with his enemies and destroy him. Such was her power over Ægeus that she was able to persuade him to invite the stranger youth to a feast in the palace, and to give him a cup that would have poison in it.

Theseus came to the palace. He sat down to the banquet with the king. But before the cup was brought something moved him to stand up and draw forth the sword that he carried. Fearfully the king looked upon the sword. Then he saw the heavy ivory hilt with the curious carving on it, and he knew that this was the sword that he had once laid under the stone near the palace of the King of Trœzen. He questioned Theseus as to how he had come by the sword, and Theseus told him how Æthra, his mother, had shown him where it was hidden, and how he had been able to take it from under the stone before he was grown a youth. More and more Ægeus questioned him, and he came to know that the youth before him was his son indeed. He dashed down the cup that had been brought to the table, and he shook all over with the thought of how near he had been to a terrible crime. The witchwoman watched all that passed; mounting on a car drawn by dragons she made flight from Athens.

And now the people of the city, knowing that it was he who had slain the robbers Sinnias and Procrustes, rejoiced to have Theseus amongst them. When he appeared as their prince they rejoiced still more. Soon he was able to bring to an end the wars in the city and the troubles that afflicted Athens.

II

The greatest king in the world at that time was Minos, King of Crete. Minos had sent his son to Athens to make peace and friendship between his kingdom and the kingdom of King Ægeus. But the people of Athens slew the son of King Minos, and because Ægeus had not given him the protection that a king should have given a stranger come upon such an errand he was deemed to have some part in the guilt of his slaying.

Minos, the great king, was wroth, and he made war on Athens, wreaking great destruction upon the country and the people. Moreover, the gods themselves were wroth with Athens; they punished the people with famine, making even the rivers dry up. The Athenians went to the oracle and asked Apollo what they should do to have their guilt taken away. Apollo made answer that they should make peace with Minos and fulfill all his demands.

All this Theseus now heard, learning for the first time that behind the wars and troubles in Athens there was a deed of evil that Ægeus, his father, had some guilt in.

The demands that King Minos made upon Athens were terrible. He demanded that the Athenians should send into Crete every year seven youths and seven maidens as a price for the life of his son. And these youths and maidens were not to meet death merely, nor were they to be reared in slavery—they were to be sent that a monster called the Minotaur might devour them.

Youths and maidens had been sent, and for the third time the messengers of King Minos were coming to Athens. The tribute for the Minotaur was to be chosen by lot. The fathers and mothers were in fear and trembling, for each man and woman thought that his or her son or daughter would be taken for a prey for the Minotaur.

They came together, the people of Athens, and they drew the lots fearfully. And on the throne above them all sat their pale-faced king, Ægeus, the father of Theseus.

Before the first lot was drawn Theseus turned to all of them and said, "People of Athens, it is not right that your children should go and that I, who am the son of King Ægeus, should remain behind. Surely, if any of the youths of Athens should face the dread monster of Crete, I should face it. There is one lot that you may leave undrawn. I will go to Crete."

His father, on hearing the speech of Theseus, came down from his throne and pleaded with him, begging him not to go. But the will of Theseus was set; he would go with the others and face the Minotaur. And he reminded his father of how the people had complained, saying that if Ægeus had done the duty of a king, Minos's son would not have been slain and the tribute to the Minotaur would have not been demanded. It was the passing about of such complaints that had led to the war and troubles that Theseus found on his coming to Athens.

Also Theseus told his father and told the people that he had hope in his hands—that the hands that were strong enough to slay Sinnias and Procrustes, the giant robbers, would be strong enough to slay the dread monster of Crete. His father at last consented to his going. And Theseus was able to make the people willing to believe that he would be able to overcome the Minotaur, and so put an end to the terrible tribute that was being exacted from them.

With six other youths and seven maidens Theseus went on board of the ship that every year brought to Crete the grievous tribute. This ship always sailed with black sails.

But before it sailed this time King Ægeus gave to Nausitheus, the master of the ship, a white sail to take with him. And he begged Theseus, that in case he should be able to overcome the monster, to hoist the white sail he had given. Theseus promised he would do this. His father would watch for the return of the ship, and if the sail were black he would know that the Minotaur had dealt with his son as it had dealt with the other youths who had gone from Athens. And if the sail were white Ægeus would have indeed cause to rejoice.

<h2 style="text-align:center">III</h2>

And now the black-sailed ship had come to Crete, and the youths and maidens of Athens looked from its deck on Knossos, the marvelous city that Dædalus the builder had built for King Minos. And they saw the palace of the king, the red and black palace in which was the labyrinth, made also by Dædalus, where the dread Minotaur was hidden.

In fear they looked upon the city and the palace. But not in fear did Theseus look, but in wonder at the magnificence of it all—the harbor with its great steps leading up into the city, the far-spreading palace all red and black, and the crowds of ships with their white and red sails. They were brought through the city of Knossos to the palace of the king. And there Theseus looked upon Minos. In a great red chamber on which was painted the sign of the axe, King Minos sat.

On a low throne he sat, holding in his hand a scepter on which a bird was perched. Not in fear, but steadily, did Theseus look upon the king. And he saw that Minos had the face of one who has thought long upon troublesome things, and that his eyes were strangely dark and deep. The king noted that the eyes of Theseus were upon him, and he made a sign with his head to an attendant and the attendant laid his hand upon him and brought Theseus to stand beside the king. Minos questioned him as to who he was and what lands he had been in, and when he learned that Theseus was the son of Ægeus, the King of Athens, he said the name of his son who had been slain, "Androgeus, Androgeus," over and over again, and then spoke no more.

While he stood there beside the king there came into the chamber three maidens; one of them, Theseus knew, was the daughter of Minos. Not like the maidens of Greece were the princess and her two attendants: instead of having on flowing garments and sandals and wearing their hair bound, they had on dresses of gleaming material that were tight at the waists and bell-shaped; the hair that streamed on their shoulders was made wavy; they had on high shoes of a substance that shone like glass. Never had Theseus looked upon maidens who were so strange.

They spoke to the king in the strange Cretan language; then Minos's daughter made reverence to her father, and they went from the chamber. Theseus watched them as they went through a long passage, walking slowly on their high-heeled shoes.

Through the same passage the youths and maidens of Athens were afterward brought. They came into a great hall. The walls were red and on them were paintings in black—pictures of great bulls with girls and slender youths struggling with them. It was a place for games and shows, and Theseus stood with the youths and maidens of Athens and with the people of the palace and watched what was happening.

They saw women charming snakes; then they saw a boxing match, and afterward they all looked on a bout of wrestling. Theseus looked past the wrestlers and he saw, at the other end of the hall, the daughter of King Minos and her two attendant maidens.

One broad-shouldered and bearded man overthrew all the wrestlers who came to grips with him. He stood there boastfully, and Theseus was made angry by the man's arrogance. Then, when no other wrestler would come against him, he turned to leave the arena.

But Theseus stood in his way and pushed him back. The boastful man laid hands upon him and pulled him into the arena. He strove to throw Theseus as he had

Very adroit was the Cretan wrestler, and Theseus had to use all his strength to keep upon his feet; but soon he mastered the tricks that the wrestler was using against him. *See page 175*.

thrown the others; but he soon found that the youth from Greece was a wrestler, too, and that he would have to strive hard to overthrow him.

More eagerly than they had watched anything else the people of the palace and the youths and maidens of Athens watched the bout between Theseus and the lordly wrestler. Those from Athens who looked upon him now thought that they had never seen Theseus look so tall and so conquering before; beside the slender, dark-haired people of Crete he looked like a statue of one of the gods.

Very adroit was the Cretan wrestler, and Theseus had to use all his strength to keep upon his feet; but soon he mastered the tricks that the wrestler was using against him. Then the Cretan left aside his tricks and began to use all his strength to throw Theseus.

Steadily Theseus stood and the Cretan wrestler was spent and gasping in the effort to throw him. Then Theseus made him feel his grip. He bent him backward, and then, using all his strength suddenly, forced him to the ground. All were filled with wonder at the strength and power of this youth from overseas.

Food and wine were given the youths and maidens of Athens, and they with Theseus were let wander through the grounds of the palace. But they could make no escape, for guards followed them and the way to the ships was filled with strangers who would not let them pass. They talked to each other about the Minotaur, and there was fear in every word they said. But Theseus went from one to the other, telling them that perhaps there was a way by which he could come to the monster and destroy it. And the youths and maidens, remembering how he had overthrown the lordly wrestler, were comforted a little, thinking that Theseus might indeed be able to destroy the Minotaur and so save all of them.

IV

Theseus was awakened by some one touching him. He arose and he saw a dark-faced servant, who beckoned to him. He left the little chamber where he had been sleeping, and then he saw outside one who wore the strange dress of the Cretans.

When Theseus looked full upon her he saw that she was none other than the daughter of King Minos. "I am Ariadne," she said, "and, O youth from Greece, I have come to save you from the dread Minotaur."

He looked upon Ariadne's strange face with its long, dark eyes, and he wondered how this girl could think that she could save him and save the youths and maidens of Athens from the Minotaur. Her hand rested upon his arm, and she led him into the chamber where Minos had sat. It was lighted now by many little lamps.

"I will show the way of escape to you," said Ariadne.

Then Theseus looked around, and he saw that none of the other youths and maidens were near them, and he looked on Ariadne again, and he saw that the strange princess had been won to help him, and to help him only.

"Who will show the way of escape to the others?" asked Theseus.

"Ah," said the Princess Ariadne, "for the others there is no way of escape."

"Then," said Theseus, "I will not leave the youths and maidens of Athens who came with me to Crete to be devoured by the Minotaur."

"Ah, Theseus," said Ariadne, "they cannot escape the Minotaur. One only may escape, and I want you to be that one. I saw you when you wrestled with Deucalion, our great wrestler, and since then I have longed to save you."

"I have come to slay the Minotaur," said Theseus, "and I cannot hold my life as my own until I have slain it."

Said Ariadne, "If you could see the Minotaur, Theseus, and if you could measure its power, you would know that you are not the one to slay it. I think that only Talos, that giant who was all of bronze, could have slain the Minotaur."

"Princess," said Theseus, "can you help me to come to the Minotaur and look upon it so that I can know for certainty whether this hand of mine can slay the monster?"

"I can help you to come to the Minotaur and look upon it," said Ariadne.

"Then help me, princess," cried Theseus; "help me to come to the Minotaur and look upon it, and help me, too, to get back the sword that I brought with me to Crete."

"Your sword will not avail you against the Minotaur," said Ariadne; "when you look upon the monster you will know that it is not for your hand to slay."

"Oh, but bring me my sword, princess," cried Theseus, and his hands went out to her in supplication.

"I will bring you your sword," said she.

She took up a little lamp and went through a doorway, leaving Theseus standing by the low throne in the chamber of Minos. Then after a little while she came back, bringing with her Theseus's great ivory-hilted sword.

"It is a great sword," she said; "I marked it before because it is your sword, Theseus. But even this great sword will not avail against the Minotaur."

"Show me the way to come to the Minotaur, O Ariadne," cried Theseus.

He knew that she did not think that he would deem himself able to strive with the Minotaur, and that when he looked upon the dread monster he would return to her and then take the way of his escape.

She took his hand and led him from the chamber of Minos. She was not tall, but she stood straight and walked steadily, and Theseus saw in her something of the strange majesty that he had seen in Minos the king.

They came to high bronze gates that opened into a vault. "Here," said Ariadne, "the labyrinth begins. Very devious is the labyrinth, built by Dædalus, in which the Minotaur is hidden, and without the clue none could find a way through the passages. But I will give you the clue so that you may look upon the Minotaur and then come back to me. Theseus, now I put into your hand the thread that will guide you through all the windings of the labyrinth. And outside the place where the Minotaur is you will find another thread to guide you back."

A cone was on the ground and it had a thread fastened to it.
Ariadne gave Theseus the thread and the cone to wind it around.
See page 179.

A cone was on the ground and it had a thread fastened to it. Ariadne gave Theseus the thread and the cone to wind it around. The thread as he held it and wound it around the cone would bring him through all the windings and turnings of the labyrinth.

She left him, and Theseus went on. Winding the thread around the cone he went along a wide passage in the vault. He turned and came into a passage that was very long. He came to a place in this passage where a door seemed to be, but within the frame of the doorway there was only a blank wall. But below that doorway there was a flight of six steps, and down these steps the thread led him. On he went, and he crossed the marks that he himself had made in the dust, and he thought he must have come back to the place where he had parted from Ariadne. He went on, and he saw before him a flight of steps. The thread did not lead up the steps; it led into the most winding of passages. So sudden were the turnings in it that one could not see three steps before one. He was dazed by the turnings of this passage, but still he went on. He went up winding steps and then along a narrow wall. The wall overhung a broad flight of steps, and Theseus had to jump to them. Down the steps he went and into a wide, empty hall that had doorways to the right hand and to the left hand. Here the thread had its end. It was fastened to a cone that lay on the ground, and beside this cone was another—the clue that was to bring him back.

Now Theseus, knowing he was in the very center of the labyrinth, looked all around for sight of the Minotaur. There was no sight of the monster here. He went to all the doors and pushed at them, and some opened and some remained fast. The middle door opened. As it did Theseus felt around him a chilling draft of air.

That chilling draft was from the breathing of the monster. Theseus then saw the Minotaur. It lay on the ground, a strange, bull-faced thing.

When the thought came to Theseus that he would have to fight that monster alone and in that hidden and empty place all delight left him; he grew like a stone; he groaned, and it seemed to him that he heard the voice of Ariadne calling him back. He could find his way back through the labyrinth and come to her. He stepped back, and the door closed on the Minotaur, the dread monster of Crete.

In an instant Theseus pushed the door again. He stood within the hall where the Minotaur was, and the heavy door shut behind him. He looked again on that dark, bull-faced thing. It reared up as a horse rears and Theseus saw that it would crash down on him and tear him with its dragon claws. With a great bound he went far away from where the monster crashed down. Then Theseus faced it: he saw its thick lips and its slobbering mouth; he saw that its skin was thick and hard.

He drew near the monster, his sword in his hand. He struck at its eyes, and his sword made a great dint. But no blood came, for the Minotaur was a bloodless monster. From its mouth and nostrils came a draft that covered him with a chilling slime.

Then it rushed upon him and overthrew him, and Theseus felt its terrible weight upon him. But he thrust his sword upward, and it reared up again, screaming with pain. Theseus drew himself away, and then he saw it searching around and around, and he knew he had made it sightless. Then it faced him; all the more fearful it was because from its wounds no blood came.

Anger flowed into Theseus when he saw the monster standing frightfully before him; he thought of all the youths and maidens that this bloodless thing had destroyed, and all the youths and maidens that it would destroy if he did not slay it now. Angrily he rushed upon it with his great sword. It clawed and tore him, and it opened wide its most evil mouth as if to draw him into it. But again he sprang at it; he thrust his great sword through its neck, and he left his sword there.

With the last of his strength he pulled open the heavy door and he went out from the hall where the Minotaur was. He picked up the thread and he began to wind it as

Then Theseus faced it: he saw its thick lips and its slobbering mouth; he saw that its skin was thick and hard. He drew near the monster, his sword in his hand. *See page 180.*

he had wound the other thread on his way down. On he went, through passage after passage, through chamber after chamber. His mind was dizzy, and he had little thought for the way he was going. His wounds and the chill that the monster had breathed into him and his horror of the fearful and bloodless thing made his mind almost forsake him. He kept the thread in his hand and he wound it as he went on through the labyrinth. He stumbled and the thread broke. He went on for a few steps and then he went back to find the thread that had fallen out of his hands. In an instant he was in a part of the labyrinth that he had not been in before.

He walked a long way, and then he came on his own footmarks as they crossed themselves in the dust. He pushed open a door and came into the air. He was now by the outside wall of the palace, and he saw birds flying by him. He leant against the wall of the palace, thinking that he would strive no more to find his way through the labyrinth.

V

That day the youths and maidens of Athens were brought through the labyrinth and to the hall where the Minotaur was. They went through the passages weeping and lamenting. Some cried out for Theseus, and some said that Theseus had deserted them. The heavy door was opened. Then those who were with the youths and maidens saw the Minotaur lying stark and stiff with Theseus's sword through its neck. They shouted and blew trumpets and the noise of their trumpets filled the labyrinth. Then they turned back, bringing the youths and maidens with them, and a whisper went through the whole palace that the Minotaur had been slain. The youths and maidens were lodged in the chamber where Minos gave his judgments.

VI

Theseus, wearied and overcome, fell into a deep sleep by the wall of the palace. He awakened with a feeling that the claw of the Minotaur was upon him. There were stars in the sky above the high palace wall, and he saw a dark-robed and ancient man standing beside him. Theseus knew that this was Dædalus, the builder of the palace and the labyrinth. Dædalus called and a slim youth came— Icarus, the son of Dædalus. Minos had set father and son apart from the rest of the palace, and Theseus had come near the place where they were confined. Icarus came and brought him to a winding stairway and showed him a way to go.

A dark-faced servant met and looked him full in the face. Then, as if he knew that Theseus was the one whom he had been searching for, he led him into a little chamber where there were three maidens. One started up and came to him quickly, and Theseus again saw Ariadne.

She hid him in the chamber of the palace where her singing birds were, and she would come and sit beside him, asking about his own country and telling him that she would go with him there. "I showed you how you might come to the Minotaur," she said, "and you went there and you slew the monster, and now I may not stay in my father's palace."

And Theseus thought all the time of his return, and of how he might bring the youths and maidens of Athens back to their own people. For Ariadne, that strange princess, was not dear to him as Medea was dear to Jason, or Atalanta the Huntress to young Meleagrus.

One sunset she led him to a roof of the palace and she showed him the harbor with the ships, and she showed him the ship with the black sail that had brought him to Knossos. She told him she would take him aboard that ship, and that the youths and maidens of Athens could go with them. She would bring to the master of the ship the seal of King Minos, and the master, seeing it, would set sail for whatever place Theseus desired to go.

Then did she become dear to Theseus because of her great kindness, and he kissed her eyes and swore that he would not go from the palace unless she would come with him to his own country. The strange princess smiled and wept as if she doubted what he said. Nevertheless, she led him from the roof and down into one of the palace gardens. He waited there, and the youths and maidens of Athens were led into the garden, all wearing cloaks that hid their forms and faces. Young Icarus led them from the grounds of the palace and down to the ships. And Ariadne went with them, bringing with her the seal of her father, King Minos.

And when they came on board of the black-sailed ship they showed the seal to the master, Nausitheus, and the master of the ship let the sail take the breeze of the evening, and so Theseus went away from Crete.

VII

To the Island of Naxos they sailed. And when they reached that place the master of the ship, thinking that what had been done was not in accordance with the will of King Minos, stayed the ship there. He waited until other ships came from Knossos. And when they came they brought word that Minos would not slay nor demand back Theseus nor the youths and maidens of Athens. His daughter, Ariadne, he would have back, to reign with him over Crete.

Then Ariadne left the black-sailed ship, and went back to Crete from Naxos. Theseus let the princess go, although he might have struggled to hold her. But more strange than dear did Ariadne remain to Theseus.

And all this time his father, Ægeus, stayed on the tower of his palace, watching for the return of the ship that had sailed for Knossos. The life of the king wasted since the departure of Theseus, and now it was but a thread. Every day he watched for the return of the ship, hoping against hope that Theseus would return alive to him. Then a ship came into the harbor. It had black sails. Ægeus did not know that Theseus was aboard of it, and that Theseus in the hurry of his flight and in the sadness of his parting from Ariadne had not thought of taking out the white sail

But the king, his father, saw the black sails on his ship, and straightway the thread of his life broke, and he died on the roof of the tower which he had built to look out on the sea. *See page 186.*

that his father had given to Nausitheus.

Joyously Theseus sailed into the harbor, having slain the Minotaur and lifted for ever the tribute put upon Athens. Joyously he sailed into the harbor, bringing back to their parents the youths and maidens of Athens. But the king, his father, saw the black sails on his ship, and straightway the thread of his life broke, and he died on the roof of the tower which he had built to look out on the sea.

Theseus landed on the shore of his own country. He had the ship drawn up on the beach and he made sacrifices of thanksgiving to the gods. Then he sent messengers to the city to announce his return. They went toward the city, these joyful messengers, but when they came to the gate they heard the sounds of mourning and lamentation. The mourning and the lamentation were for the death of the king, Theseus's father. They hurried back and they came to Theseus where he stood on the beach. They brought a wreath of victory for him, but as they put it into his hand they told him of the death of his father. Then Theseus left the wreath on the ground, and he wept for the death of Ægeus—of Ægeus, the hero, who had left the sword under the stone for him before he was born.

The men and women who came to the beach wept and laughed as they clasped in their arms the children brought back to them. And Theseus stood there, silent and bowed; the memory of his last moments with his father, of his fight with the Minotaur, of his parting with Ariadne—all flowed back upon him. He stood there with head bowed, the man who might not put upon his brows the wreath of victory that had been brought to him.

VIII

There had come into the city a youth of great valor whose name was Peirithous: from a far country he had come, filled with a desire of meeting Theseus, whose fame had come to him. The youth was in Athens at the time Theseus returned. He went down to the beach with the townsfolk, and he saw Theseus standing alone with his head bowed down. He went to him and he spoke, and Theseus lifted his head and he saw before him a young man of strength and beauty. He looked upon him, and the thought of high deeds came into his mind again. He wanted this young man to be his comrade in dangers and upon quests. And Peirithous looked upon Theseus, and he felt that he was greater and nobler than he had thought. They became friends and sworn brothers, and together they went into far countries.

Now there was in Epirus a savage king who had a very fair daughter. He had named this daughter Persephone, naming her thus to show that she was held as fast by him as that other Persephone was held who ruled in the Underworld. No man might see her, and no man might wed her. But Peirithous had seen the daughter of this king, and he desired above all things to take her from her father and make her his wife. He begged Theseus to help him enter that king's palace and carry off the maiden.

So they came to Epirus, Theseus and Peirithous, and they entered the king's palace, and they heard the bay of the dread hound that was there to let no one out who had once come within the walls. Suddenly the guards of the savage king came upon them, and they took Theseus and Peirithous and they dragged them down into dark dungeons.

Two great chairs of stone were there, and Theseus and Peirithous were left seated in them. And the magic powers that were in the chairs of stone were such that the heroes could not lift themselves out of them. There they stayed, held in the great stone chairs in the dungeons of that savage king.

Then it so happened that Heracles came into the palace of the king. The harsh king feasted Heracles and abated his savagery before him. But he could not forbear boasting of how he had trapped the heroes who had come to carry off Persephone. And he told how they could not get out of the stone chairs and how they were held captive in his dark dungeon. Heracles listened, his heart full of pity for the heroes from Greece who had met with such a harsh fate. And when the king mentioned that one of the heroes was Theseus, Heracles would feast no more with him until he had promised that the one who had been his comrade on the *Argo* would be let go.

The king said he would give Theseus his liberty if Heracles would carry the stone chair on which he was seated out of the dungeon and into the outer world. Then Heracles went down into the dungeon. He found the two heroes in the great chairs of stone. But one of them, Peirithous, no longer breathed. Heracles took the great chair of stone that Theseus was seated in, and he carried it up, up, from the dungeon and out into the world. It was a heavy task even for Heracles. He broke the chair in pieces, and Theseus stood up, released.

Thereafter the world was before Theseus. He went with Heracles, and in the deeds that Heracles was afterward to accomplish Theseus shared.

IV. The Life and Labors of Heracles

I

HERACLES was the son of Zeus, but he was born into the family of a mortal king. When he was still a youth, being overwhelmed by a madness sent upon him by one of the goddesses, he slew the children of his brother Iphicles. Then, coming to know what he had done, sleep and rest went from him: he went to Delphi, to the shrine of Apollo, to be purified of his crime.

At Delphi, at the shrine of Apollo, the priestess purified him, and when she had purified him she uttered this prophecy: "From this day forth thy name shall be, not Alcides, but Heracles. Thou shalt go to Eurystheus, thy cousin, in Mycenæ, and serve him in all things. When the labors he shall lay upon thee are accomplished, and when the rest of thy life is lived out, thou shalt become one of the immortals." Heracles, on hearing these words, set out for Mycenæ.

He stood before his cousin who hated him; he, a towering man, stood before a king who sat there weak and trembling. And Heracles said, "I have come to take up the labors that you will lay upon me; speak now, Eurystheus, and tell me what you would have me do."

Eurystheus, that weak king, looking on the young man who stood as tall and as firm as one of the immortals, had a heart that was filled with hatred. He lifted up his head and he said with a frown:

"There is a lion in Nemea that is stronger and more fierce than any lion known before. Kill that lion, and bring the lion's skin to me that I may know that you have truly performed your task." So Eurystheus said, and Heracles, with neither shield nor arms, went forth from the king's palace to seek and to combat the dread lion of Nemea.

He went on until he came into a country where the fences were overthrown and the fields wasted and the houses empty and fallen. He went on until he came to the waste around that land: there he came on the trail of the lion; it led up the side of a mountain, and Heracles, without shield or arms, followed the trail.

He heard the roar of the lion. Looking up he saw the beast standing at the mouth of a cavern, huge and dark against the sunset. The lion roared three times, and then it went within the cavern.

Around the mouth were strewn the bones of creatures it had killed and carried there. Heracles looked upon them when he came to the cavern. He went within. Far into the cavern he went, and then he came to where he saw the lion. It was sleeping.

Heracles viewed the terrible bulk of the lion, and then he looked upon his own knotted hands and arms. He remembered that it was told of him that, while still a child of eight months, he had strangled a great serpent that had

Then the lion yawned. Heracles sprang on it and put his great hands upon its throat. *See page 191.*

come to his cradle to devour him. He had grown and his strength had grown too.

So he stood, measuring his strength and the size of the lion. The breath from its mouth and nostrils came heavily to him as the beast slept, gorged with its prey. Then the lion yawned. Heracles sprang on it and put his great hands upon its throat. No growl came out of its mouth, but the great eyes blazed while the terrible paws tore at Heracles. Against the rock Heracles held the beast; strongly he held it, choking it through the skin that was almost impenetrable. Terribly the lion struggled; but the strong hands of the hero held around its throat until it struggled no more.

Then Heracles stripped off that impenetrable skin from the lion's body; he put it upon himself for a cloak. Then, as he went through the forest, he pulled up a young oak tree and trimmed it and made a club for himself. With the lion's skin over him—that skin that no spear or arrow could pierce—and carrying the club in his hand he journeyed on until he came to the palace of King Eurystheus.

The king, seeing coming toward him a towering man all covered with the hide of a monstrous lion, ran and hid himself in a great jar. He lifted the lid up to ask the servants what was the meaning of this terrible appearance. And the servants told him that it was Heracles come back with the skin of the lion of Nemea. On hearing this Eurystheus hid himself again.

He would not speak with Heracles nor have him come near him, so fearful was he. But Heracles was content to be left alone. He sat down in the palace and feasted himself.

The servants came to the king; Eurystheus lifted the lid of the jar and they told him how Heracles was feasting and devouring all the goods in the palace. The king flew into a rage, but still he was fearful of having the hero before him. He issued commands through his heralds ordering Heracles to go forth at once and perform the second of his tasks.

It was to slay the great water snake that made its lair in

It grew into such a rage that it came through the swamp to attack him. Heracles swung his club. As the Hydra came near he knocked head after head off its body. *See page 193.*

the swamps of Lerna. Heracles stayed to feast another day, and then, with the lion's skin across his shoulders and the great club in his hands, he started off. But this time he did not go alone; the boy Iolaus went with him.

Heracles and Iolaus went on until they came to the vast swamp of Lerna. Right in the middle of the swamp was the water snake that was called the Hydra. Nine heads it had, and it raised them up out of the water as the hero and his companion came near. They could not cross the swamp to come to the monster, for man or beast would sink and be lost in it.

The Hydra remained in the middle of the swamp belching mud at the hero and his companion. Then Heracles took up his bow and he shot flaming arrows at its heads. It grew into such a rage that it came through the swamp to attack him. Heracles swung his club. As the Hydra came near he knocked head after head off its body.

But for every head knocked off two grew upon the Hydra. And as he struggled with the monster a huge crab came out of the swamp, and gripping Heracles by the foot tried to draw him in. Then Heracles cried out. The boy Iolaus came; he killed the crab that had come to the Hydra's aid.

Then Heracles laid hands upon the Hydra and drew it out of the swamp. With his club he knocked off a head and he had Iolaus put fire to where it had been, so that two heads might not grow in that place. The life of the Hydra was in its middle head; that head he had not been able to knock off with his club. Now, with his hands he tore it off, and he placed this head under a great stone so that it could not rise into life again. The Hydra's life was now destroyed. Heracles dipped his arrows into the gall of the monster, making his arrows deadly; no thing that was struck by these arrows afterward could keep its life.

Again he came to Eurystheus's palace, and Eurystheus, seeing him, ran again and hid himself in the jar. Heracles ordered the servants to tell the king that he had returned and that the second labor was accomplished.

Eurystheus, hearing from the servants that Heracles was mild in his ways, came out of the jar. Insolently he spoke. "Twelve labors you have to accomplish for me," said he to Heracles, "and eleven yet remain to be accomplished."

"How?" said Heracles. "Have I not performed two of the labors? Have I not slain the lion of Nemea and the great water snake of Lerna?"

"In the killing of the water snake you were helped by Iolaus," said the king, snapping out his words and looking at Heracles with shifting eyes. "That labor cannot be allowed you."

Heracles would have struck him to the ground. But then he remembered that the crime that he had committed in his madness would have to be expiated by labors performed at the order of this man. He looked full upon Eurystheus and he said, "Tell me of the other labors, and I will go forth from Mycenæ and accomplish them."

Then Eurystheus bade him go and make clean the stables of King Augeias. Heracles came into that king's country. The smell from the stables was felt for miles around. Countless herds of cattle and goats had been in the stables for years, and because of the uncleanness and the smell that came from it the crops were withered all around. Heracles told the king that he would clean the stables if he were given one tenth of the cattle and the goats for a reward.

The king agreed to this reward. Then Heracles drove the cattle and the goats out of the stables; he broke through the foundations and he made channels for the two rivers Alpheus and Peneius. The waters flowed through the stables, and in a day all the uncleanness was washed away. Then Heracles turned the rivers back into their own courses.

He was not given the reward he had bargained for, however.

He went back to Mycenæ with the tale of how he had

cleaned the stables. "Ten labors remain for me to do now," he said.

"Eleven," said Eurystheus. "How can I allow the cleaning of King Augeias's stables to you when you bargained for a reward for doing it?"

Then while Heracles stood still, holding himself back from striking him, Eurystheus ran away and hid himself in the jar. Through his heralds he sent word to Heracles, telling him what the other labors would be.

He was to clear the marshes of Stymphalus of the man-eating birds that gathered there; he was to capture and bring to the king the golden-horned deer of Coryneia; he was also to capture and bring alive to Mycenæ the boar of Erymanthus.

Heracles came to the marshes of Stymphalus. The growth of jungle was so dense that he could not cut his way through to where the man-eating birds were; they sat upon low bushes within the jungle, gorging themselves upon the flesh they had carried there.

For days Heracles tried to hack his way through. He could not get to where the birds were. Then, thinking he might not be able to accomplish this labor, he sat upon the ground in despair.

It was then that one of the immortals appeared to him; for the first and only time he was given help from the gods.

It was Athena who came to him. She stood apart from Heracles, holding in her hands brazen cymbals. These she clashed together. At the sound of this clashing the Stymphalean birds rose up from the low bushes behind the jungle. Heracles shot at them with those unerring arrows of his. The man-eating birds fell, one after the other, into the marsh.

Then Heracles went north to where the Coryneian deer took her pasture. So swift of foot was she that no hound nor hunter had ever been able to overtake her. For the whole of a year Heracles kept Golden Horns in chase, and at last, on the side of the Mountain Artemision, he caught her. Artemis, the goddess of the wild things, would have punished Heracles for capturing the deer, but the hero pleaded with her, and she relented and agreed to let him bring the deer to Mycenæ and show her to King Eurystheus. And Artemis took charge of Golden Horns while Heracles went off to capture the Erymanthean boar.

He came to the city of Psophis, the inhabitants of which were in deadly fear because of the ravages of the boar. Heracles made his way up the mountain to hunt it. Now on this mountain a band of centaurs lived, and they, knowing him since the time he had been fostered by Chiron, welcomed Heracles. One of them, Pholus, took Heracles to the great house where the centaurs had their wine stored.

Seldom did the centaurs drink wine; a draft of it made them wild, and so they stored it away, leaving it in the charge of one of their band. Heracles begged Pholus to give him a draft of wine; after he had begged again and again the centaur opened one of his great jars.

Heracles drank wine and spilled it. Then the centaurs that were without smelt the wine and came hammering at the door, demanding the drafts that would make them wild. Heracles came forth to drive them away. They attacked him. Then he shot at them with his unerring arrows and he drove them away. Up the mountain and away to far rivers the centaurs raced, pursued by Heracles with his bow.

One was slain, Pholus, the centaur who had entertained him. By accident Heracles dropped a poisoned arrow on his foot. He took the body of Pholus up to the top of the mountain and buried the centaur there. Afterward, on the snows of Erymanthus, he set a snare for the boar and caught him there.

Upon his shoulders he carried the boar to Mycenæ and he led the deer by her golden horns. When Eurystheus had looked upon them the boar was slain, but the deer was loosed and she fled back to the Mountain Artemision.

King Eurystheus sat hidden in the great jar, and he

thought of more terrible labors he would make Heracles engage in. Now he would send him oversea and make him strive with fierce tribes and more dread monsters. When he had it all thought out he had Heracles brought before him and he told him of these other labors.

He was to go to savage Thrace and there destroy the man-eating horses of King Diomedes; afterward he was to go amongst the dread women, the Amazons, daughters of Ares, the god of war, and take from their queen, Hippolyte, the girdle that Ares had given her; then he was to go to Crete and take from the keeping of King Minos the beautiful bull that Poseidon had given him; afterward he was to go to the Island of Erytheia and take away from Geryoneus, the monster that had three bodies instead of one, the herd of red cattle that the two-headed hound Orthus kept guard over; then he was to go to the Garden of the Hesperides, and from that garden he was to take the golden apples that Zeus had given to Hera for a marriage gift—where the Garden of the Hesperides was no mortal knew.

So Heracles set out on a long and perilous quest. First he went to Thrace, that savage land that was ruled over by Diomedes, son of Ares, the war god. Heracles broke into the stable where the horses were; he caught three of them by their heads, and although they kicked and bit and trampled he forced them out of the stable and down to the seashore, where his companion, Abderus, waited for him. The screams of the fierce horses were heard by the men of Thrace, and they, with their king, came after Heracles. He left the horses in charge of Abderus while he fought the Thracians and their savage king. Heracles shot his deadly arrows amongst them, and then he fought with their king. He drove them from the seashore, and then he came back to where he had left Abderus with the fierce horses.

They had thrown Abderus upon the ground, and they were trampling upon him. Heracles drew his bow and he shot the horses with the unerring arrows that were dipped with the gall of the Hydra he had slain. Screaming, the horses of King Diomedes raced toward the sea, but one fell and another fell, and then, as it came to the line of the foam, the third of the fierce horses fell. They were all slain with the unerring arrows.

Then Heracles took up the body of his companion and he buried it with proper rites, and over it he raised a column. Afterward, around that column a city that bore the name of Heracles's friend was built.

Then toward the Euxine Sea he went. There, where the River Themiscyra flows into the sea he saw the abodes of the Amazons. And upon the rocks and the steep place he saw the warrior women standing with drawn bows in their hands. Most dangerous did they seem to Heracles. He did not know how to approach them; he might shoot at them with his unerring arrows, but when his arrows were all shot away, the Amazons, from their steep places, might be able to kill him with the arrows from their bows.

While he stood at a distance, wondering what he might do, a horn was sounded and an Amazon mounted upon a white stallion rode toward him. When the warrior-woman came near she cried out, "Heracles, the Queen Hippolyte permits you to come amongst the Amazons. Enter her tent and declare to the queen what has brought you amongst the never-conquered Amazons."

Heracles came to the tent of the queen. There stood tall Hippolyte with an iron crown upon her head and with a beautiful girdle of bronze and iridescent glass around her waist. Proud and fierce as a mountain eagle looked the queen of the Amazons: Heracles did not know in what way he might conquer her. Outside the tent the Amazons stood; they struck their shields with their spears, keeping up a continuous savage din.

"For what has Heracles come to the country of the Amazons?" Queen Hippolyte asked.

"For the girdle you wear," said Heracles, and he held his hands ready for the struggle.

"Is it for the girdle given me by Ares, the god of war, that you have come, braving the Amazons, Heracles?" asked the queen.

"For that," said Heracles.

"I would not have you enter into strife with the Amazons," said Queen Hippolyte. And so saying she drew off the girdle of bronze and iridescent glass, and she gave it into his hands.

Heracles took the beautiful girdle into his hands. Fearful he was that some piece of guile was being played upon him, but then he looked into the open eyes of the queen and he saw that she meant no guile. He took the girdle and he put it around his great brows; then he thanked Hippolyte and he went from the tent. He saw the Amazons standing on the rocks and the steep places with bows bent; unchallenged he went on, and he came to his ship and he sailed away from that country with one more labor accomplished.

The labor that followed was not dangerous. He sailed over sea and he came to Crete, to the land that King Minos ruled over. And there he found, grazing in a special pasture, the bull that Poseidon had given King Minos. He laid his hands upon the bull's horns and he struggled with him and he overthrew him. Then he drove the bull down to the seashore.

His next labor was to take away the herd of red cattle that was owned by the monster Geryoneus. In the Island of Erytheia, in the middle of the Stream of Ocean, lived the monster, his herd guarded by the two-headed hound Orthus—that hound was the brother of Cerberus, the three-headed hound that kept guard in the Underworld.

Mounted upon the bull given Minos by Poseidon, Heracles fared across the sea. He came even to the straits that divide Europe from Africa, and there he set up two pillars as a memorial of his journey—the Pillars of Heracles that stand to this day. He and the bull rested there. Beyond him stretched the Stream of Ocean; the Island of Erytheia was there, but Heracles thought that the bull would not be able to bear him so far.

And there the sun beat upon him, and drew all strength away from him, and he was dazed and dazzled by the rays of the sun. He shouted out against the sun, and in his anger he wanted to strive against the sun. Then he drew his bow and shot arrows upward. Far, far out of sight the arrows of Heracles went. And the sun god, Helios, was filled with admiration for Heracles, the man who would attempt the impossible by shooting arrows at him; then did Helios fling down to Heracles his great golden cup.

Down, and into the Stream of Ocean fell the great golden cup of Helios. It floated there wide enough to hold all the men who might be in a ship. Heracles put the bull of Minos into the cup of Helios, and the cup bore them away, toward the west, and across the Stream of Ocean.

Thus Heracles came to the Island of Erytheia. All over the island straggled the red cattle of Geryoneus, grazing upon the rich pastures. Heracles, leaving the bull of Minos in the cup, went upon the island; he made a club for himself out of a tree and he went toward the cattle.

The hound Orthus bayed and ran toward him; the two-headed hound that was the brother of Cerberus sprang at Heracles with poisonous foam upon his jaws. Heracles swung his club and struck the two heads off the hound. And where the foam of the hound's jaws dropped down a poisonous plant sprang up. Heracles took up the body of the hound, and swung it around and flung it far out into the Ocean.

Then the monster Geryoneus came upon him. Three bodies he had instead of one; he attacked Heracles by hurling great stones at him. Heracles was hurt by the stones. And then the monster beheld the cup of Helios, and he began to hurl stones at the golden thing, and it seemed that he might sink it in the sea, and leave Heracles without a way of getting from the island. Heracles took up his bow and he shot arrow after arrow at the monster, and he left him dead in the deep grass of the pastures.

Then he rounded up the red cattle, the bulls and the cows, and he drove them down to the shore and into the

Then the monster Geryoneus came upon him. Three bodies he had
instead of one; he attacked Heracles by hurling great stones at him.
. . . Heracles took up his bow and he shot arrow after arrow
at the monster. . . . *See page 200.*

golden cup of Helios where the bull of Minos stayed. Then back across the Stream of Ocean the cup floated, and the bull of Crete and the cattle of Geryoneus were brought past Sicily and through the straits called the Hellespont. To Thrace, that savage land, they came. Then Heracles took the cattle out, and the cup of Helios sank in the sea. Through the wild lands of Thrace he drove the herd of Geryoneus and the bull of Minos, and he came into Mycenæ once more.

But he did not stay to speak with Eurystheus. He started off to find the Garden of the Hesperides, the Daughters of the Evening Land. Long did he search, but he found no one who could tell him where the garden was. And at last he went to Chiron on the Mountain Pelion, and Chiron told Heracles what journey he would have to make to come to the Hesperides, the Daughters of the Evening Land.

Far did Heracles journey; weary he was when he came to where Atlas stood, bearing the sky upon his weary shoulders. As he came near he felt an undreamt-of perfume being wafted toward him. So weary was he with his journey and all his toils that he would fain sink down and dream away in that evening land. But he roused himself, and he journeyed on toward where the perfume came from. Over that place a star seemed always about to rise.

He came to where a silver lattice fenced a garden that was full of the quiet of evening. Golden bees hummed through the air, and there was the sound of quiet waters. How wild and laborious was the world he had come from, Heracles thought! He felt that it would be hard for him to return to that world.

He saw three maidens. They stood with wreaths upon their heads and blossoming branches in their hands. When the maidens saw him they came toward him crying out: "O man who has come into the Garden of the Hesperides, go not near the tree that the sleepless dragon guards!" Then they went and stood by a tree as if to keep guard over it. All around were trees that bore flowers and fruit, but this tree had golden apples amongst its bright green leaves.

Then he saw the guardian of the tree. Beside its trunk a dragon lay, and as Heracles came near the dragon showed its glittering scales and its deadly claws.

The apples were within reach, but the dragon, with its glittering scales and claws, stood in the way. Heracles shot an arrow; then a tremor went through Ladon, the sleepless dragon; it screamed and then lay stark. The maidens cried in their grief; Heracles went to the tree, and he plucked the golden apples and he put them into the pouch he carried. Down on the ground sank the Hesperides, the Daughters of the Evening Land, and he heard their laments as he went from the enchanted garden they had guarded.

Back from the ends of the earth came Heracles, back from the place where Atlas stood holding the sky upon his weary shoulders. He went back through Asia and Libya and Egypt, and he came again to Mycenæ and to the palace of Eurystheus.

He brought to the king the herd of Geryoneus; he brought to the king the bull of Minos; he brought to the king the girdle of Hippolyte; he brought to the king the golden apples of the Hesperides. And King Eurystheus, with his thin white face, sat upon his royal throne and he looked over all the wonderful things that the hero had brought him. Not pleased was Eurystheus; rather was he angry that one he hated could win such wonderful things.

He took into his hands the golden apples of the Hesperides. But this fruit was not for such as he. An eagle snatched the branch from his hand, and the eagle flew and flew until it came to where the Daughters of the Evening Land wept in their garden. There the eagle let fall the branch with the golden apples, and the maidens set it back upon the tree, and behold! it grew as it had been growing before Heracles plucked it.

The next day the heralds of Eurystheus came to Heracles and they told him of the last labor that he would have to set out to accomplish—this time he would have to go down into the Underworld, and bring up from King Aidoneus's realm Cerberus, the three-headed hound.

Heracles put upon him the impenetrable lion's skin and set forth once more. This might indeed be the last of his life's labors: Cerberus was not an earthly monster, and he who would struggle with Cerberus in the Underworld would have the gods of the dead against him.

But Heracles went on. He journeyed to the cave Tainaron, which was an entrance to the Underworld. Far into that dismal cave he went, and then down, down, until he came to Acheron, that dim river that has beyond it only the people of the dead. Cerberus bayed at him from the place where the dead cross the river. Knowing that he was no shade, the hound sprang at Heracles, but he could neither bite nor tear through that impenetrable lion's skin. Heracles held him by the neck of his middle head so that Cerberus was neither able to bite nor tear nor bellow.

Then to the brink of Acheron came Persephone, queen of the Underworld. She declared to Heracles that the gods of the dead would not strive against him if he promised to bring Cerberus back to the Underworld, carrying the hound downward again as he carried him upward.

This Heracles promised. He turned around and he carried Cerberus, his hands around the monster's neck while foam dripped from his jaws. He carried him on and upward toward the world of men. Out through a cave that was in the land of Trœzen Heracles came, still carrying Cerberus by the neck of his middle head.

From Trœzen to Mycenæ the hero went and men fled before him at the sight of the monster that he carried. On he went toward the king's palace. Eurystheus was seated outside his palace that day, looking at the great jar that he had often hidden in, and thinking to himself that Heracles would never appear to affright him again. Then Heracles appeared. He called to Eurystheus, and when the king looked up he held the hound toward him. The three heads grinned at Eurystheus; he gave a cry and scrambled into

Knowing that he was no shade, the hound sprang at Heracles, but he could neither bite nor tear through that impenetrable lion's skin. Heracles held him by the neck of his middle head so that Cerberus was neither able to bite nor tear nor bellow. *See page 204.*

the jar. But before his feet touched the bottom of it Eurystheus was dead of fear. The jar rolled over, and Heracles looked upon the body that was all twisted with fright. Then he turned around and made his way back to the Underworld. On the brink of Acheron he loosed Cerberus, and the bellow of the three-headed hound was heard again.

II

It was then that Heracles was given arms by the gods— the sword of Hermes, the bow of Apollo, the shield made by Hephæstus; it was then that Heracles joined the Argonauts and journeyed with them to the edge of the Caucasus, where, slaying the vulture that preyed upon Prometheus's liver, he, at the will of Zeus, liberated the Titan. Thereafter Zeus and Prometheus were reconciled, and Zeus, that neither might forget how much the enmity between them had cost gods and men, had a ring made for Prometheus to wear; that ring was made out of the fetter that had been upon him, and in it was set a fragment of the rock that the Titan had been bound to.

The Argonauts had now won back to Greece. But before he saw any of them he had been in Oichalia, and had seen the maiden Iole.

The king of Oichalia had offered his daughter Iole in marriage to the hero who could excel himself and his sons in shooting with arrows. Heracles saw Iole, the blue-eyed and childlike maiden, and he longed to take her with him to some place near the Garden of the Hesperides. And Iole looked on him, and he knew that she wondered to see him so tall and so strongly knit even as he wondered to see her so childlike and delicate.

Then the contest began. The king and his sons shot wonderfully well, and none of the heroes who stood before Heracles had a chance of winning. Then Heracles shot his arrows. No matter how far away they moved the mark, Heracles struck it and struck the very center of it. The people wondered who this great archer might be.

And then a name was guessed at and went around—Heracles!

When the king heard the name of Heracles he would not let him strive in the contest any more. For the maiden Iole would not be given as a prize to one who had been mad and whose madness might afflict him again. So the king said, speaking in judgment in the market place.

Rage came on Heracles when he heard this judgment given. He would not let his rage master him lest the madness that was spoken of should come with his rage. So he left the city of Oichalia declaring to the king and the people that he would return.

It was then that, wandering down to Crete, he heard of the Argonauts being near. And afterward he heard of them being in Calydon, hunting the boar that ravaged Œneus's country. To Calydon Heracles went. The heroes had departed when he came into the country, and all the city was in grief for the deaths of Prince Meleagrus and his two uncles.

On the steps of the temple where Meleagrus and his uncles had been brought Heracles saw Deianira, Meleagrus's sister. She was pale with her grief, this tall woman of the mountains; she looked like a priestess, but also like a woman who could cheer camps of men with her counsel, her bravery, and her good companionship; her hair was very dark and she had dark eyes.

Straightway she became friends with Heracles; and when they saw each other for a while they loved each other. And Heracles forgot Iole, the childlike maiden whom he had seen in Oichalia.

He made himself a suitor for Deianira, and those who protected her were glad of Heracles's suit, and they told him they would give him the maiden to marry as soon as the mourning for Prince Meleagrus and his uncles was over. Heracles stayed in Calydon, happy with Deianira, who had so much beauty, wisdom, and bravery.

But then a dreadful thing happened in Calydon; by an accident, while using his strength unthinkingly, Heracles killed a lad who was related to Deianira. He might not marry her now until he had taken punishment for slaying one who was close to her in blood.

As a punishment for the slaying it was judged that Heracles should be sold into slavery for three years. At the end of his three years' slavery he could come back to Calydon and wed Deianira.

And so Heracles and Deianira were parted. He was sold as a slave in Lydia; the one who bought him was a woman, a widow named Omphale. To her house Heracles went, carrying his armor and wearing his lion's skin. And Omphale laughed to see this tall man dressed in a lion's skin coming to her house to do a servant's tasks for her.

She and all in her house kept up fun with Heracles. They would set him to do housework, to carry water, and set vessels on the tables, and clear the vessels away. Omphale set him to spin with a spindle as the women did. And often she would put on Heracles's lion skin and go about dragging his club, while he, dressed in woman's garb, washed dishes and emptied pots.

But he would lose patience with these servant's tasks, and then Omphale would let him go away and perform some great exploit. Often he went on long journeys and stayed away for long times. It was while he was in slavery to Omphale that he liberated Theseus from the dungeon in which he was held with Peirithous, and it was while he still was in slavery that he made his journey to Troy.

At Troy he helped to repair for King Laomedon the great walls that years before Apollo and Poseidon had built around the city. As a reward for this labor he was offered the Princess Hesione in marriage; she was the daughter of King Laomedon, and the sister of Priam, who was then called, not Priam but Podarces. He helped to repair the wall, and two of the Argonauts were there to aid him: one was Peleus and the other was Telamon. Peleus did not stay for long: Telamon stayed, and to reward Telamon Heracles withdrew his own claim for the hand of the Princess Hesione. It was not hard on Heracles to do this, for his thoughts were ever upon Deianira.

But Telamon rejoiced, for he loved Hesione greatly. On the day they married Heracles showed the two an eagle in the sky. He said it was sent as an omen to them—an omen for their marriage. And in memory of that omen Telamon named his son "Aias"; that is, "Eagle."

Then the walls of Troy were repaired and Heracles turned toward Lydia, Omphale's home. Not long would he have to serve Omphale now, for his three years' slavery was nearly over. Soon he would go back to Calydon and wed Deianira.

As he went along the road to Lydia he thought of all the pleasantries that had been made in Omphale's house and he laughed at the memory of them. Lydia was a friendly country, and even though he had been in slavery Heracles had had his good times there.

He was tired with the journey and made sleepy with the heat of the sun, and when he came within sight of Omphale's house he lay down by the side of the road, first taking off his armor, and laying aside his bow, his quiver, and his shield. He wakened up to see two men looking down upon him; he knew that these were the Cercopes, robbers who waylaid travelers upon this road. They were laughing as they looked down on him, and Heracles saw that they held his arms and his armor in their hands.

They thought that this man, for all his tallness, would yield to them when he saw that they had his arms and his armor. But Heracles sprang up, and he caught one by the waist and the other by the neck, and he turned them upside down and tied them together by the heels. Now he held them securely and he would take them to the town and give them over to those whom they had waylaid and robbed. He hung them by their heels across his shoulders and marched on.

But the robbers, as they were being bumped along, began to relate pleasantries and mirthful tales to each other, and Heracles, listening, had to laugh. And one said to the other, "O my brother, we are in the position of the frogs when the mice fell upon them with such fury." And the other said, "Indeed nothing can save us if Zeus does not send an ally to us as he sent an ally to the frogs." And the first robber said, "Who began that conflict, the frogs or the mice?" And thereupon the second robber, his head reaching down to Heracles's waist, began:

THE BATTLE OF THE FROGS AND MICE

A warlike mouse came down to the brink of a pond for no other reason than to take a drink of water. Up to him hopped a frog. Speaking in the voice of one who had rule and authority, the frog said:

"Stranger to our shore, you may not know it, but I am Puff Jaw, king of the frogs. I do not speak to common mice, but you, as I judge, belong to the noble and kingly sort. Tell me your race. If I know it to be a noble one I shall show you my kingly friendship."

The mouse, speaking haughtily, said: "I am Crumb Snatcher, and my race is a famous one. My father is the heroic Bread Nibbler, and he married Quern Licker, the lovely daughter of a king. Like all my race I am a warrior who has never been wont to flinch in battle. Moreover, I have been brought up as a mouse of high degree, and figs and nuts, cheese and honeycakes is the provender that I have been fed on."

Now this reply of Crumb Snatcher pleased the kingly frog greatly. "Come with me to my abode, illustrious Crumb Snatcher," said he, "and I shall show you such entertainment as may be found in the house of a king."

But the mouse looked sharply at him. "How may I get to your house?" he asked. "We live in different elements, you and I. We mice want to be in the driest of dry places, while you frogs have your abodes in the water."

"Ah," answered Puff Jaw, "you do not know how favored the frogs are above all other creatures. To us alone the gods have given the power to live both in the water and on the land. I shall take you to my land palace that is the other side of the pond."

"How may I go there with you?" asked Crumb Snatcher the mouse, doubtfully.

"Upon my back," said the frog. "Up now, noble Crumb Snatcher. And as we go I will show you the wonders of the deep."

He offered his back and Crumb Snatcher bravely mounted. The mouse put his forepaws around the frog's neck. Then Puff Jaw swam out. Crumb Snatcher at first was pleased to feel himself moving through the water. But as the dark waves began to rise his mighty heart began to quail. He longed to be back upon the land. He groaned aloud.

"How quickly we get on," cried Puff Jaw; "soon we shall be at my land palace."

Heartened by this speech, Crumb Snatcher put his tail into the water and worked it as a steering oar. On and on they went, and Crumb Snatcher gained heart for the adventure. What a wonderful tale he would have to tell to the clans of the mice!

But suddenly, out of the depths of the pond, a water snake raised his horrid head. Fearsome did that head seem to both mouse and frog. And forgetful of the guest that he carried upon his back, Puff Jaw dived down into the water. He reached the bottom of the pond and lay on the mud in safety.

But far from safety was Crumb Snatcher the mouse. He sank and rose, and sank again. His wet fur weighed him down. But before he sank for the last time he lifted up his voice and cried out and his cry was heard at the brink of the pond:

"Ah, Puff Jaw, treacherous frog! An evil thing you have done, leaving me to drown in the middle of the pond. Had you faced me on the land I should have shown you which of us two was the better warrior. Now I must lose my life in the water. But I tell you my death shall not go unavenged—the cowardly frogs will be punished for the ill they have done to me who am the son of the king of the mice."

Then Crumb Snatcher sank for the last time. But Lick Platter, who was at the brink of the pond, had heard his words. Straightway this mouse rushed to the hole of Bread Nibbler and told him of the death of his princely son.

Bread Nibbler called out the clans of the mice. The warrior mice armed themselves, and this was the grand way of their arming:

First, the mice put on greaves that covered their forelegs. These they made out of bean shells broken in two. For shield, each had a lamp's centerpiece. For spears they had the long bronze needles that they had carried out of the houses of men. So armed and so accoutered they were ready to war upon the frogs. And Bread Nibbler, their king, shouted to them: "Fall upon the cowardly frogs, and leave not one alive upon the bank of the pond. Henceforth that bank is ours, and ours only. Forward!"

And, on the other side, Puff Jaw was urging the frogs to battle. "Let us take our places on the edge of the pond," he said, "and when the mice come amongst us, let each catch hold of one and throw him into the pond. Thus we will get rid of these dry bobs, the mice."

The frogs applauded the speech of their king, and straightway they went to their armor and their weapons. Their legs they covered with the leaves of mallow. For breastplates they had the leaves of beets. Cabbage leaves, well cut, made their strong shields. They took their spears from the pond side—deadly pointed rushes they were, and they placed upon their heads helmets that were empty snail shells. So armed and so accoutered they were ready to meet the grand attack of the mice.

When the robber came to this part of the story Heracles halted his march, for he was shaking with laughter. The robber stopped in his story. Heracles slapped him on the leg and said: "What more of the heroic exploits of the mice?" The second robber said, "I know no more, but perhaps my brother at the other side of you can tell you of the mighty combat between them and the frogs." Then Heracles shifted the first robber from his back to his front, and the first robber said: "I will tell you what I know about the heroical combat between the frogs and the mice." And thereupon he began:

The gnats blew their trumpets. This was the dread signal for war.

Bread Nibbler struck the first blow. He fell upon Loud Crier the frog, and overthrew him. At this Loud Crier's friend, Reedy, threw down spear and shield and dived into the water. This seemed to presage victory for the mice. But then Water Larker, the most warlike of the frogs, took up a great pebble and flung it at Ham Nibbler who was then pursuing Reedy. Down fell Ham Nibbler, and there was dismay in the ranks of the mice.

Then Cabbage Climber, a great-hearted frog, took up a clod of mud and flung it full at a mouse that was coming furiously upon him. That mouse's helmet was knocked off and his forehead was plastered with the clod of mud, so that he was well-nigh blinded.

It was then that victory inclined to the frogs. Bread Nibbler again came into the fray. He rushed furiously upon Puff Jaw the king.

Leeky, the trusted friend of Puff Jaw, opposed Bread Nibbler's onslaught. Mightily he drove his spear at the king of the mice. But the point of the spear broke upon Bread Nibbler's shield, and then Leeky was overthrown.

Bread Nibbler came upon Puff Jaw, and the two great kings faced each other. The frogs and the mice drew aside, and there was a pause in the combat. Bread Nibbler the mouse struck Puff Jaw the frog terribly upon the toes.

Puff Jaw drew out of the battle. Now all would have been lost for the frogs had not Zeus, the father of the gods, looked down upon the battle.

"Dear, dear," said Zeus, "what can be done to save the frogs? They will surely be annihilated if the charge of yonder mouse is not halted."

For the father of the gods, looking down, saw a warrior mouse coming on in the most dreadful onslaught of the whole battle. Slice Snatcher was the name of this warrior. He had come late into the field. He waited to split a chestnut in two and to put the halves upon his paws. Then, furiously dashing amongst the frogs, he cried out that he would not leave the ground until he had destroyed the race, leaving the bank of the pond a playground for the mice and for the mice alone.

To stop the charge of Slice Snatcher there was nothing for Zeus to do but to hurl the thunderbolt that is the terror of gods and men.

Frogs and mice were awed by the thunder and the flame. But still the mice, urged on by Slice Snatcher, did not hold back from their onslaught upon the frogs.

Now would the frogs have been utterly destroyed; but, as they dashed on, the mice encountered a new and a dreadful army. The warriors in these ranks had mailed backs and curving claws. They had bandy legs and long-stretching arms. They had eyes that looked behind them. They came on sideways. These were the crabs, creatures until now unknown to the mice. And the crabs had been sent by Zeus to save the race of the frogs from utter destruction.

Coming upon the mice they nipped their paws. The mice turned around and they nipped their tails. In vain the boldest of the mice struck at the crabs with their sharpened spears. Not upon the hard shells on the backs of the crabs did the spears of the mice make any dint. On and on, on their queer feet and with their terrible nippers, the crabs went. Bread Nibbler could not rally them any more, and Slice Snatcher ceased to speak of the monument of victory that the mice would erect upon the bank of the pond.

With their heads out of the water they had retreated to, the frogs watched the finish of the battle. The mice threw down their spears and shields and fled from the battleground. On went the crabs as if they cared nothing for their victory, and the frogs came out of the water and sat upon the bank and watched them in awe.

Heracles had laughed at the diverting tale that the robbers had told him; he could not bring them then to a place where they would meet with captivity or death. He let them loose upon the highway, and the robbers thanked him with high-flowing speeches, and they declared that if they should ever find him sleeping by the roadway again they would let him lie. Saying this they went away, and Heracles, laughing as he thought upon the great exploits of the frogs and mice, went on to Omphale's house.

Omphale, the widow, received him mirthfully, and then set him to do tasks in the kitchen while she sat and talked to him about Troy and the affairs of King Laomedon. And afterward she put on his lion's skin, and went about in the courtyard dragging the heavy club after her. Mirthfully and pleasantly she made the rest of his time in Lydia pass for Heracles, and the last day of his slavery soon came, and he bade good-by to Omphale, that pleasant widow, and to Lydia, and he started off for Calydon to claim his bride Deianira.

Beautiful indeed Deianira looked now that she had ceased to mourn for her brother, for the laughter that had been under her grief always now flashed out even while she looked priestesslike and of good counsel; her dark eyes shone like stars, and her being had the spirit of one who wanders from camp to camp, always greeting friends and leaving friends behind her. Heracles and Deianira wed, and they set out for Tiryns, where a king had left a kingdom to Heracles.

They came to the River Evenus. Heracles could have crossed the river by himself, but he could not cross it at the part he came to, carrying Deianira. He and she went along the river, seeking a ferry that might take them across. They wandered along the side of the river, happy with each other, and they came to a place where they had sight of a centaur.

Heracles knew this centaur. He was Nessus, one of the

centaurs whom he had chased up the mountain the time when he went to hunt the Erymanthean boar. The centaurs knew him, and Nessus spoke to Heracles as if he had friendship for him. He would, he said, carry Heracles's bride across the river.

Then Heracles crossed the river, and he waited on the other side for Nessus and Deianira. Nessus went to another part of the river to make his crossing. Then Heracles, upon the other bank, heard screams—the screams of his wife, Deianira. He saw that the centaur was savagely attacking her.

Then Heracles leveled his bow and he shot at Nessus. Arrow after arrow he shot into the centaur's body. Nessus loosed his hold on Deianira, and he lay down on the bank of the river, his lifeblood streaming from him.

Then Nessus, dying, but with his rage against Heracles unabated, thought of a way by which the hero might be made to suffer for the death he had brought upon him. He called to Deianira, and she, seeing he could do her no more hurt, came close to him. He told her that in repentance for his attack upon her he would bestow a great gift upon her. She was to gather up some of the blood that flowed from him; his blood, the centaur said, would be a love philter, and if ever her husband's love for her waned it would grow fresh again if she gave to him something from her hands that would have this blood upon it.

Deianira, who had heard from Heracles of the wisdom of the centaurs, believed what Nessus told her. She took a phial and let the blood pour into it. Then Nessus plunged into the river and died there as Heracles came up to where Deianira stood.

She did not speak to him about the centaur's words to her, nor did she tell him that she had hidden away the phial that had Nessus's blood in it. They crossed the river at another point and they came after a time to Tiryns and to the kingdom that had been left to Heracles.

There Heracles and Deianira lived, and a son who was named Hyllos was born to them. And after a time Heracles

Then Nessus, dying, but with his rage against Heracles unabated, thought of a way by which the hero might be made to suffer for the death he had brought upon him. He called to Deianira, and she, seeing he could do her no more hurt, came close to him. *See page 216.*

was led into a war with Eurytus—Eurytus who was king of Oichalia.

Word came to Deianira that Oichalia was taken by Heracles, and that the king and his daughter Iole were held captive. Deianira knew that Heracles had once tried to win this maiden for his wife, and she feared that the sight of Iole would bring his old longing back to him.

She thought upon the words that Nessus had said to her, and even as she thought upon them messengers came from Heracles to ask her to send him a robe—a beautifully woven robe that she had—that he might wear it while making a sacrifice. Deianira took down the robe; through this robe, she thought, the blood of the centaur could touch Heracles and his love for her would revive. Thinking this she poured Nessus's blood over the robe.

Heracles was in Oichalia when the messengers returned to him. He took the robe that Deianira sent, and he went to a mountain that overlooked the sea that he might make the sacrifice there. Iole went with him. Then he put on the robe that Deianira had sent. When it touched his flesh the robe burst into flame. Heracles tried to tear it off, but deeper and deeper into his flesh the flames went. They burned and burned and none could quench them.

Then Heracles knew that his end was near. He would die by fire, and knowing that he piled up a great heap of wood and he climbed upon it. There he stayed with the flaming robe burning into him, and he begged of those who passed to fire the pile that his end might come more quickly.

None would fire the pile. But at last there came that way a young warrior named Philoctetes, and Heracles begged of him to fire the pile. Philoctetes, knowing that it was the will of the gods that Heracles should die that way, lighted the pile. For that Heracles bestowed upon him his great bow and his unerring arrows. And it was this bow and these arrows, brought from Philoctetes, that afterward helped to take Priam's city.

The pile that Heracles stood upon was fired. High up,

above the sea, the pile burned. All who were near that burning fled—all except Iole, that childlike maiden. She stayed and watched the flames mount up and up. They wrapped the sky, and the voice of Heracles was heard calling upon Zeus. Then a great chariot came and Heracles was borne away to Olympus. Thus, after many labors, Heracles passed away, a mortal passing into an immortal being in a great burning high above the sea.

V. Admetus

I

IT happened once that Zeus would punish Apollo, his son. Then he banished him from Olympus, and he made him put off his divinity and appear as a mortal man. And as a mortal Apollo sought to earn his bread amongst men. He came to the house of King Admetus and took service with him as his herdsman.

For a year Apollo served the young king, minding his herds of black cattle. Admetus did not know that it was one of the immortal gods who was in his house and in his fields. But he treated him in friendly wise, and Apollo was happy whilst serving Admetus.

Afterward people wondered at Admetus's ever-smiling face and ever-radiant being. It was the god's kindly thought of him that gave him such happiness. And when Apollo was leaving his house and his fields he revealed himself to Admetus, and he made a promise to him that when the god of the Underworld sent Death for him he would have one more chance of baffling Death than any mortal man.

That was before Admetus sailed on the *Argo* with Jason and the companions of the quest. The companionship of Admetus brought happiness to many on the voyage, but the hero to whom it gave the most happiness was Heracles. And often Heracles would have Admetus beside him to tell him about the radiant god Apollo, whose bow and arrows Heracles had been given.

After that voyage and after the hunt in Calydon Admetus went back to his own land. There he wed that fair and loving woman, Alcestis. He might not wed her until he had yoked lions and leopards to the chariot that drew her. This was a feat that no hero had been able to accomplish. With Apollo's aid he accomplished it. Thereafter Admetus, having the love of Alcestis, was even more happy than he had been before.

One day as he walked by fold and through pasture field he saw a figure standing beside his herd of black cattle. A radiant figure it was, and Admetus knew that this was Apollo come to him again. He went toward the god and he made reverence and began to speak to him. But Apollo turned to Admetus a face that was without joy.

"What years of happiness have been mine, O Apollo, through your friendship for me," said Admetus. "Ah, as I walked my pasture land to-day it came into my mind how much I loved this green earth and the blue sky! And all that I know of love and happiness has come to me through you."

But still Apollo stood before him with a face that was without joy. He spoke and his voice was not that clear and vibrant voice that he had once in speaking to Admetus. "Admetus, Admetus," he said, "it is for me to tell you that you may no more look on the blue sky nor walk upon the green earth. It is for me to tell you that the god of the Underworld will have you come to him. Admetus, Admetus, know that even now the god of the Underworld is sending Death for you."

Then the light of the world went out for Admetus, and he heard himself speaking to Apollo in a shaking voice: "O Apollo, Apollo, thou art a god, and surely thou canst save me! Save me now from this Death that the god of the Underworld is sending for me!"

But Apollo said, "Long ago, Admetus, I made a bargain

with the god of the Underworld on thy behalf. Thou hast been given a chance more than any mortal man. If one will go willingly in thy place with Death, thou canst still live on. Go, Admetus. Thou art well loved, and it may be that thou wilt find one to take thy place."

Then Apollo went up unto the mountaintop and Admetus stayed for a while beside the cattle. It seemed to him that a little of the darkness had lifted from the world. He would go to his palace. There were aged men and women there, servants and slaves, and one of them would surely be willing to take the king's place and go with Death down to the Underworld.

So Admetus thought as he went toward the palace. And then he came upon an ancient woman who sat upon stones in the courtyard, grinding corn between two stones. Long had she been doing that wearisome labor. Admetus had known her from the first time he had come into that courtyard as a little child, and he had never seen aught in her face but a heavy misery. There she was sitting as he had first known her, with her eyes bleared and her knees shaking, and with the dust of the courtyard and the husks of the corn in her matted hair. He went to her and spoke to her, and he asked her to take the place of the king and go with Death.

But when she heard the name of Death horror came into the face of the ancient woman, and she cried out that she would not let Death come near her. Then Admetus left her, and he came upon another, upon a sightless man who held out a shriveled hand for the food that the servants of the palace might bestow upon him. Admetus took the man's shriveled hand, and he asked him if he would not take the king's place and go with Death that was coming for him. The sightless man, with howls and shrieks, said he would not go.

Then Admetus went into the palace and into the chamber where his bed was, and he lay down upon the bed and he lamented that he would have to go with Death that was coming for him from the god of the Underworld, and he lamented that none of the wretched ones around the palace would take his place.

A hand was laid upon him. He looked up and he saw his tall and grave-eyed wife, Alcestis, beside him. Alcestis spoke to him slowly and gravely. "I have heard what you have said, O my husband," said she. "One should go in your place, for you are the king and have many great affairs to attend to. And if none other will go, I, Alcestis, will go in your place, Admetus."

It had seemed to Admetus that ever since he had heard the words of Apollo that heavy footsteps were coming toward him. Now the footsteps seemed to stop. It was not so terrible for him as before. He sprang up, and he took the hands of Alcestis and he said, "You, then, will take my place?"

"I will go with Death in your place, Admetus," Alcestis said.

Then, even as Admetus looked into her face, he saw a pallor come upon her; her body weakened and she sank down upon the bed. Then, watching over her, he knew that not he but Alcestis would go with Death. And the words he had spoken he would have taken back—the words that had brought her consent to go with Death in his place.

Paler and weaker Alcestis grew. Death would soon be here for her. No, not here, for he would not have Death come into the palace. He lifted Alcestis from the bed and he carried her from the palace. He carried her to the temple of the gods. He laid her there upon the bier and waited there beside her. No more speech came from her. He went back to the palace where all was silent—the servants moved about with heads bowed, lamenting silently for their mistress.

II

As Admetus was coming back from the temple he heard a great shout; he looked up and saw one standing at the palace doorway. He knew him by his lion's skin and his

A hand was laid upon him. He looked up and he saw his tall
and grave-eyed wife, Alcestis, beside him. Alcestis spoke
to him slowly and gravely. *See page 222.*

great height. This was Heracles—Heracles come to visit him, but come at a sad hour. He could not now rejoice in the company of Heracles. And yet Heracles might be on his way from the accomplishment of some great labor, and it would not be right to say a word that might turn him away from his doorway; he might have much need of rest and refreshment.

Thinking this Admetus went up to Heracles and took his hand and welcomed him into his house. "How is it with you, friend Admetus?" Heracles asked. Admetus would only say that nothing was happening in his house and that Heracles, his hero-companion, was welcome there. His mind was upon a great sacrifice, he said, and so he would not be able to feast with him.

The servants brought Heracles to the bath, and then showed him where a feast was laid for him. And as for Admetus, he went within the chamber, and knelt beside the bed on which Alcestis had lain, and thought of his terrible loss.

Heracles, after the bath, put on the brightly colored tunic that the servants of Admetus brought him. He put a wreath upon his head and sat down to the feast. It was a pity, he thought, that Admetus was not feasting with him. But this was only the first of many feasts. And thinking of what companionship he would have with Admetus, Heracles left the feasting hall and came to where the servants were standing about in silence.

"Why is the house of Admetus so hushed to-day?" Heracles asked.

"It is because of what is befalling," said one of the servants.

"Ah, the sacrifice that the king is making," said Heracles. "To what god is that sacrifice due?"

"To the god of the Underworld," said the servant. "Death is coming to Alcestis the queen where she lies on a bier in the temple of the gods."

Then the servant told Heracles the story of how Alcestis had taken her husband's place, going in his stead with

When Death entered the temple Heracles laid hands upon him. . . .
In Death's grip there was a strength beyond strength. *See page 226.*

Death. Heracles thought upon the sorrow of his friend, and of the great sacrifice that his wife was making for him. How noble it was of Admetus to bring him into his house and give entertainment to him while such sorrow was upon him. And then Heracles felt that another labor was before him.

"I have dragged up from the Underworld," he thought, "the hound that guards those whom Death brings down into the realm of the god of the Underworld. Why should I not strive with Death? And what a noble thing it would be to bring back this faithful woman to her house and to her husband! This is a labor that has not been laid upon me, and it is a labor I will undertake." So Heracles said to himself.

He left the palace of Admetus and he went to the temple of the gods. He stood inside the temple and he saw the bier on which Alcestis was laid. He looked upon the queen. Death had not touched her yet, although she lay so still and so silent. Heracles would watch beside her and strive with Death for her.

Heracles watched and Death came. When Death entered the temple Heracles laid hands upon him. Death had never been gripped by mortal hands and he strode on as if that grip meant nothing to him. But then he had to grip Heracles. In Death's grip there was a strength beyond strength. And upon Heracles a dreadful sense of loss came as Death laid hands upon him—a sense of the loss of light and the loss of breath and the loss of movement. But Heracles struggled with Death although his breath went and his strength seemed to go from him. He held that stony body to him, and the cold of that body went through him, and its stoniness seemed to turn his bones to stone, but still Heracles strove with him, and at last he overthrew him and he held Death down upon the ground.

"Now you are held by me, Death," cried Heracles. "You are held by me, and the god of the Underworld will be made angry because you cannot go about his business— either this business or any other business. You are held by me, Death, and you will not be let go unless you promise to go forth from this temple without bringing one with you." And Death, knowing that Heracles could hold him there, and that the business of the god of the Underworld would be left undone if he were held, promised that he would leave the temple without bringing one with him. Then Heracles took his grip off Death, and that stony shape went from the temple.

Soon a flush came into the face of Alcestis as Heracles watched over her. Soon she arose from the bier on which she had been laid. She called out to Admetus, and Heracles went to her and spoke to her, telling her that he would bring her back to her husband's house.

III

Admetus left the chamber where his wife had lain and stood before the door of his palace. Dawn was coming, and as he looked toward the temple he saw Heracles coming to the palace. A woman came with him. She was veiled, and Admetus could not see her features.

"Admetus," Heracles said, when he came before him, "Admetus, there is something I would have you do for me. Here is a woman whom I am bringing back to her husband. I won her from an enemy. Will you not take her into your house while I am away on a journey?"

"You cannot ask me to do this, Heracles," said Admetus. "No woman may come into the house where Alcestis, only yesterday, had her life."

"For my sake take her into your house," said Heracles. "Come now, Admetus, take this woman by the hand."

A pang came to Admetus as he looked at the woman who stood beside Heracles and saw that she was the same stature as his lost wife. He thought that he could not bear to take her hand. But Heracles pleaded with him, and he took her by the hand.

"Now take her across your threshold, Admetus," said Heracles.

Hardly could Admetus bear to do this—hardly could he bear to think of a strange woman being in his house and his own wife gone with Death. But Heracles pleaded with him, and by the hand he held he drew the woman across his threshold.

"Now raise her veil, Admetus," said Heracles.

"This I cannot do," said Admetus. "I have had pangs enough. How can I look upon a woman's face and remind myself that I cannot look upon Alcestis's face ever again?"

"Raise her veil, Admetus," said Heracles.

Then Admetus raised the veil of the woman he had taken across the threshold of his house. He saw the face of Alcestis. He looked again upon his wife brought back from the grip of Death by Heracles, the son of Zeus. And then a deeper joy than he had ever known came to Admetus. Once more his wife was with him, and Admetus the friend of Apollo and the friend of Heracles had all that he cared to have.

VI. How Orpheus the Minstrel Went Down to the World of the Dead

MANY were the minstrels who, in the early days, went through the world, telling to men the stories of the gods, telling of their wars and their births. Of all these minstrels none was so famous as Orpheus who had gone with the Argonauts; none could tell truer things about the gods, for he himself was half divine.

But a great grief came to Orpheus, a grief that stopped his singing and his playing upon the lyre. His young wife Eurydice was taken from him. One day, walking in the garden, she was bitten on the heel by a serpent, and straightway she went down to the world of the dead.

Then everything in this world was dark and bitter for the minstrel Orpheus; sleep would not come to him, and for him food had no taste. Then Orpheus said: "I will do that which no mortal has ever done before; I will do that

Then Orpheus went on his way to the valley of Acherusia
which goes down, down into the world of the dead . . . as he went
along Orpheus played upon his lyre and sang. . . . *See page 230.*

which even the immortals might shrink from doing: I will go down into the world of the dead, and I will bring back to the living and to the light my bride Eurydice."

Then Orpheus went on his way to the valley of Acherusia which goes down, down into the world of the dead. He would never have found his way to that valley if the trees had not shown him the way. For as he went along Orpheus played upon his lyre and sang, and the trees heard his song and they were moved by his grief, and with their arms and their heads they showed him the way to the deep, deep valley of Acherusia.

Down, down by winding paths through that deepest and most shadowy of all valleys Orpheus went. He came at last to the great gate that opens upon the world of the dead. And the silent guards who keep watch there for the rulers of the dead were affrighted when they saw a living being, and they would not let Orpheus approach the gate.

But the minstrel, knowing the reason for their fear, said: "I am not Heracles come again to drag up from the world of the dead your three-headed dog Cerberus. I am Orpheus, and all that my hands can do is to make music upon my lyre."

And then he took the lyre in his hands and played upon it. As he played, the silent watchers gathered around him, leaving the gate unguarded. And as he played the rulers of the dead came forth, Aidoneus and Persephone, and listened to the words of the living man.

"The cause of my coming through the dark and fearful ways," sang Orpheus, "is to strive to gain a fairer fate for Eurydice, my bride. All that is above must come down to you at last, O rulers of the most lasting world. But before her time has Eurydice been brought here. I have desired strength to endure her loss, but I cannot endure it. And I come before you, Aidoneus and Persephone, brought here by Love."

When Orpheus said the name of Love, Persephone, the queen of the dead, bowed her young head, and bearded Aidoneus, the king, bowed his head also. Persephone remembered how Demeter, her mother, had sought her all through the world, and she remembered the touch of her mother's tears upon her face. And Aidoneus remembered how his love for Persephone had led him to carry her away from the valley in the upper world where she had been gathering flowers. He and Persephone bowed their heads and stood aside, and Orpheus went through the gate and came amongst the dead.

Still upon his lyre he played. Tantalus—who, for his crimes, had been condemned to stand up to his neck in water and yet never be able to assuage his thirst—Tantalus heard, and for a while did not strive to put his lips toward the water that ever flowed away from him; Sisyphus—who had been condemned to roll up a hill a stone that ever rolled back—Sisyphus heard the music that Orpheus played, and for a while he sat still upon his stone. And even those dread ones who bring to the dead the memories of all their crimes and all their faults, even the Eumenides had their cheeks wet with tears.

In the throng of the newly come dead Orpheus saw Eurydice. She looked upon her husband, but she had not the power to come near him. But slowly she came when Aidoneus called her. Then with joy Orpheus took her hands.

It would be granted them—no mortal ever gained such privilege before—to leave, both together, the world of the dead, and to abide for another space in the world of the living. One condition there would be—that on their way up through the valley of Acherusia neither Orpheus nor Eurydice should look back.

They went through the gate and came amongst the watchers that are around the portals. These showed them the path that went up through the valley of Acherusia. That way they went, Orpheus and Eurydice, he going before her.

Up and up through the darkened ways they went, Orpheus knowing that Eurydice was behind him, but never looking back upon her. But as he went, his heart was filled with things to tell—how the trees were blossoming in the garden she had left; how the water was sparkling in the fountain; how the doors of the house stood open, and how they, sitting together, would watch the sunlight on the laurel bushes. All these things were in his heart to tell her, to tell her who came behind him, silent and unseen.

And now they were nearing the place where the valley of Acherusia opened on the world of the living. Orpheus looked on the blue of the sky. A white-winged bird flew by. Orpheus turned around and cried, "O Eurydice, look upon the world that I have won you back to!"

He turned to say this to her. He saw her with her long dark hair and pale face. He held out his arms to clasp her. But in that instant she slipped back into the depths of the valley. And all he heard spoken was a single word, "Farewell!" Long, long had it taken Eurydice to climb so far, but in the moment of his turning around she had fallen back to her place amongst the dead.

Down through the valley of Acherusia Orpheus went again. Again he came before the watchers of the gate. But now he was not looked at nor listened to, and, hopeless, he had to return to the world of the living.

The birds were his friends now, and the trees and the stones. The birds flew around him and mourned with him; the trees and stones often followed him, moved by the music of his lyre. But a savage band slew Orpheus and threw his severed head and his lyre into the River Hebrus. It is said by the poets that while they floated in midstream the lyre gave out some mournful notes and the head of Orpheus answered the notes with song.

And now that he was no longer to be counted with the living, Orpheus went down to the world of the dead, not going now by that steep descent through the valley of Acherusia, but going down straightway. The silent watchers let him pass, and he went amongst the dead and saw his Eurydice in the throng. Again they were together, Orpheus and Eurydice, and as they went through the place that King Aidoneus ruled over, they had no fear of looking back, one upon the other.

VII. Jason and Medea

JASON and Medea, unable to win to Iolcus, stayed at Corinth, at the court of King Creon. Creon was proud to have Jason in his city, but of Medea the king was fearful, for he had heard how she had brought about the death of Apsyrtus, her brother.

Medea wearied of this long waiting in the palace of King Creon. A longing came upon her to exercise her powers of enchantment. She did not forget what Queen Arete had said to her—that if she wished to appease the wrath of the gods she should have no more to do with enchantments. She did not forget this, but still there grew in her a longing to use all her powers of enchantment.

And Jason, at the court of King Creon, had his longings, too. He longed to enter Iolcus and to show the people the Golden Fleece that he had won; he longed to destroy Pelias, the murderer of his mother and father; above all he longed to be a king, and to rule in the kingdom that Cretheus had founded.

Once Jason spoke to Medea of his longing. "O Jason," Medea said, "I have done many things for thee and this thing also I will do. I will go into Iolcus, and by my enchantments I will make clear the way for the return of the *Argo* and for thy return with thy comrades—yea, and for thy coming to the kingship, O Jason."

He should have remembered then the words of Queen Arete to Medea, but the longing that he had for his triumph and his revenge was in the way of his remembering. He said, "O Medea, help me in this with all thine enchantments and thou wilt be more dear to me than ever before thou wert."

Medea then went forth from the palace of King Creon and she made more terrible spells than ever she had made in Colchis. All night she stayed in a tangled place weaving her spells. Dawn came, and she knew that the spells she had woven had not been in vain, for beside her

As for Medea, she placed in a heap beside her the magic herbs and grasses she had gathered. Then she put them in a bronze pot and boiled them in water from the stream. *See page 235.*

there stood a car that was drawn by dragons.

Medea the Enchantress had never looked on these dragon shapes before. When she looked upon them now she was fearful of them. But then she said to herself, "I am Medea, and I would be a greater enchantress and a more cunning woman than I have been, and what I have thought of, that will I carry out." She mounted the car drawn by the dragons, and in the first light of the day she went from Corinth.

To the places where grew the herbs of magic Medea journeyed in her dragon-drawn car—to the Mountains Ossa, Pelion, Œthrys, Pindus, and Olympus; then to the rivers Apidanus, Enipeus, and Peneus. She gathered herbs on the mountains and grasses on the rivers' banks; some she plucked up by the roots and some she cut with the curved blade of a knife. When she had gathered these herbs and grasses she went back to Corinth on her dragon-drawn car.

Then Jason saw her; pale and drawn was her face, and her eyes were strange and gleaming. He saw her standing by the car drawn by the dragons, and a terror of Medea came into his mind. He went toward her, but in a harsh voice she bade him not come near to disturb the brewing that she was going to begin. Jason turned away. As he went toward the palace he saw Glauce, King Creon's daughter; the maiden was coming from the well and she carried a pitcher of water. He thought how fair Glauce looked in the light of the morning, how the wind played with her hair and her garments, and how far away she was from witcheries and enchantments.

As for Medea, she placed in a heap beside her the magic herbs and grasses she had gathered. Then she put them in a bronze pot and boiled them in water from the stream. Soon froth came on the boiling, and Medea stirred the pot with a withered branch of an apple tree. The branch was withered—it was indeed no more than a dry stick, but as she stirred the herbs and grasses with it, first leaves, then flowers, and lastly, bright gleaming apples came on it. And when the pot boiled over and drops from it fell upon the ground, there grew up out of the dry earth soft grasses and flowers. Such was the power of renewal that was in the magical brew that Medea had made.

She filled a phial with the liquid she had brewed, and she scattered the rest in the wild places of the garden. Then, taking the phial and the apples that had grown on the withered branch, she mounted the car drawn by the dragons, and she went once more from Corinth.

On she journeyed in her dragon-drawn car until she came to a place that was near to Iolcus. There the dragons descended. They had come to a dark pool. Medea, making herself naked, stood in that dark pool. For a while she looked down upon herself, seeing in the dark water her white body and her lovely hair. Then she bathed herself in the water. Soon a dread change came over her: she saw her hair become scant and gray, and she saw her body become bent and withered. She stepped out of the pool a withered and witchlike woman; when she dressed herself the rich clothes that she had worn before hung loosely upon her, and she looked the more forbidding because of them. She bade the dragons go, and they flew through the air with the empty car. Then she hid in her dress the phial with the liquid she had brewed and the apples that had grown upon the withered branch. She picked up a stick to lean upon, and with the gait of an ancient woman she went hobbling upon the road to Iolcus.

On the streets of the city the fierce fighting men that Pelias had brought down from the mountains showed themselves; few of the men or women of the city showed themselves even in the daytime. Medea went through the city and to the palace of King Pelias. But no one might enter there, and the guards laid hands upon her and held her.

Medea did not struggle with them. She drew from the folds of her dress one of the gleaming apples that she carried and she gave it to one of the guards. "It is for King Pelias," she said. "Give the apple to him and then do with me as the king would have you do."

The guards brought the gleaming apple to the king. When he had taken it into his hand and had smelled its fragrance, old trembling Pelias asked where the apple had come from. The guards told him it had been brought by an ancient woman who was now outside seated on a stone in the courtyard.

He looked on the shining apple and he felt its fragrance and he could not help thinking, old trembling Pelias, that this apple might be the means of bringing him back to the fullness of health and courage that he had had before. He sent for the ancient woman who had brought it that she might tell him where it had come from and who it was that had sent it to him. Then the guards brought Medea before him.

She saw an old man, white-faced and trembling, with shaking hands and eyes that looked on her fearfully. "Who are you," he asked, "and from whence came the apple that you had them bring me?"

Medea, standing before him, looked a withered and shrunken beldame, a woman bent with years, but yet with eyes that were bright and living. She came near him and she said: "The apple, O King, came from the garden that is watched over by the Daughters of the Evening Land. He who eats it has a little of the weight of old age taken from him. But things more wonderful even than the shining apples grow in that far garden. There are plants there the juices of which make youthful again all aged and failing things. The apple would bring you a little way toward the vigor of your prime. But the juices I have can bring you to a time more wonderful—back even to the strength and the glory of your youth."

When the king heard her say this a light came into his heavy eyes, and his hands caught Medea and drew her to him. "Who are you?" he cried, "who speak of the garden watched over by the Daughters of the Evening Land? Who are you who speak of juices that can bring back one to the strength and glory of his youth?"

Medea answered: "I am a woman who has known many

and great griefs, O king. My griefs have brought me through the world. Many have searched for the garden watched over by the Daughters of the Evening Land, but I came to it unthinkingly, and without wanting them I gathered the gleaming apples and took from the plants there the juices that can bring youth back."

Pelias said: "If you have been able to come by those juices, how is it that you remain in woeful age and decrepitude?"

She said: "Because of my many griefs, king, I would not renew my life. I would be ever nearer death and the end of all things. But you are a king and have all things you desire at your hand—beauty and state and power. Surely if any one would desire it, you would desire to have youth back to you."

Pelias, when he heard her say this, knew that besides youth there was nothing that he desired. After crimes that had gone through the whole of his manhood he had secured for himself the kingdom that Cretheus had founded. But old age had come on him, and the weakness of old age, and the power he had won was falling from his hands. He would be overthrown in his weakness, or else he would soon come to die, and there would be an end then to his name and to his kingship.

How fortunate above all kings he would be, he thought, if it could be that some one should come to him with juices that would renew his youth! He looked longingly into the eyes of the ancient-seeming woman before him, and he said: "How is it that you show no gains from the juices that you speak of? You are old and in woeful decrepitude. Even if you would not win back to youth you could have got riches and state for that which you say you possess."

Then Medea said: "I have lost so much and have suffered so much that I would not have youth back at the price of facing the years. I would sink down to the quiet of the grave. But I hope for some ease before I die—for the ease that is in king's houses, with good food to eat, and rest, and servants to wait upon one's aged body. These are the things I desire, O Pelias, even as you desire youth. You can give me such things, and I have come to you who desire youth eagerly rather than to kings who have a less eager desire for it. To you I will give the juices that bring one back to the strength and the glory of youth."

Pelias said: "I have only your word for it that you possess these juices. Many there are who come and say deceiving things to a king."

Said Medea: "Let there be no more words between us, O king. To-morrow I will show you the virtue of the juices I have brought with me. Have a great vat prepared—a vat that a man could lay himself in with the water covering him. Have this vat filled with water, and bring to it the oldest creature you can get—a ram or a goat that is the oldest of their flock. Do this, O king, and you will be shown a thing to wonder at and to be hopeful over."

So Medea said, and then she turned around and left the king's presence. Pelias called to his guards and he bade them take the woman into their charge and treat her considerately. The guards took Medea away. Then all day the king mused on what had been told him and a wild hope kept beating about his heart. He had the servants prepare a great vat in the lower chambers, and he had his shepherd bring him a ram that was the oldest in the flock.

Only Medea was permitted to come into that chamber with the king; the ways to it were guarded, and all that took place in it was secret. Medea was brought to the closed door by her guard. She opened it and she saw the king there and the vat already prepared; she saw a ram tethered near the vat.

Medea looked upon the king. In the light of the torches his face was white and fierce and his mouth moved gaspingly. She spoke to him quietly, and said: "There is no need for you to hear me speak. You will watch a great miracle, for behold! the ram which is the oldest and feeblest in the flock will become young and invigorated when it comes forth from this vat."

She untethered the ram, and with the help of Pelias
drew it to the vat. This was not hard to do, for the beast
was very feeble; its feet could hardly bear it upright, its
wool was yellow and stayed only in patches on its
shrunken body. Easily the beast was forced into the vat.
Then Medea drew the phial out of her bosom and poured
into the water some of the brew she had made in Creon's
garden in Corinth. The water in the vat took on a strange
bubbling, and the ram sank down.

Then Medea, standing beside the vat, sang an incantation.

"O Earth," she sang, "O Earth who dost provide wise
men with potent herbs, O Earth help me now. I am she
who can drive the clouds; I am she who can dispel the
winds; I am she who can break the jaws of serpents with
my incantations; I am she who can uproot living trees and
rocks; who can make the mountains shake; who can bring
the ghosts from their tombs. O Earth, help me now." At
this strange incantation the mixture in the vat boiled and
bubbled more and more. Then the boiling and bubbling
ceased. Up to the surface came the ram. Medea helped it
to struggle out of the vat, and then it turned and smote
the vat with its head.

Pelias took down a torch and stood before the beast.
Vigorous indeed was the ram, and its wool was white and
grew evenly upon it. They could not tether it again, and
when the servants were brought into the chamber it took
two of them to drag away the ram.

The king was most eager to enter the vat and have
Medea put in the brew and speak the incantation over it.
But Medea bade him wait until the morrow. All night the
king lay awake, thinking of how he might regain his youth
and his strength and be secure and triumphant thereafter.

At the first light he sent for Medea and he told her that
he would have the vat made ready and that he would go
into it that night. Medea looked upon him, and the help-
lessness that he showed made her want to work a greater
evil upon him, or, if not upon him, upon his house. How

soon it would have reached its end, all her plot for the destruction of this king! But she would leave in the king's house a misery that would not have an end so soon.

So she said to the king: "I would say the incantation over a beast of the field, but over a king I could not say it. Let those of your own blood be with you when you enter the vat that will bring such change to you. Have your daughters there. I will give them the juice to mix in the vat, and I will teach them the incantation that has to be said."

So she said, and she made Pelias consent to having his daughters and not Medea in the chamber of the vat. They were sent for and they came before Medea, the daughters of King Pelias.

They were women who had been borne down by the tyranny of their father; they stood before him now, two dim-eyed creatures, very feeble and fearful. To them Medea gave the phial that had in it the liquid to mix in the vat; also she taught them the words of the incantation, but she taught them to use these words wrongly.

The vat was prepared in the lower chambers; Pelias and his daughters went there, and the chamber was guarded, and what happened there was in secret. Pelias went into the vat; the brew was thrown into it, and the vat boiled and bubbled as before. Pelias sank down in it. Over him then his daughters said the magic words as Medea had taught them.

Pelias sank down, but he did not rise again. The hours went past and the morning came, and the daughters of King Pelias raised frightened laments. Over the sides of the vat the mixture boiled and bubbled, and Pelias was to be seen at the bottom with his limbs stiffened in death.

Then the guards came, and they took King Pelias out of the vat and left him in his royal chamber. The word went through the palace that the king was dead. There was a hush in the palace then, but not the hush of grief. One by one servants and servitors stole away from the palace that was hated by all. Then there was clatter in the streets as the fierce fighting men from the mountains galloped away with what plunder they could seize. And through all this the daughters of King Pelias sat crouching in fear above the body of their father.

And Medea, still an ancient woman seemingly, went through the crowds that now came on the streets of the city. She told those she went amongst that the son of Æson was alive and would soon be in their midst. Hearing this the men of the city formed a council of elders to rule the people until Jason's coming. In such way Medea brought about the end of King Pelias's reign.

In triumph she went through the city. But as she was passing the temple her dress was caught and held, and turning around she faced the ancient priestess of Artemis, Iphias. "Thou art Æetes's daughter," Iphias said, "who in deceit didst come into Iolcus. Woe to thee and woe to Jason for what thou hast done this day! Not for the slaying of Pelias art thou blameworthy, but for the misery that thou hast brought upon his daughters by bringing them into the guilt of the slaying. Go from the city, daughter of King Æetes; never, never wilt thou come back into it."

But little heed did Medea pay to the ancient priestess, Iphias. Still in the guise of an old woman she went through the streets of the city, and out through the gate and along the highway that led from Iolcus. To that dark pool she came where she had bathed herself before. But now she did not step into the pool nor pour its water over her shrinking flesh; instead she built up two altars of green sods—an altar to Youth and an altar to Hecate, queen of the witches; she wreathed them with green boughs from the forest, and she prayed before each. Then she made herself naked, and she anointed herself with the brew she had made from the magical herbs and grasses. All marks of age and decrepitude left her, and when she stood over the dark pool and looked down on herself she saw that her body was white and shapely as before, and that her hair was soft and lovely.

She stayed all night between the tangled wood and the

She stayed all night between the tangled wood and the dark pool, and with the first light the car drawn by the scaly dragons came to her. She mounted the car, and she journeyed back to Corinth. *See page 242.*

dark pool, and with the first light the car drawn by the
scaly dragons came to her. She mounted the car, and she
journeyed back to Corinth.

Into Jason's mind a fear of Medea had come since the
hour when he had seen her mount the car drawn by the
scaly dragons. He could not think of her any more as
the one who had been his companion on the *Argo*. He
thought of her as one who could help him and do wonderful things for him, but not as one whom he could talk
softly and lovingly to. Ah, but if Jason had thought less of
his kingdom and less of his triumphing with the Fleece of
Gold, Medea would not have had the dragons come to her.

And now that his love for Medea had altered, Jason
noted the loveliness of another—of Glauce, the daughter
of Creon, the King of Corinth. And Glauce, who had red
lips and the eyes of a child, saw in Jason who had brought
the Golden Fleece out of Colchis the image of every hero
she had heard about in stories. Creon, the king, often
brought Jason and Glauce together, for his hope was that
the hero would wed his daughter and stay in Corinth and
strengthen his kingdom. He thought that Medea, that
strange woman, could not keep a companionship with
Jason.

Two were walking in the king's garden, and they were
Jason and Glauce. A shadow fell between them, and when
Jason looked up he saw Medea's dragon car. Down flew
the dragons, and Medea came from the car and stood between Jason and the princess. Angrily she spoke to him.
"I have made the kingdom ready for your return," she
said, "but if you would go there you must first let me deal
in my own way with this pretty maiden." And so fiercely
did Medea look upon her that Glauce shrank back and
clung to Jason for protection. "O, Jason," she cried, " thou
didst say that I am such a one as thou didst dream of
when in the forest with Chiron, before the adventure of
the Golden Fleece drew thee away from the Grecian lands.
Oh, save me now from the power of her who comes in the

dragon car." And Jason said: "I said all that thou hast said, and I will protect thee, O Glauce."

And then Medea thought of the king's house she had left for Jason, and of the brother whom she had let be slain, and of the plot she had carried out to bring Jason back to Iolcus, and a great fury came over her. In her hand she took foam from the jaws of the dragons, and she cast the foam upon Glauce, and the princess fell back into the arms of Jason with the dragon foam burning into her.

Then, seeing in his eyes that he had forgotten all that he owed to her—the winning of the Golden Fleece, and the safety of *Argo,* and the destruction of the power of King Pelias—seeing in his eyes that Jason had forgotten all this, Medea went into her dragon-borne car and spoke the words that made the scaly dragons bear her aloft. She flew from Corinth, leaving Jason in King Creon's garden with Glauce dying in his arms. He lifted her up and laid her upon a bed, but even as her friends came around her the daughter of King Creon died.

And Jason? For long he stayed in Corinth, a famous man indeed, but one sorrowful and alone. But again there grew in him the desire to rule and to have possessions. He called around him again the men whose home was in Iolcus—those who had followed him as bright-eyed youths when he first proclaimed his purpose of winning the Fleece of Gold. He called them around him, and he led them on board the *Argo*. Once more they lifted sails, and once more they took the *Argo* into the open sea.

Toward Iolcus they sailed; their passage was fortunate, and in a short time they brought the *Argo* safely into the harbor of Pagasæ. Oh, happy were the crowds that came thronging to see the ship that had the famous Fleece of Gold upon her masthead, and green and sweet smelling were the garlands that the people brought to wreathe the heads of Jason and his companions! Jason looked upon the throngs, and he thought that much had gone from him, but he thought that whatever else had gone something remained to him—to be a king and a great ruler over a people.

And so Jason came back to Iolcus. The *Argo* he made a blazing pile of in sacrifice to Poseidon, the god of the sea. The Golden Fleece he hung in the temple of the gods. Then he took up the rule of the kingdom that Cretheus had founded, and he became the greatest of the kings of Greece.

And to Iolcus there came, year after year, young men who would look upon the gleaming thing that was hung there in the temple of the gods. And as they looked upon it, young man after young man, the thought would come to each that he would make himself strong enough and heroic enough to win for his country something as precious as Jason's GOLDEN FLEECE. And for all their lives they kept in mind the words that Jason had inscribed upon a pillar that was placed beside the Fleece of Gold—the words that Triton spoke to the Argonauts when they were fain to win their way out of the inland sea:—

THAT IS THE OUTLET TO THE SEA, WHERE THE DEEP WATER LIES UNMOVED AND DARK; ON EACH SIDE ROLL WHITE BREAKERS WITH SHINING CRESTS; AND THE WAY BETWEEN FOR YOUR PASSAGE OUT IS NARROW. BUT GO IN JOY, AND AS FOR LABOR LET THERE BE NO GRIEVING THAT LIMBS IN YOUTHFUL VIGOR SHOULD STILL TOIL.